BRICKS AND MORTAR

CW01496181

Persephone Book N° 49
Published by Persephone Books Ltd 2004

First published 1932 by Victor Gollancz Ltd and
by Doubleday, Doran in 1933
© The Estate of Helen Ashton

Endpapers taken from a 1930 block-printed linen
furnishing fabric, 'Welwyn Garden City', designed
by Doris Gregg for Footprints Ltd.
© the Trustees of the Victoria & Albert Museum, London

Typeset in ITC Baskerville by Keystroke,
Jacaranda Lodge, Wolverhampton

Colour by Banbury Litho

Printed and bound by Biddles, King's Lynn

ISBN 1 903155 398

Persephone Books Ltd
59 Lamb's Conduit Street
London WC1N 3NB
020 7242 9292

www.persephonebooks.co.uk

BRICKS AND MORTAR

by

HELEN ASHTON

✳✳✳✳✳✳✳

'Lie heavy on him, Earth, for he
Laid many a heavy load on thee.'

Epitaph for Sir John Vanbrugh, architect

PERSEPHONE BOOKS
LONDON

for Leigh and Kitty

PUBLISHER'S NOTE

※※※※※※※※

Helen Ashton was one of the numerous early twentieth-century novelists beloved of the circulating libraries who received little critical attention but were consistently adept at what they set out to do – to write an entertaining but interesting novel which leaves the reader something to think about.

She was best-known for the 'hospital' novels drawing on her medical background: these were *Dr Serrocold*: A Page from his Day-book (1930), which was a Book-of-the-Month Selection in the US and a Book Society Choice in England, and *Yeoman's Hospital* (1944), on which the film *White Corridors* (1955) was based. But architecture and furniture were two of her great interests – her brother Leigh became director of the Victoria and Albert Museum and later married Madge Garland, Fashion Editor of *Vogue* – and *Bricks and Mortar* is one of the few novels ever written (the most famous example being Ayn Rand's *The Fountainhead*) about the life of an architect. It is also a perceptive novel about someone with dignity, commonsense and kindness making the best of a marriage entered into (in romantic, Forsterian Italy) with more impetuousness than judgement, who has children he does not understand but again tries to make the best of.

****

Bricks and Mortar was published in a peak year for women writers: a curiously large number of them published books in 1932. Like several other Persephone novels, it was published by Victor Gollancz. It did respectably, but in America was a bestseller and had a much larger print run: we have used the 1933 Doubleday, Doran version because it has been impossible to find a copy of the English edition other than in the British Library.

The ephemeral nature of these novels is apparent from the frontispiece of the English edition. It quotes glowing reviews of *Mackerel Sky* (1930); but although *Bricks and Mortar* came out barely two years later, *Mackerel Sky* is by now 'Out of Print'. By 1933 *Mackerel Sky* and *Bricks and Mortar* had the accolade of being in a Tauchnitz edition; but none of Helen Ashton's novels were ever in Penguin.

The Times Literary Supplement's review appeared on 11 February 1932. The anonymous reviewer, whom we now know to be Orlo Williams the literary critic, wrote:

> "The Lovells were a typical family of the professional classes in their time, reasonably prosperous, respectably if not brilliantly connected, rather more cultivated than the average, friendly, interested and given to much simple hospitality." These words, which occur about half way through Helen Ashton's novel *Bricks and Mortar*, are a very true description of Martin Lovell, architect, his wife Letty, his son Aubrey, and his daughter Stacy, whose life forms the whole of this quiet but attractive novel.

BRICKS AND MORTAR

I

MARTIN LOVELL met Letty Stapleford in Rome, in the autumn of 1892. He was twenty-four years old at that date and as innocent as he looked, a very decent, simple, sweet-minded creature, sensitive and easily distressed or shocked, very earnest about the things in which he believed, ambitious, as his age demanded, but rather because he wished to create than to possess. In person he was tall and rather awkward, with long, powerful limbs which were not yet altogether under his own control, so that he strode when he walked, sprawled when he sat, and was no use at any kind of game. He had grey, honest, visionary eyes, which stared happily upon the world from under a bumpy, intelligent forehead; his mouth was amiable and wide, his hair long, untidy and bright brown. His clothes were old and shabby, he obviously needed some woman to look after them. He talked with an enthusiastic stammer and an engaging humble deference; and on his own subjects he could be eloquent. His hands were his best feature, large, powerful, well-shaped, and very delicate in their movements. Their readiness with pencil and paper and a certain glancing excitement in his eye made the old ladies in his pension take him at first for an art-student; in point of fact he was an architect, and very much in love with his profession.

He had arrived in Rome on a wet April morning, dazed with sleep, after sitting through a night-journey between a snuffy priest and a cigar-smoking commercial traveller. The air of the third-class carriage had become intolerably foul and thick: Martin was not able to get the window open until the express slowed down to encircle the city, then he stuck his head out into the cold, raw morning, expecting he knew not what magnificence of ruin. His hot young eyes perceived a dull confusion of flat brown hollow-tiled roofs and smoking chimneys gathered together under wet heavy rain-clouds, a low hill or two, crowned with cypress-trees behind garden walls, an unexpected and unexplained little pyramid, innumerable gas-works and factory chimneys, and the backs of many shabby stuccoed houses with closed unpainted shutters and laundry drying on their balconies. Then came a passing, bewildering vision of what seemed no more than a range of railway arches, one on top of another; he thought too late, "That couldn't really have been an aqueduct, could it?" Then he was carried on between hoardings covered with peeling advertisements and under a station roof, and descended into a crowd of shouting, gesticulating foreigners, who shouldered him in all directions and impressed his insignificance upon him.

He emerged from the station into pouring rain, which spouted from the tramlines and ran down the glistening umbrellas over the little carriages, and darkened the coats of the patient waiting cab horses; he might have been in London except for that enormous, tumbledown heap of Roman brickwork across the square, behind the blowing spray from the fountain, which looked so like a piece of modern house-breakers' work and yet was the Baths of Diocletian.

The pension to which he drove was the usual tall, bare, comfortless haunt of poor and simple persons like himself: it was in a street of trams going up to the Pincian Hill and afforded him a stifling attic bedroom under the tiles with a leaky roof, a red brick floor, some elaborately carved and hideous black-walnut furniture, a hard, uncomfortable bed and a breath-taking view of the domes and roofs and chimneys and triumphal columns of the city, all glistening together in the rain, and the dome of St. Peter's looming under a tearful sky beyond. He dumped his luggage and rushed out enthusiastically into the wet with his maps and his guide-book; he was too young to waste an hour of his first day in Rome.

He wandered for hours, confused, tongue-tied and ecstatic, through the cold, dripping, crowded streets, staring down into the monstrous hollows of excavations, up at the gesticulating statues on church and column, and into the yellow vortices of Tiber, chafing at his bridges and swollen with rain. All that was pure bliss, but when he came back in the evening, footsore and dazed, it became immediately obvious that the evening meal at the pension was going to be an alarming function. He had not realised the importance of punctuality; the long table was full, and the harassed waiter was already clearing the first course. Martin stumbled to his place in the far corner past a line of critical, accusing eyes; he was blushingly conscious of plain and elderly ladies, of a thin clergyman with a straggling beard and a stout German with his napkin tucked

into his collar. Too shy to realise his immediate neighbours, the boy fell over a pair of feet, slid into his
place, took a spoonful of cold macaroni and choked on
it, then looked up and found himself sitting opposite
to the prettiest girl in the world.

In theory, he fell in love with Letty Stapleford at
that moment, and when this view of the matter was
suggested to him later he accepted it with enthusiasm.
Actually, of course, he was far too confused to do
more than stare at her helplessly, hope that he need
not talk to her, and turn for refuge to her mother, who
sat beside him, and asked politely whether this was
his first visit to Rome.

Lady Stapleford had been the wife of a certain Sir
Aubrey Stapleford, an unsuccessful barrister who had
compromised on an Indian jùdgeship and died before
he had earned his pension. His widow was a thin, elegant, obstinate little woman, well-connected, poor, skilful at concealing her economies, and quietly, desperately determined to marry her pretty daughter to the
first eligible comer. It would have taken a more resolute young man than Martin Lovell to oppose her in
this or any other matter on which she had set her heart.
Letty Stapleford was eighteen years old, small, sweet,
rosy and delicious, with forget-me-not eyes and smooth
golden hair. Martin thought her just like one of those
blue-and-white Della Robbia Madonnas whose glazed
smile flowers above the altar of a Florentine church.
She had very little to say for herself, and indeed she
seldom got a chance to open her soft lips when her
mother was about; but her voice was so musical in its
young cadence, so gentle in its hesitations, that you
could not but take pleasure in provoking her to speech.

She had pretty, caressing ways and an affectionate nature, and she had been early slapped and scolded into what now seemed a native docility; she was good, sweet, and sensible and gave her mother no trouble. Lady Stapleford put her very skilfully through her paces in public, criticised her unmercifully in private for any schoolgirl clumsiness, economised constantly to give her clothes, education and opportunities, and was prepared to sacrifice herself and everyone else to secure her child's future. She did not intend Letty to wait about for two years or three years and become critical and fanciful; she believed that any girl could be married off in her first season if handled properly: after that the matter became progressively more difficult and uncertain, and she had laid her plans accordingly. She pounced with the precision of social experience upon the defenceless and unpractised Martin and extracted from him in the simplest and easiest manner, during the progress of the interminable meal, every detail that was to her purpose.

"No, I don't paint," said Martin. "I haven't come for the galleries. I want to go round the excavations and measure up the buildings and all that. You see, I'm going to be an architect." He admitted it with a lover's blush, which was lost on both of them. Lady Stapleford said, rather disparagingly, "A very useful profession." Letty, who had profited by her mother's maxims and knew that it was her business to sympathise with young men when they talked about their work, raised her Madonna lids, and ventured, "It must be very interesting to build a house."

"It's f-frightfully interesting," the boy stammered, turning round incautiously, and losing himself in the

spell of blue eyes which had been bred and trained
for that very end. "P-people think," stuttered Martin,
"that it's all very dull and stupid, but it isn't. Bricks
and mortar are the most fascinating things in the
world." He really thought so, and it did not occur to
him that the pretty girl who listened so dutifully to
his inarticulate exposition had really very little notion
of what he was talking about. Lady Stapleford listened
watchfully, slipped in a deft word or two when Letty
fumbled her answers and encouraged the boy to
blunder on, exposing his defenceless innocence and ar-
dent youth. She got him back quite easily from Roman
architecture to himself and his circumstances, his
orphaned, independent state, his enthusiasms and his
future. "Yes," explained Martin at intervals, "my
father was a parson, but he's dead, and my mother
died when I was a baby. Yes, those Wiltshire Lovells
are cousins of mine. No, the old general was only a distant relation. I suppose you met him in India. It was
his cousin, the solicitor, who brought me up. But I'm
on my own now; and I can do what I like. I always told
Uncle Dick that I wanted to be an architect, and he
gave way in the end. He couldn't stop me. The money
came to me absolutely, anyhow, when I was twenty-
one, so he made the best of a bad job. Yes, I'm through
my articles now. I've been with a firm in Manchester
since I was eighteen. No, I'm not going back there
again. I've finished all my R. I. B. A. exams, and I've
got an assistant's job in London. I'm going into Nicholas Barford's office." He was evidently proud of this;
it meant more to him that it did to Letty, who knew
nothing about these matters, but said politely, "How
splendid!" and made him colour.

Lady Stapleford assimilated his information, so transparently and evidently genuine, so easily checked by familiar names and details. He was obviously in her own class and respectably, if not brilliantly, connected, as obviously malleable, unsuspicious, easy to handle and already attracted by her daughter. It would have been folly to neglect so unforeseen and promising an opportunity in this manless desert of the cheaper Italian pensions, where they were concluding a last educational winter before Letty's début. He would do for Letty to practise upon, even if he were of no more permanent value. To a woman of Lady Stapleford's experience there was a hopeful promise in the eager youthful voice which was now asking Letty whether she had seen the super-imposed basilicas of San Clemente, and the lost waters running through the wet chapel of Mithras in the cellars below them. "I think we went there last Thursday," said Letty, doubtfully, not remembering the name.

"Of course we did," her mother swiftly interrupted, "but we were late, and they were just shutting up. We couldn't get inside. We shall have to go again and see the place properly, it was much too interesting to hurry over. Perhaps we might make an expedition together."

"I should l-love that," stammered Martin fervently, and the matter was arranged before they parted for the night.

"Mr. Lovell seems a very pleasant young man," Lady Stapleford told her daughter in their bedroom, burnishing the golden hair with its brisk nightly hundred strokes. "We shall find him useful to go about with. But you'll have to take more trouble about reading up your Baedeker, child, or you'll never be able to keep up an intelligent conversation with him. You were perfectly ridiculous and stupid about that church of his and I was quite ashamed of you." She brushed out a tangle with a determination which brought tears into her daughter's eyes.

2

Martin fell in love with Letty quite simply and immediately, without any suspicion that the matter was being arranged for him. He mooned about after her, watched her across the dinner-table with unconcealed adoration, and manœuvred constantly for a chance to go with her and her domineering, efficient little mother to visit some church or gallery or ruin. The whole business interfered very considerably with the plan of study which he had made for himself before he came, but he was far too bemused and blissful to regret the fact: it never occurred to him that Lady Stapleford had the whole delicate situation well in hand, that she would have planned the expeditions if he had not done so, or that Letty was given no chance of escaping from them. He did not even suspect that the girl found them a little exhausting. She tired easily in the hot September weather, turned pale and silent at the end of a long afternoon, and found it difficult to respond to all Martin's enthusiasms, for, although there was a theory that she had come to Rome to study Italian Art, like other young ladies of the period, such things did not really mean much to her. At the bottom of her childish heart she found the cats that slunk about in the grass-grown pit of Trajan's Forum more amusing than the whole white company of statues in the Vatican. She would have preferred a shop window on the sunny side of the Corso to any of the cold Roman palaces with their ceilings coloured like the morning sky and their hard, echoing, interminable marble floors. She longed for the English tea-rooms in the Piazza di Spagna all through the long afternoons in the churches, which all seemed to her exactly alike, with their flaring candles, gilt mosaics, salvaged antique porphyry and jasper columns, crowded monuments and smell of stale incense and dirt. She enjoyed her one picnic among the blue distances of the Campagna, between a striding aqueduct and a broken tomb, better than all her rattling drives over the cobbles of the dirty, smelly, narrow streets, between the tumble-down slum-houses, patched with antique stone and marble, and roofed with the romantic hollow tiles, which were Martin's delight. Secretly, she would have preferred a young man who bought her chocolates, or gloves, or scented roses from the flower-stalls at the street corners to a discreet, clumsy youth like Martin, who talked to her about matters which she did not understand, and lent her books which made her head ache. However, she was too gentle and simple to find any fault with the boy for ignoring her preferences. She thought him very clever to know as much as he did and she submitted with the sweetest docility to interminable lectures on "firmness, commodity, and delight" and all other principles of the mistress Art. She did not dislike him; indeed, she liked him as well as she would have liked any personable young man who found her beautiful, and conveyed it with just that tremor of uncontrolled devotion. It was her first experience of the kind, and she accepted

it placidly enough: if she had been forbidden to love
him she would have cried and obeyed; when she was
told to love him she would smile and find it easy. As
for Martin, his case was obvious and satisfactory.
Lady Stapleford decided that point at her leisure, following the two of them discreetly round excavations
and museums, and consoling herself for any necessary
tedium which she endured by reminding herself that
her penniless, pretty, foolish daughter might have gone
much further, and fared much worse, in her search for
a suitable husband. "I can never be too thankful to
Margaret Grey for recommending that pension," reflected Lady Stapleford ten days later as she waited
for the two young people under the encircling gaze of
the empty eye-sockets of the Colosseum, and decided
that another week should settle the matter.

Martin was as unconscious as the girl herself at first,
and hardly knew what was the matter with him; when
he began to realise his own state he plunged himself
into unnecessary anxieties by supposing that he was unworthy of his delicious Letty, and would never be allowed to marry her. Indeed the idea of marriage had
as yet hardly occurred to him; it was something that
happened to grown-up people, and he hardly thought
of himself yet as grown-up. He was young for his years
and only at the beginning of his career; he had vaguely
supposed that in five or ten years' time he would be
ready to find himself a wife and a home. Lady Stapleford, however, knew his business better than he did,
and he was not permitted to stand in the way of her
arrangements. She took him for a walk on an appointed
afternoon, among the moss-corroded, sun-flecked altars
and terminal statues of the Borghese Gardens, and sit-

ting on a stone seat, under the dry, warm rustle of an ilex-tree, she told him, with a good deal of point, that his delays were making Letty unhappy.

"I thought," said she, in her high, light, rather petu-lant tones, going straight to the heart of the matter, "that you were so devoted to Letty."

Martin protested with truth that he was very much in love with Letty. It was the first time that he had put the fact into words and the colour came up all over his honest young face: he stammered a good deal over the admission, and Lady Stapleford felt annoyed by his incompetence. However, his answer was satisfac-tory enough, as far as it went, and she concealed her impatience with a maternal smile. "Well, my dear boy, why don't you tell her so?" she demanded. Martin stammered more than ever. "You can't expect a child like Letty to guess these things," said Lady Stapleford, with a little more edge to her voice; and she added, so that there should be no mistake in his mind, "Of course I saw how you felt about her from the very first."

Martin had been so ignorant of his own feelings that his breath was quite taken away: he could only stutter, "Letty would never look at me."

"You can't be certain of that till you ask her," said Lady Stapleford, pinning down her captive with a smile which appeared to him extremely sympathetic. "Of course I shall leave her to make up her own mind about marrying you; but I think—mind you, I only say I *think*—that the child is very fond of you." She gave a little genuine, effective sigh, and breathed, "I don't know what I shall do without her," and she looked anxiously out of the corners of her eyes to see whether she had made her effect. She dared not risk any slip at this point: there was everything at stake for pretty, silly, useless Letty, and she was hardly able to breathe while she waited for the boy's answer.

Martin did not know whether he was on his head or his heels. He accepted her deft introduction of the marriage-notion without a protest, it appeared to him by this time that he had thought of it for himself. "Of course I'd give anything to marry Letty," he murmured weakly, "if only she'd have me."

Lady Stapleford allowed an incautious, unconscious sigh of relief to escape her, but Martin did not notice it: he was bemused by dreams of his Della Robbia Madonna and her young, lovely smile.

"In that case," promised Lady Stapleford, fortifying the captured position lest he should indulge in second thoughts, "I'll see that you get a chance to talk to her to-morrow and you shall tell her all about it. I know you'll be glad to have everything settled"; and she concluded with alarming graciousness, "You've made me very happy, Martin. There's nobody I'd rather have for a son-in-law."

Martin nodded gravely. He was appalled and fascinated by his prospects, they gave him what in those days he regarded as a sleepless night. Lady Stapleford had kept him cunningly at a distance all that evening and shown him Letty talking to a couple of newly-arrived friends from England, too busy to notice him; she had taken the girl up to bed with only a public good night, and had left him to fret himself into a fever at his window, staring, through long hours of the hot September moonlight, at the shining roofs of the city and the motionless cypresses on the Palatine Hill, and trying to realise what was happening to him.

They had planned to go to the Forum, and Martin shyly and dutifully took his place with them after breakfast in a dirty little open cab with a sheepskin rug, a striped umbrella, and red pompons on the tasselled harness. They were rattled away over the cobblestones at a pace which made conversation impossible. Martin, sliding about on the little seat, with his back to the raw-boned horse and the vociferous driver, had more opportunity than courage to steal glances at the girl, who seemed not unlikely to spend the rest of her life in his company. She wore an absurd blue and white striped dress, tight-laced and flounced at the hips and shoulders in the fashion of the time; she had bought a flat, tilted hat of Italian straw, and underneath it, where her skin took on a faint, golden glow, there was a trembling, reflected light upon the contours of her childish face. She kept her long lashes down. The young man noticed for the first time that their infantile gold was tipped with brown, and this detail had an exquisite significance for him; it was one of a thousand things in her which he might presently claim the right to discover. Her blue-and-white striped parasol had not preserved her from two or three delicious cowslip freckles across the bridge of her little, turned-up nose. The boy could imagine kissing them much more easily than he could imagine kissing her fresh red lips. He adored her, and he was terrified of her, and he could think of nothing at all to say to her. He fixed his eyes, dazed and fascinated, upon Lady Stapleford, sitting as straight as a queen in her brown holland coat and skirt, holding her green-lined sunshade above the stiff tilt of her sailor hat to defy the Roman sun, and compressing her nostrils in disgust at the smell of the narrow, dirty streets. They got out of the little carriage at the turnstiles of the Forum, and descended into the immense rubbish-heap of fallen columns, crumbling walls, broken vaults and lost masses of brickwork and marble, tumbled together in the flowery grass. They had repelled the importunities of the chattering guides, but Martin set himself most earnestly to point out the foundation-plan of the different buildings. His chief wish and dread was that he might be left alone with Letty.

It was a fine autumn morning, there was a light air blowing but the sunshine was hot and beat back from the dusty stones. Martin stammered and gesticulated with his usual characteristic enthusiasm, arguing dates and styles with a text-book in his hand and his long hair dishevelled on his forehead, as he stared up at the tiers of classic, mediæval and Renaissance masonry which sheathe the precipice of the Capitol. Letty listened politely with her blue eyes fixed upon him, but he did not look at her; he was absorbed in his own subject, and the girl began to droop. Lady Stapleford understood her daughter's mournful look, and decided that Martin had wasted enough of the morning. She glanced impatiently at the three monstrous coffered brick half-domes of the Basilica of Constantine as they approached it, yawned, tapped her foot, and interrupted briskly, "My dear Martin, this heat is too much for me; I shall have to sit down and rest. Take Letty round to look at that triumphal arch we missed before and then we really must go home. It doesn't do to be out too long in the sun at this time of year."

"I thought we might go closer and look at the vaulting," stammered Martin, arrested in full career, and terrified by the final approach of his interview with Letty.

Lady Stapleford gave a little shriek of horror. "You mustn't take Letty in among those cold ruins when she's been standing about in the sun. It's the very way to give her a chill. No, just a stroll down to the arch and back, and then we must go home." She added with significance, "No need to hurry and get overheated. I shall be perfectly happy sitting here by myself in the shade, thinking over what you told us." She furled her parasol with a decisive snap, and seated herself like a resolute little general upon a dusty bench under the Temple of Romulus, just where a twisted fig-tree clung to its circular wall.

Martin and Letty walked dutifully and unhappily back to look at the little yellow Arch of Titus. There did not seem to be anything particular to say about it when they got there; and after they had made a circle round it, keeping carefully a pace or two apart, and had identified the seven-branched candlestick from Jerusalem on the soffit of the arch, Letty, who was much too inexperienced to control the situation, supposed, with a certain melancholy, that they had better go back to her mother.

Martin opened his lips to assent, but found himself begging hastily, "Don't do that yet. Let's sit down in the shade."

She gave him a fluttering, captive look, which betrayed her knowledge of his thoughts; but the boy was too much in earnest to enjoy her confusion, it merely added to his own distress. He found her a place, on a broken Corinthian capital, where she perched and preened like a bird, settling her blue and white flounces

about her; then he dropped on the grass at her feet.
She looked down at him, shy and considering; it would
have been evident to an observer that she did not know
what to do with him. They were as ill at ease as a couple of children who have never met before. They were
in the shade of the ivied terraces on the red Palatine
cliff, and the grass about them was full of little bright
coloured flowers. Martin picked three of them, very
solemnly, to occupy his unsteady fingers, then put them
in Letty's lap, as if he felt that they belonged to her.
A lizard came out of a crevice between the ancient
stones, and remained motionless, staring at them out of
its bright eyes, its green throat trembling with terror.
Martin touched Letty's hand stealthily to show her the
creature; it vanished on the instant, but the girl looked
at him with just the same startled eyes and tremulous
throat and he felt that in a moment she too would dart
away from him. His grip tightened and for the first
time he thought of her as a possession to be attained.
"Letty," he besought her, "don't go away!"

Her hand trembled and was still; he relaxed his
fingers a little but hers were not withdrawn, and his
courage grew.

"You must listen," he commanded, stumbling in his
speech, "I can't do without you. I never thought there
could be anybody like you. I want you to marry me,
but I suppose you never could." He bungled the whole
business horribly, he was stammering, embarrassed, his
honest eyes were fixed imploringly upon her, he clung
tightly and agonisingly to her fingers. "I do love you—
I do love you," he told her, as if he needed to convince
himself and her by the repetition, and then, as she

trembled and did not answer, he burst out desperately:
"Oh! Letty, couldn't you marry me?"

She turned the flower-blue eyes to his; her lips
trembled, she nodded as gravely as a child, and seemed
not to know what to do next. They stared at each
other, innocently afraid, lost together in a strange
country. The boy put out a groping hand, the girl lifted
an uncertain mouth towards her first embrace. Drawing back from it, Martin could see the wet, golden-
brown lashes as near as he chose, but they hid the blue
eyes from him, and he whispered, "Look at me." She
obeyed him meekly; a quicker pupil than she, he kissed
again, and this time found it pleasure. His arms learnt
confidence, and taught submission; he discovered the
vigour of his own youth. Letty showed him an infantile
tenderness, faltering and sweet: she smiled and sighed
and listened while he planned a boastful future, she believed everything that he told her. They were perfectly
happy among the flowering grasses, while their hour
lasted, in a world of their own.

Under the writhing roots of the dead fig-tree that
grew out of what had been the Temple of Romulus,
Letty's mother blinked resolutely through the midday
glare at the dusty imperial ruins and watched the passage of time, and realised, with a slow sense of exhaustion, that her campaign had succeeded.

3

Next day Martin had a further confusing talk with
his chosen mother-in-law about money matters. Lady
Stapleford began with an artistic and deliberate vague-

ness, "My dear husband used to manage all these
things for me. I find it so difficult to get on without
him. He would have told me what was best to do. I
only want my girl to be happy." She had satisfied herself already, by discreet enquiries, about Martin's private means and prospects, but she did not know how
practical or miserly his temper might be. She soon perceived, however, that he was as indefinite and generous
as any mother could wish, and it became perfectly easy
for her to glide over the central fact that pretty Letty
had no money of her own at present, and very little
to expect.

"Dear Aubrey left me a life-interest in everything,"
said Lady Stapleford, "but it all goes to Letty after
my death. Of course, he knew he could trust me to do
everything in my power for her, but you've no idea
how difficult things have been. Aubrey was so unfor-
tunate with all his investments, and a judge's salary is
really quite inadequate in India, with all the entertaining one has to do, and the exchange getting worse and
worse. It simply wasn't possible for us to lay anything
by. But I shall make Letty as large a dress allowance
as I possibly can," promised Lady Stapleford, carefully evading the figures which Martin was far too
inexperienced and embarrassed to require. "I only wish
I could do more for you both, but it really does young
people no harm to start in a small way," maintained
Lady Stapleford, and she continued with a certain
touching candour, "I've done my best to train Letty in
economical ways. We've always had to be careful. She's
content with quite simple pleasures, and she's very
clever at making her own frocks."

Martin was distressed by the apology in her voice.

It almost seemed as if the poor lady were making a belated, remorseful protest against her own conviction that she had treated him unfairly.

"I'm so thankful," admitted Lady Stapleford, in one of her rare defenceless moments of candour, "that Letty's found a good husband. She terribly needs to be looked after. She's such an inexperienced, childish little thing, and she's always depended on me for everything. I know you'll shelter her in every way." She gave Martin a queer desperate look, as if he were her only hope: the boy caught a glimpse of some struggle which he did not understand. It actually frightened him, he clenched his fists, and drew a deep breath, which seemed to choke him; he could not express the surge of protective pity which overcame him. "I'll do my best," he muttered.

Lady Stapleford gave him one of her quick considering looks, which made him feel inadequately young; then, apparently satisfied, dismissed him to the less exacting company of her daughter.

Letty was even more happily vague in her notions than Martin himself; she had been brought up to shy away from the mention of money as if there were something rather disgraceful about it.

"I'm sure everything will be lovely," was her refrain when Martin tried to be definite. "We shall have to be very economical to start with," Martin pointed out without any very clear idea of how this object was to be attained. "Of course I'm very lucky to have got this job under old Nick Barford, but he won't pay me much for a year or two. I'm supposed to be going there for the sake of the experience. It's a great thing for me to be in the office of a man like that."

Letty did not know very much about that eminent
architect, Nicholas Barford, with his large commer-
cialised practice, his office in Bedford Row, his various assistants and draughtsmen, and his peculiar personality.

"I'm afraid I never heard of him before," she murmured, lifting a dove-like glance which pleaded for indulgence.

Martin laughed and did not seem annoyed. "No
earthly reason why you should, darling, even if you'd
spent your life in London instead of at school and out
here." And he added cheerfully, "Nobody ever knows
the name of an architect. We don't sign our buildings
and we belong to the Cinderella of the professions.
People go cheerfully about, shutting their eyes to
everything we put up. The most you ever hear said is,
"There's some sort of new building going up at the
corner of Regent Street; I don't think I like it much.
Why can't they leave London alone?" Letty laughed
as dutifully at this as she did when her mother made
fun of the other guests in the pension, and Martin, encouraged, continued, "All the same, Old Nick is rather
a big fellow in his way."

"What's he like himself?" asked Letty with feminine curiosity.

"Oh! a queer old boy, vigorous, excitable, always in
a hurry. I've only met him once. I get on with him all
right," said Martin carelessly, and reverted to an
aspect of his chief which interested him more. "He
builds banks and town halls and things of that kind, a
lot of important stuff. I think his work is rather ugly
myself, but he's in quite a big way and he can teach me
all sorts of things I don't know about the practical side

of the business. When I've been with him a year or two
I shall try and get away on my own, and build houses.
That's what I like best, you know." If Letty did not
know by this time, it was not for want of telling; but
she listened as sympathetically as ever while he abused
the inconvenient houses of the time, and described, with
youthful and unpractical fervour, the kind of home that
he would like to build. "And as soon as we can possibly
afford it I'll build us one for ourselves," he told her
fondly.

Letty appreciated that plan much more readily, and
even made little suggestions which delighted him; on
this plane she could satisfy him much more easily than
over his classical jargon of pedestal, and shaft and
entablature, or the pilasters and cornices of his Renaissance façades. She had her share of the nest-building
instinct, and everything else Martin fondly supposed
that he could teach her when he had her to himself.
"Because I do want," Letty assured him wistfully, "to
understand all about your work if I can." It was easy
for him to believe that possible, and he was not after
all such a pedantic young fool as to criticise too closely
whatever was spoken by that sweet, trailing, hesitating
voice, or with that little timid, appealing, delicious
smile. Letty might have been much more foolish than
she was before Martin at this stage would have noticed
any defect in her.

A little later the question of the wedding was intro-
duced. Martin had vaguely supposed that they would
be engaged for some months, or even a year, that he
would return to Mr. Barford's office and console himself for the delay by hard work and a delicious correspondence with Letty, and that in due course he would

find himself, by some process which he did not fully
understand, possessed of an income, a circle of clients
and a shrine in which to place his Madonna. It presently appeared, however, that he had mistaken the position entirely. "You see, my dear boy," Letty's mother
explained to him, "Letty and I have no home for her
to be married from. Aubrey died just when we were
going to retire, and since then she and I have been wandering about the Continent trying to economise and to
finish Letty's education. I was to take Letty to London
this summer and present her and get her aunts to take
her about to a few parties; but what's the use of that
now? She doesn't want to meet any other young men,
she's quite satisfied with you." Her sweet, finished,
slightly insincere smile, as it wandered over Martin,
concealed her relief at having been spared the necessity for this hazardous campaign. "Now I don't believe," said Lady Stapleford with deceptive candour,
"in keeping young people waiting about after they've
made up their minds to marry each other. Parents
ought to make every sacrifice, and give their children
their happiness while they're young enough to enjoy
it. You're twenty-five and independent and all alone
in the world, and Letty has no one to consider except
me. I should not dream of standing in her way. It
would be extremely selfish of me," said the judge's
widow, who did not mean to incur the expense of a
London wedding, or risk the sobering effect of a
change of scene and the likelihood of a young man's
inconstancy. "It really seems to me that the best thing
you both can do is to have a quiet wedding out here in
the English Church, and a little honeymoon on the
way home to England, and then you can settle down

without any more waste of time, and get on with your work." Martin was in no case to quarrel with any plan which would place his yielding, lovely virgin so promptly and unexpectedly in his arms. He stammered, of course, and hesitated, and felt as if there were something obscurely and fatally illegal about the whole matter, but he brought forward no objections which Lady Stapleford could not demolish. His own sense of guilt and insecurity was manifestly absurd, and he argued himself out of it in one warm sleepless Roman night. He adored his Letty and she was obviously there for the taking; he was his own master, and there was no evident reason for delay. "Give him time to get used to the idea," reflected Lady Stapleford, "and he's bound to give in." She was perfectly right in her calculations: Martin took fire, and began to chafe at even the slight delays which were caused by legal formalities and by the acquisition of Letty's small, convent-made trousseau. But in spite of his impatience the days ran out; the two young people paid their last visit to their own corner of the Forum and saw their last sunset from the hanging Pincian terraces, and sighed perfunctorily over Martin's list of unvisited monuments as they flung their votive pence on their last evening into the dashing, spouting stream of Trevi.

"But we can come back again in a year or two when we've made our fortunes, and do all the things we haven't had time for," declared Martin with confidence. His penny dropped into the foaming turmoil beneath the chariot of Neptune, far out of reach of recovery, under the stony gaze of the nymphs and Tritons in their artificial grottoes, and he added with a laugh, "That makes it certain."

"Mine didn't go far enough," confessed Letty, rather mournfully. "One of those boys has just waded in and fished it out again. I suppose that means I shan't come back." She gave an odd, premonitory shiver. Martin, however, squeezed her arm in his, and declared stoutly, "I'm not coming back here without you. After to-morrow we shall do everything together for the rest of our lives." She clung to his arm rather forlornly, shivered again, said that the sunset air made her feel chilly, and begged to be taken home.

She gave her mother a little trouble that night: the poor child was worn out by Martin's exhausting enthusiasms, her mother's activity, and the confusion of her own feelings: she cried and shuddered, and protested that she did not want to marry anybody yet. However, these inconvenient emotions were not allowed to interfere with her mother's plans. Lady Stapleford took her firmly in hand, gave her, unknown to Martin, such a good slapping and shaking as her eighteen years still occasionally received with meekness, and put her to bed to recover herself. By the morning of the wedding-day she was her own smiling, tearful, tremulous self again, delighted with her trailing flounced white muslin gown, her Leghorn hat, and her bunch of orange-blossom, excited by finding herself the central figure of the day, and not ill-pleased by the prospect of exchanging her mother's domination for the company of a young man who would, she felt instinctively, be wax in her small, uncertain hands. Martin was unusually tidy and very nervous and bewildered. The few acquaintances from the pension chattered and congratulated, and Lady Stapleford managed the whole business with extreme efficiency, from the first dressing and counselling of her daughter, through the meagre ceremonies and the confusion of a festal meal at the pension, to the final packing of her daughter's boxes and the tearful drive to the railway station.

Martin found time to look out of the window as the cab rattled over the tram-lines and Letty dried her tears against her mother's shoulder. He saw the brown brick fragments of the Baths of Diocletian, crowded between the shops and the railway station, looking completely dilapidated, incredible and forlorn; he remembered how dramatic his first sight of them had been when he emerged from that same station a few weeks earlier. Now he was going back to England with this soft, warm, helpless young creature, who had just been handed over to him like a kitten with its eyes shut, and the whole of his life had been upset and changed, by an event which as yet he hardly realised. He had a sudden queer regret for a hundred things which he had meant to do and see by himself in Rome.

He had been lost and drowned in the blue eyes of Letty and the days had gone by him and been wasted. The whole imperial confusion of domes and towers, of obelisks and columns, of temples and colonnades and fountains, lay behind him in an accusing golden sunset. He wondered whether he would ever come back again and make up for all that he had missed: for a moment he was full of regrets, then came the shouting and disturbance of the station, and the climb into the express, and Letty's agitated farewells through the window were interrupted by the unexpected, inadequate sound of the little tin horn. The train moved and hesitated and started, the perspective of the platform receded, it changed with startling rapidity to the backs of tall, tumbledown, patched, brick and stucco tenements, to an unexpected fragment of an aqueduct, to a distant group of statues gesticulating from the portico of the Lateran across a wilderness of flat, brown hollow-tiled roofs, smoky chimneys, gas-works, goods yards, and shunting trucks. Then the carriage began to sway as the train gathered speed for the journey, the hot draught from the open window scattered cinders over the white antimacassars on the cushion, and Martin found himself shut up alone with a frightened, forlorn, beloved creature whose eyes implored him for protection against himself and her destiny.

He did not remember to look out of the window as the city was left behind. He was kissing his wife, and promising her, over and over, "I will be good to you, I will make you happy."

II

MARTIN had had a fanciful notion of spending his
honeymoon in Greece, a sufficiently adventurous proposal for the 'nineties; and had told Letty a great deal
about sun-browned marble columns, rosemary bushes,
black figs, peasant costumes and the blue and delicate
serrations of the mountains, to all of which she listened
open-eyed. However, Lady Stapleford had extin-
guished the project rapidly and mysteriously, though
Martin could never quite discover afterwards with
what arguments she had done it; and he had found
himself committed to a quiet ten days in Hampshire,
and perhaps a little fishing.

They had an emotional, uncomfortable and tiring
journey back to England by way of Genoa, Avignon,
and Paris, in which Letty showed herself helpless and
easily alarmed, and Martin betrayed his inexperience
with porters, hotel-clerks, lost luggage, and foreign
languages. The young couple told each other that
foreign travel was delightful, but both of them were
secretly relieved to find themselves at Romsey, in a
pleasant, dilapidated inn, darkened by unexpectedly
massive and crooked oak beams. Their room had some
fragments of well-proportioned Tudor panelling, and

gave upon an outside gallery overhanging the courtyard. Letty's candle used to gutter in the draught as
she went along this gallery at night, and make her
shadow and her heart jump menacingly together. She
was afraid of the dark, and used to wake Martin up
in the night with alarm when mice scuffled and scam-
pered behind the panelling. But she was altogether in
a timid, tearful state; she fluttered like a caught bird,
she cried and clung to Martin, or cried and pushed him
from her, for no reason that he could discover. Sometimes everything that he did hurt and vexed her, he
felt himself blundering and slow beside her, she pined
and sulked and cried in homesick fits for her mother.
Then, for as little reason, she turned sweet and sunny,
teased him into bewilderment, and left him fascinated
and disheartened. He accepted each mood as final, was
tormented by her petulance, and adored her infrequent
gaiety. They were young, ignorant, and very deeply in
love; both were perplexed to find that their happiness
was not immediate or perfect. From these uncertainties
Martin at least could escape to quiet himself with the
masculine solidity of the Norman abbey. His mind was
refreshed by the squat, chubby columns and the squared
effect of the stilted arches high in the clerestories of
the transepts, by the intricate system of shaft and vault
in the triforium, by the rich, incrusted, geometrical
lines of ornament and by the great perspective of pillars along the stony desert of the nave. The place had
meaning and restraint, it followed a rule, there was no
caprice in its nobility, its image satisfied him and remained with him when the small frets and fervours of
those days were forgotten.

The honeymoon, after all, was much like other

honeymoons. The young couple wandered about and explored the country, made love to each other, discovered differences in taste, and perhaps found time hang a little heavily on their hands. They had the usual contests of unselfishness; Martin would have liked to measure and sketch details in the abbey, but found this kept him too long away from Letty, who soon lost interest when she had to watch him. He wanted to walk, but she dropped behind, limping in her absurd, pretty shoes, along the hot autumn roads, and complained of feeling tired: even when a friend offered him a day's trout-fishing in the water-meadows there was somehow less pleasure in it than he had expected. Letty started out cheerfully enough at his side, in her clean holland dress and her sailor hat, with the pink ribbon round it. She had a satchel full of sketching-things, and Martin carried her camp-stool and umbrella, the food and his own fishing-gear.

They intended to stay out all day, have tea at a cottage, and perhaps wait for the evening rise. It was a lovely autumn morning, the grass of the water-meadows was pale, sunburnt, ragged and heavy with dew, the blackberry hedges under their silver veil of cobwebs had been touched by a frosty finger: the air was cool and very still. They walked a couple of miles up the valley, and Martin established Letty on the step of a stile between a stubble field and a riverside group of elm-trees, with two thatched cottages to occupy her pencil, and the lichened roof of a church. Then, reprieved, he struck off upstream, whistling cheerfully as he went.

It was too bright a day for fishing, actually, and the season was just at an end, but there was always the

chance of a big fish moving up. He went creeping and
crouching, keeping his eyes open for the quiet dimpled
circle off the mouth of a black carrier, or the bubble
breaking under the overhanging grasses of the bank.
He was perfectly and unconsciously happy, but two
hours later, when he returned, he found Letty sitting
very miserably under the green umbrella. She had soon
wearied of her sketch when there was no one to praise
and encourage her. The edges of her clouds had dried
hard, the sky had run down into the roof of the church,
the perspective of the foreground had entirely defeated
her, so that her river ran uphill, and the reflections in
the water had been worked over until they looked
more solid than the trees above them. She was inclined
to sulk at first, to magnify adventures with cows, and
to reproach Martin for neglecting her so long.

"Of course you knew I shouldn't begin lunch without you. I do think you might have come back a little
sooner."

However, these were after all the early days, and
her vexation was diverted by the sight of a brace of fat
and speckled trout shining in their bed of grasses. She
cheered up again and made a nursery picnic of their
lunch, ham sandwiches and chocolate, although the ket-
tle would not boil. There was plenty of laughter under
the green umbrella, and afterwards companionable
idleness; the sketch blew away, unregarded, and perhaps this was as well, for she would never have made
anything of it.

Later she walked up the bank with Martin, and took
a lesson in casting, but she had not the patience to per-
severe with it; and they went home before the evening

rise, because the damp chill of the water-meadows displeased her.

However, it had been a good day, on the whole; and so was the day when they went to Salisbury, and walked on the shaven lawns of the Close, between the comfortable red Georgian houses, and stared up at the delicate worn grey detail of the tremendous spire.

"Nobody knows the name of the man who built that," said Martin to his wife, uttering the last word of a silent meditation: and he added, innocently, "When I was a small boy, you know, I always wanted to build a cathedral. I promised myself that I'd do it when I grew up. I suppose it was because I'd admired my father's church. It was very lovely, you know; a big, lost, useless place on top of the Cotswolds, much too large for the village, typical Perpendicular, light and lovely and empty, 'more glass than wall.' We'll go and see it one of these days, darling, it made an immense impression on me."

"I don't see why you shouldn't build a cathedral," Letty stoutly declared, clinging to his arm.

"I don't suppose I shall ever get the chance," said Martin. "I expect I shall spend my life building semi-detached villas."

He laughed, and so did she; they neither of them thought it likely.

2

They went back to London in the autumn of 1892, and settled into what proved at first a very happy domesticity.

Nicholas Barford's office was in Bedford Row, where he occupied the first floor of a dignified brown eighteenth century house with tall sash-windows, wrought iron balconies and railings of the classic honeysuckle pattern and a fanlight under a hood, supported by console brackets. Within were elaborate plaster ceilings, a staircase with a florid iron balustrade, and some dilapidated pine-panelling which looked as if it had not been repainted for a very long time.

Mr. Barford interviewed his clients in the front room, an elegant but rather dirty saloon with raised panels, a pediment over the door-way, and a marble chimney-piece whose overmantel was surrounded by festoons of carved flowers: its refinement conflicted a little with Mr. Barford's roll-top desk, Victorian horsehair chairs, open bookshelves stacked with dusty letterfiles and framed photographs of completed houses. Behind this room was the drawing-office, very untidy and dirty, with more framed photographs and dilapidated cardboard models of the principal's less successful houses; and many more files in cardboard cylinders, and trays and shallow drawers, full of plans and tracings and working drawings of current jobs. There were three trestle-tables pushed up to the window, an inadequate gas-bracket overhead for night-work, and a perpetual confusion of blue prints and catalogues and samples of bricks and tiles and marble which the inefficient charwoman obediently did not disturb.

The young Lovells had decided to settle round the corner from this office, and had found chambers on a top floor on the north side of Gray's Inn Square. The set was not really very well planned for their purposes;

it had a small bright room looking into the square, which faced south and should have been their living-room, but had unfortunately been fitted up as a kitchen. It had an immense, draughty sitting-room, whose three north windows peeped down through the tasselled branches and freckled, peeling trunks of the plane-trees in the gardens. When these windows were open in the summer you heard the roar of the traffic in Theobald's Road. Between the two rooms, in the middle of the building, was an awkwardly-shaped bedroom with a skylight, very cold in winter and very hot in summer; and across the passage was a kind of cupboard, called his dressing-room, in which Martin kept the hip-bath which was all the place afforded at that date. The rooms were reached by a common staircase, with twisted balusters, and worn treads of silvery oak; the rooms were panelled, and over the sitting-room chimney-piece were heavy swags of beribboned foliage, carved in high relief. Martin loved this room, but Letty found it chilly, and seldom sat in it unless he was at home: she preferred to spend her time in the kitchen.

After an interval of gentility they sank into having their meals there, and Martin's drawings began to invade the sitting-room because of its north light. Letty proved contentedly domestic, though she was neither as skilful nor as economical as Martin had been led to expect. She cut down the hours of their first bleary, dirty, dishonest charwoman, and finally dismissed her; she started out with Martin in the mornings through the postern-gate into Jockey's Fields, and went marketing with a basket in Red Lion Street: she made an absurd picnic out of her cooking and sewing. She was not very successful at first, but she improved with practice. She smartened up her young husband, made him cut his untidy hair, brush his old clothes, and discard a flowing artistic tie to which he had been addicted. They were asked out to one or two formal dinners, and Letty returned wedding-calls in the velvet bonnet and sealskin jacket which were her best clothes in those days. Martin came home to lunch every day and was not at first too busy to spend his evenings at home. He was able to share each little domestic adventure, to laugh at Letty's experiments and extravagances, to enjoy the decoration and furnishing of their rooms and to spend his Saturday afternoons and Sundays exploring the City with his wife on his arm, tracing the line of its old walls and gates, collecting Wren churches, or exploring the archways and gardens of the Inns of Court.

It was as exciting and amusing as their Roman expeditions had been, and it had all the fuller savour because they need not part politely at the end of the afternoon, but could go back up their carved staircase, and shut their outer door on the world and draw the curtains to shut in the light of their own fire.

Lady Stapleford had gone back, with a good deal more tact than Martin expected, to her Italian pension for the winter: and the young couple were left as hidden and insignificant as a pair of pigeons, nesting under the tiles and rafters of Gray's Inn.

3

Nicholas Barford, Old Nick, hardly came up to Martin's preconceived notions of a distinguished architect. He was at that time about fifty-seven or fifty-eight, and he proved to be a robust, cheerful, vulgar, untidy little man, with a ragged tobacco-stained grey moustache, a loud voice and a taste for coarsely humorous anecdote. He looked like a successful builder, and in fact that was what his father had been. Nick had been trained in the best traditions of the Gothic revival. He had assimilated the dictates of Ruskin, professed an apparently genuine admiration for the cardboard intricacies and exhausting detail of the Houses of Parliament, imitated the ornament, but not the religious fervour of Pugin, swore by Sir Gilbert Scott as the flower of the profession and had succeeded in remaining through everything a vigorous, hard-headed and practical individual, with no artistic nonsense about him. His original line had been the clerical-domestic; he had specialised in vicarages, and had turned out an immense number of the substantial dwellings of an earlier period, solid, well-built, uncomfortable and hideous. He had luxuriated in red-and-purple glazed brickwork with terra-cotta trimmings, in plate-glass sash windows framed by groups of lancet arches, in sticky varnished deal woodwork and in orange and claret-coloured stained glass. His houses had combined the maximum of ornament with the minimum of comfort; they had contained high-ceiled, ill-proportioned rooms inadequately warmed by little cast-iron fireplaces, gaslit, beetle-haunted underground kitchens, steep back-breaking stairs and a quantity of labour-making decorative features; but they had satisfied the taste of the time. In addition he had, in his later and more distinguished phase, erected a fair number of public buildings, banks and offices, adorned with the marble discs, grotesque animal capitals, polished pink granite columns and "streaky-bacon" masonry of the bastard Venetian Gothic in which his youth had been instructed. His high-water mark had been a peculiarly hideous town hall somewhere in Wales. It was the pride of his heart; and a framed and coloured perspective of the front elevation hung in the drawing-office at Bedford Row, and afflicted Martin daily with the suspicion that Mr. Barford could not be such a very good architect after all.

In point of fact Old Nick was, as Martin eventually realised, a thoroughly sensible and efficient person, whose mind was preoccupied by a thousand practical details; he did not worry himself at all over questions of æsthetics. He was reasonably honest, or at any rate expensive to bribe, and not easily hoodwinked: his lazy good humour concealed an immense capacity for hard work, and he spared himself as little as he spared others: but he managed his large practice with a casual unconcern which was apt to shock the beginner, who might have supposed that Mr. Barford gave personal attention to all his work. Nick had an affable way with clients, and was no mean diplomatist; he understood how to handle men and he usually got his own way. In private life he was a kindly, amusing old fellow, with no pretensions to gentility. He was a bachelor, lived by himself in a large, cold, comfortless house in Mecklenburgh Square, and had his own amusements.

He came round at an early stage to see what kind of a wife Martin was keeping in Gray's Inn. Letty was alarmed by this visit. She tried to make an occasion of it, and insisted on preparing an unnecessarily elaborate, unpunctual and not very successful lunch, of which

Nick ate largely, joking and teasing her meanwhile. He thought her a pretty girl, but stiff and awkward; she was not his type. He liked a young woman who had something to say for herself, and did not turn thorny when he flirted with her in a fatherly way, pinched her arm or knee, and hinted that he wished he were younger. Letty visibly resented the familiarity of his jokes, and put on a little air of schoolgirl dignity which amused and vexed the old fellow; he praised her looks to Martin afterwards in his own broad and jocular fashion, but he did not come again as often as Letty had feared he might; their acquaintance remained formal.

At the office, however, he and Martin got on excellently, in spite of their temperamental dissimilarity. Nick took a fancy to his shy and awkward assistant, laughed at his youthful enthusiasms, and detected the greed for work which was their only common characteristic. He loaded the young man with drawing, which kept him away from Letty half the night, sent him round London, and into the suburbs and provinces to inspect his various jobs, gave him dull measuring and surveying work to finish, and would say to him constantly, with his cheerful wink: "Good experience for you to see how things look when they're half done. This kind of thing will teach you how to keep the contractor up to his work when you're building something of your own."

However, as the whole office, and later Martin, perfectly well realised, Mr. Barford no longer had the head for scaffolding, especially in the mornings; he preferred to keep off the stagings and wait until there was a solid staircase for him to climb. Martin himself

was never very good at scaffolding, especially in windy
weather. It was to be a handicap to him all his life.
He was obliged to keep his eyes firmly fixed on the
rungs of a ladder, or the planks of the staging, or the
wall in front of him, or the face of the foreman accompanying him, for if he looked sideways or down into
empty air he got an uncertain feeling in the back of
his head, the joints of his knees were loosened and his
damp fingers clutched and slipped on the nearest hold.

However, he contrived to put a fairly good face on
these sensations, though he never became independent
of them, and he learnt to make himself useful in innumerable ways to Mr. Barford, but did not forget his
own ambitions. After six months he passed into the
inevitable stage when he aspired to make his name and
fortune by winning a public competition. Mr. Barford
was cheerfully contemptuous of the notion, which was
an old story to him.

"This isn't the sort of firm that goes in for hundred-
and-fifty-thousand pound competitions for new town
halls," he pointed out to his assistant. "That kind of
thing doesn't pay. You win one, and get a job that lasts
you ten years, perhaps; and you spend the rest of your
life whistling for another one. We prefer to make our
money out of good solid domestic stuff. However, I
don't mind your going in for a little one if you like,
so long as you don't waste too much time on it. You'll
have a lot of fun for your entrance-fee, and it'll keep
you out of my way, and give you a bit of practice in
designing. You'll advertise the office too, if you get any
sort of prize or mention. But you won't do that," he
concluded, rolling about in his chair in his usual manner, and wheezing and laughing. Martin laughed too,

quite politely and cheerfully; he thought Nick was trying to be funny.

"Better try this here church at Little Puddlington, or Snodlington, or whatever it is," advised Nick, turning over the papers on his desk.

"Now where the devil did I put the particulars? Here you are: I knew I'd got 'em somewhere. They send these things all round the big offices. Yes, that's the right sort of job for you to start on, my lad. Any ass can design a church, or a cathedral, for that matter; 'tisn't like a house. The thing's perfectly simple and straightforward. You only stick to the Latin cross, and you can't go wrong. The plan's all settled for you —a nave and a choir and a couple of transepts—some sort of a tower at the crossing to take the bells—leave room for the organ-loft and the vestry—don't forget the heating-apparatus—shove in a few trimmings and the thing's done. Simple as kiss your hand. You're in luck, my boy; it might have been a post-office on a sloping three-cornered site."

Martin took the papers and enquired with diffidence, "Where is the place?"

"Oh! somewhere in Staffordshire or Derbyshire or thereabouts. I forget exactly; but it's one of these bright, respectable suburbs that develop outside manufacturing towns. You go ahead," advised Old Nick, "and stick up something really handsome. It's not your business how they're going to pay for it. You'll get your fees all right, and they can work off the debt with bazaars and so on."

"What's the local style?"

"God knows, I don't! Blue brick with terra-cotta trimmings, I should think," said Mr. Barford. "Give 'em plenty of gargoyles and crockets and a lychgate. It always pays to stick to copy-book Gothic, committees like something they can recognise. Besides, it gives you a chance for windows. You could build any church three times over with the money people will give for memorial windows. They'll shell out, too, for a screen or a reredos, or anything they can carve their names on; but nobody wants to pay for plain bricks and mortar."

Plain bricks and mortar, however, were unfortunately just what appealed to Martin, and at this particular stage of his existence he detested Gothic architecture. So he went away and wasted some weeks of his off-time on a hopelessly inappropriate design which was his salute to Italy. His church came out oblong in plan, like a Roman basilica. The exterior was a simple design in cinnamon-coloured brick; the wide gable of the nave and the sloping roofs of the aisles were covered with pantiles. A fortunate inequality of the site allowed a flight of steps to approach the west entrance, a massive doorway, guarded by crouching lions. Internally, the nave was divided from the aisles by slender pillars supporting semi-circular arches. There was an apsidal choir, decorated with gold mosaic, and covered by a half-dome, through which the light filtered down from concealed lunettes, and these lunettes, and the narrow, round-headed windows of the aisles, were glazed by thin, streaked, cream-and-amber slices of alabaster. The only stained glass was in the great wheel-window which lighted the west end of the nave. Three steps rose to the altar, which was defended by a low alabaster balustrade; there was a yellow Sienese marble pulpit, and the font was an ala-

baster well-head surrounding a sunken pool. On the
south side of the church a double colonnade led past
a little round detached sacristy to a slender campanile,
with an open loggia at the top to release the music of
a peal of bells. Martin was extremely pleased with his
church, and was hurt when Mr. Barford roared with
laughter over the plans, then wiped his eyes and sighed
with rich enjoyment.

"Reminds me of the stuff I used to do when I was a
boy. It just shows what comes of letting you young
chaps loose on the Continent with travelling scholarships, and views on art, and so forth. I suppose you
think you've been very clever and correct. Oh! well,
this kind of thing is good practice for you, even if it
hasn't any market value. Send the design in? Oh,
Lord! Yes, if you like. That won't do you any harm,
or any good either. It'll probably come back unopened.
Committees and assessors and that lot don't bother
themselves much about competitors; they've generally
got somebody waiting behind the scenes, only it makes
the job look more reg'lar-like, to put it up for competition. I know, I've been an assessor myself once or
twice." He winked cheerfully at Martin to see whether
he would swallow the information; then said, more
kindly, "This sort of job always goes to the regular
people, my boy. You'll see when the results come out:
Highly commended, Mr. Martin Lovell, A. R. I. B. A.
Winners: Messrs. Crocket and Finial, the well-known
ecclesiastical architects: that's the ticket. Don't look
so down in the mouth; this stuff is all castles in the air,
you know. You won't take any more interest in it once
you get hold of some real bricks and mortar of your
own. We must see about finding you a little job to

play with by yourself." He grinned once more at Martin's rueful face, then said briskly, "Can't waste any more of the morning on you, my lad, got to get on with our job. Let's see what you've made of those working drawings for Thompson's place."

They returned to the consideration of a red-brick house on Wimbledon Common, in the bastard Jacobean style to which Mr. Barford had lately progressed, all angles and moulded terra-cotta trimmings, embellished within and without by a stained-glass oriel with coats of arms, a battlemented porch and a nail-studded door, a profusion of ornamental plaster work and fumed-oak panelling.

Nick was as pleased with this monstrosity in his own fashion as poor Martin had been with his undigested version of San Zeno; and by and by demanded with exuberant satisfaction, "What do you think of that for a house, eh?"

"I think it's pretty awful," blurted out Martin, still sore from Nick's condemnation of his church.

The head of the firm looked genuinely startled, perplexed, even a little hurt, though there was a characteristic lack of injured or offended dignity in his response. "Why, what's the matter with it?" said he, glancing with a momentary misgiving at the curling sketches, pinned to the bench, from which Martin's sheets of half-inch detail were being developed. The glance seemed to reassure him. "Just some of your artistic nonsense," he decided, without rancour. "There's no pleasing you young chaps. You've all got your heads full of nonsense about Webb, and Nesfield, and Norman Shaw's new houses at Bedford Park. When you're a little older you'll find out that it's the inside of a house the client cares about, not the outside. Take care of the plans and the façade will take care of itself; that's always been my motto. You're in the stage when you want to do the front elevation and fit the rooms in afterwards. I like to start with my planning and stick on the fancy bits later. That's a damned good house, let me tell you. You won't be fit to build as good a one, not for five years you won't." His scowl broke up reluctantly into a shamefaced grin. "Why should I lose my temper with a young pup who doesn't know what he's talking about," he grumbled. "Here, get out of this and find me Jenkinson's last catalogue of sanitary fittings."

Mr. Barford was, naturally, right; Martin did not win his competition nor was he selected for the short list, and the church in Staffordshire was finally erected by Messrs. Crocket and Finial, or somebody like them. Martin had the curiosity to go and look at it some twelve years later, when he was in the neighbourhood, and by that time was capable of being amused by its exact correspondence with the prophecies of Mr. Barford, whose partner he had since become. It was a dreary and pretentious building of red and blue glazed Staffordshire bricks, in a free Decorated style, with a great deal of terra-cotta tracery in the large stained-glass windows, a peculiarly ugly and elaborate sandstone reredos, encaustic floor-tiles and a pulpit and pew-ends carved in light oak. The west end was temporarily bricked up and waiting for a projected tower or spire. There was a notice in the porch of a bazaar to reduce the debt on the building fund.

4

The winter of 1892 was not so pleasant in Gray's
Inn as the autumn had been. Once the warmth of St.
Luke's summer was over there came a melancholy season of rain and fog, when the short chimney smoked,
the panelling cracked and shivered and mysterious
draughts penetrated the ill-fitting doors and windows,
and a bloom of moisture condensed on the walls of the
open staircase.

Martin caught a couple of bad colds, as he usually
did in the winter; and Letty, who had begun to carry
her first child, was sick and squeamish, sat over the
fire all day, and complained that the stairs tired her
back.

Mr. Barford's increasing confidence in Martin, and
a press of work at the office, obliged the young man to
go back there every evening when the nine-o'clock cur-
few had rung its hundred strokes, and leave Letty
lonely in her bed until one or two in the morning, unable to sleep without him, listening nervously to the
cracks and creaks of the old walls, and the fluttering,
scuffling noises of rats behind the panelling. She grew
thin and pallid, lost her bright looks and cried a good
deal for her mother.

Martin found her pitifully touching at this time. She
distracted and bewildered him by her pettishness,
amused him by her simplicity and made his heart ache
with a bruised and tender compassion. She had proved,
when he came to know her, uneducated, ignorant, vain,
weakly impressionable and yet firm in her tiny prejudices, dependent, stupid, and easily hurt: but the
gradual discovery of all these qualities hardly affected

Martin: she had become so much a part of him that it was as if he had realised these failings in himself, and vowed to conquer them. He believed that infinite patience and affection would change his Letty into all that he had once believed her to be: or if she did not change, still he would love her. She was in his mind night and day, everything that he did was done for her, would make a tale that he could tell her, or was part of the life that they had made together. She pleased him absolutely; he wanted no other company.

It could hardly be said that he looked forward to the birth of their child. He kept it out of his mind as far as possible, because he dreaded an unknown disturbance and pain for Letty, who seemed too soft and young to bear it: but his shamefaced and serious pride in the matter was undisturbed by any jealousy. It did not occur to him that the child would be more than a pleasant plaything, which would amuse Letty in his absence without disturbing his enjoyment of her when they were together.

The first invader of their solitude was Lady Stapleford, who came back to London after Christmas and troubled the peace of the little household considerably.

She settled in a boarding-house in South Kensington, full of University of London students and Anglo-Indians on leave. She talked of spending her future summers in England and her winters in Italy, for the sake of avoiding the cold. She declared that her doctor had forbidden her to settle in England permanently. "And besides, my dear Martin, why should an old woman like me trouble about running a house for herself? It isn't as though I could hope to have Letty with me all the time nowadays. I'm often very lonely, it's much better for me to be where I can have company. Besides, I can't afford the expense of buying a lot of furniture, and perhaps a house, too, for it's getting more and more difficult to find leases nowadays. It's much better for me to keep my own expenses down, so that I can help you and Letty when you need it."

Since her return she had adopted an unexpectedly plaintive tone towards Martin: apparently she had forgotten her relief when he took Letty off her hands, and merely resented the fact that it was necessary for her to help her daughter, without enjoying her uninterrupted company. She was jealous of her privileges, insisted on Letty coming to her for some part of every day, and bestowed continual criticism and patronage on the newly-married household. She could not come to a meal without bringing some extra delicacy which she presented, less with an air of affectionate generosity, than as an attempt to make an insufficient meal tolerable. Letty did not discourage these presents, she had always placidly accepted anything that her mother chose to do for her, and probably found the whole business natural and helpful; but Martin felt an underlying suggestion that he did not provide sufficiently for his wife. He was vexed, too, when Lady Stapleford criticised Letty's frocks and presented her with others.

"I like the ones you make yourself better," he blurted out once, with what was for him almost a sulky look.

However, Letty soon laughed him out of that: she, at any rate, appreciated the difference between a home-made frock and a bought one, especially when her baby began to affect her appearance.

"I shall look simply dreadful if I wear my own

clothes just now," she said with a morbid, self-conscious frown. "Besides, it tires me too much, cutting out patterns and sitting over the machine. I've got enough sewing to do as it is." She had been solemnly and childishly important over this business to begin with; but Martin's agitation and her mother's mysterious warnings had ended by frightening her, she became subdued and nervous, paid an unnecessary attention to her own discomforts, indulged in fits of melancholy and took herself very seriously altogether.

Lady Stapleford encouraged her daughter in this attitude and they had long feminine conferences together, from which Martin was pointedly excluded. They went out on innumerable shopping expeditions during which they spent a fair amount of Martin's money, and a good deal more of Lady Stapleford's. Martin vaguely resented this, but he could not forbid it. His sweet and reasonable nature told him that Lady Stapleford must naturally take a deep interest in her grandchild, and it was only her manner of doing it which made him obscurely and illogically jealous. His mind was in a turmoil of pride, disappointment, shamefaced curiosity and fear: the girl with whom he had played and whispered had been mysteriously taken away from him, and instead of her there was this tearful, clumsy, remote being who filled him with a distressed and impotent concern. She did not seem to need him and he could not think of any way to help her; the older woman stood between them, consciously or unconsciously; he could not get past her and find his own Letty again.

The child was born at the end of June, 1893, after two nights of a normal but protracted struggle, which

horrified Martin's inexperience. Lady Stapleford drove
him away from the flat whenever he appeared there,
and indeed, there was no place for him in the cramped
rooms, which rang with Letty's cries and complaints.
She did not seem to want him, or at any rate her
mother declared that she was too ill to see him: a stout
cheerful nurse and a fussy elderly doctor both discouraged his presence and he wandered back to long
nightmare sittings at the office, where Mr. Barford
grinned at him, made the kind of joke which might
have been predicted and, with true kindness, found him
some detailed drawings which occupied him for the
whole of the second night. He had the company of one
of the pupils up till midnight; after that he was alone
under the whistling gas-jets, drawing and measuring
and calculating mechanically, with his mind full of his
wife and the events of the last year. His hand slowed
and his eyes wearied as time went on, an extraordinarily desolate grey light came in by the unshaded window, towards five a drizzling rain fell and made wet
slates and pavements glisten drearily.

About six o'clock Martin's imagination became too
much for him. He convinced himself that his wife must
be dying, and that her mother had neglected to send
for him. He left his drawings and went out into the
streets, shivering in the dawn wind. The way had never
seemed so long from Bedford Row to Gray's Inn; the
postern-gate was shut in Jockey's Fields and he had
to go all the way round by Holborn and knock up the
yawning porter at the lodge.

Everything was absolutely quiet when he got to the
top of his own staircase, and the outer door was shut.
He rang and waited, and rang again; then, losing his

self-control, hammered furiously at the knocker. The door was opened then in a hurry by Lady Stapleford herself, looking extraordinarily tired and faded in a red silk dressing-gown. She was almost incoherent with rage. "Don't make that noise, you'll wake Letty. She mustn't be disturbed."

The boy stood stammering and shaking, hardly able to gasp out the words, "Is she all right?"

"All right, yes, if she's left in peace," said Lady Stapleford crossly. "For goodness' sake come in and let me get back to her." And she added in answer to another almost inaudible enquiry, "Yes, it's over half an hour ago and the doctor's gone. Nurse and I are trying to get things straight. What did you come back for? We'd have sent for you if we'd wanted you."

She pushed him into the neglected, untidy sitting-room, and left him there, giving him, over her shoulder, as she departed, the somewhat disappointed and grudging information, "It's a girl."

Martin sat down in a chair, feeling sick and shaken and conscious of a sense of whirling relief and fatigue. He was absolutely exhausted, he did not want to see Letty or anyone else, he wanted to sit where he was and recover his strength. He could have slept for a week, and perhaps he did sleep for a little time, until he was disturbed by a thin, fretful animal crying in the next room. Startled, he wondered first how Letty's voice could seem so changed and weak; then realised, with a flush of amused, amazed delight, that he was listening to the child. Immediately, he wanted to see it, to find out if it were like Letty, to talk to Letty herself, to feed and to resume a normal existence. The nightmare was over, he was tired, and hungry, and happy, and resentful of the way the women were treating him as an intruder. He opened the door cautiously and stuck his head out into the passage.

The nurse emerged at the same moment from the bed-room; she was large, red-faced, plain, and patronising in her manner, but she appeared to Martin as an angel of goodness when she showed a row of false teeth in a welcoming conspiratorial smile, and enquired with the ghost of an Irish accent, "Did ye want to see yer wife? And Baby? Well, then, why shouldn't ye?"

He did not quite know what he expected in the way of medical horrors, he went into the bedroom with his heart hammering in his throat; but Letty was lying as she lay beside him every morning, with her fair head buried in the pillow and her eyes closed; there was a smile of drowsy, infantile placidity just stirring at the corner of her mouth. He wanted to kiss her, but he had not the heart to wake her.

The baby, when he saw it, appeared to him incredibly small, crumpled, ugly and alarming; it was not at all the delightful miniature of its mother which he had expected; he hardly realised that it was human. However, Lady Stapleford and the nurse insisted that it was a fine specimen of its kind. Letty seemed a little frightened of it, and content to leave it to more professional ministrations than her own; it did not appear to compensate her for the trouble it had caused, and she was curiously disappointed that it was a girl. She alarmed Martin by her shaken apathy and fragile resentment: "I didn't know it was all going to be like this," she wailed in dispirited misery at her own discomforts.

Lady Stapleford sympathised injudiciously, sighed

and nodded, and treated Martin with a faint flavour of reproach. His triumph and relief were darkened by a sense of guilt; he said to the doctor anxiously, "I suppose my wife's had a dreadful time," and was not particularly reassured by the man's weary, professional verdict, "Nothing out of the ordinary, my dear fellow. All this is just a little nervous reaction. If she's encouraged she'll get over it."

Letty did get over it gradually; but she remained uncertain, tremulous and pitiable, and made heavy weather of the small ups-and-downs of her convalescence. She did, however, learn to take a timid, fascinated pleasure in the baby's progress from the small red monkey stage to the smiling, gurgling, contented creature which it afterwards became.

The sight of the two of them together gave Martin a mysterious pleasure, a sense of profound and personal fulfilment, which he had never anticipated and did not attempt to express. His life had struck its first, deep root, he felt himself at once older, safer, and more responsible; by a natural process his ambitions revived, he wanted to finish with Nicholas Barford's work, and get on to something of his own.

There remains, to conclude the episode, the question of the baby's name. It had been rather neglected in their preparations, there had been a tacit assumption that the baby would be a boy, and be called Martin. Martin pleaded for another Letty, but was discouraged on the score of confusion; Letty had never cared for her own name as much as he did, and there seemed to be no satisfactory variation of it available for common use.

Martin, who liked the dignity of the Roman "a"

termination, fell back from Letitia to Julia, and Lydia, and Ursula, and Barbara, the patron saint of builders and architects. However, these suggestions were disregarded in favour of Anastasia, which, it appeared, was Lady Stapleford's name, and a family inheritance. So Anastasia Letitia the baby became. It seemed an overwhelming description of anything so small and simian. "But after all," observed Martin, "we can easily call her Anstice." As a matter of fact, the little girl christened herself Stacy, as soon as she could talk plainly, and Stacy she became and remained.

III

IN THE autumn of 1893 Martin began to build his first
house. It was in the Chilterns and was creditably
abreast of its times, though afterwards he learnt to be
rather ashamed of it. The cheerful irregularities of its
weather-tiles and brick-nogging disguised an imperfectly considered ground plan in which the kitchen
offices were sacrificed to a long and excessively low
parlour. This room had an inconvenient step down in
the middle, due to a miscalculation of levels, a ceiling
crowded with oak beams, latticed casements excluding
the light, and an ingle-nook sheltering an open hearth,
which later smoked intolerably and had to be degraded
by a beaten copper canopy with blue enamel ships in
full sail on its convexities. Upstairs were a couple of
bedroom floors, where the headroom was curtailed by
a picturesque skyline treatment, involving a couple of
half-timbered flying-gables and three attic-dormers
with broad white barge-boards; a staircase turret projected above the rustic porch.

Mr. Barford laughed a good deal in his own apo-
plectic way over these youthful exuberances; but they
were thought very fine by Martin himself, who fussed
like a hen with one chicken over his first adventure into
bricks and mortar, and never grasped the fact that his

principal, with kindly cunning, had turned over to him a fidgety and self-important client, who was likely to cause more trouble than he was worth.

The man was a retired stockbroker, who had been induced by a far-sighted wife to make the building of a house his occupation for his first few idle months. He had endless conferences with the enthusiastic and innocent Martin, who went about for weeks with his pockets full of plans on the backs of old envelopes, and altered his first extravagant draft a dozen times in response to his client's natural but alarming hesitations and economies, before it was finally adopted. Then there were all the working drawings to get out, and Martin was busy for weeks with scale-plans, elevations and sections; he lingered lovingly over the phrases of his first draft-specifications; the bills of quantities and tenders were completed and the actual work began.

Martin and his client went down together by the old ·Metropolitan route from Baker Street on a raw February morning, both imperfectly concealing a schoolboy sense of excitement; and Martin, with an uncertain show of professional authority, marked out the plan of the ground-floor with tape and measuring-pegs among the hard, frozen tussocks of winter grass.

It did not look nearly as large as either of them had expected, and there was one awkward moment when it did not seem quite certain that the bow window in the dining-room would not project beyond the eastern boundary of the site, to which it had been approached in order to leave room for a tennis-court on the west: however, all was well, with a foot or so to spare. The builder's plant arrived, the concrete trenches were set out, and the walls began to rise with an unexpected and gratifying rapidity; and presently the site assumed, for the first time in Martin's experience, that delightful air of confused yet ordered activity which looks so promising to an architect and so disappointing to his clients. He was to discover later that he always liked a house best when the walls had only risen three or four feet between the scaffold-poles; when the doors and window-frames were still empty, and the trodden grass was encumbered by heaps of bricks and drain-pipes and dressed and numbered blocks of stone, inter-sected by trenches, traversed by wheeling-planks, and endangered by dumps of sand and pools of slaked lime. A building was somehow more amusing and promising then than in the later stages when the floor-boards were being hammered down on the joists, when the blind glass panes with their circles of whitewash shut out the view, and the roof was being closed in, and all the rooms looked dark and small and somehow not as pleasant as he had expected.

Everything that was possible went wrong with that first house of Martin's, or so it seemed to him at the time; though when he looked back upon it afterwards, in the light of a fuller experience, he realised that much had been spared him. The builder proved to be a kindly, sensible man, who knew his job, was indul-gent to Martin's artistic fads, and did not allow him-self to be perturbed by the contradictory and impos-sible instructions which he received. The client was easy-going and wealthy and had no pretensions to taste, but accepted what was designed for him; his wife was a sensible, motherly person, who knew what she wanted in the domestic quarters and had taken a fancy to her shy and awkward young architect.

This worthy couple did not change their minds more than half-a-dozen times over the sketch-plans, nor suggest extensive alterations after the foundations were laid, nor order extras and then disclaim them; they knew what they were prepared to spend and they were not unduly impatient to get into the house before it was finished. Naturally neither they nor Martin had realised how many untoward accidents, unforeseen expenses, and inevitable delays might occur; what trouble might arise from green mortar, sweating brickwork, unseasoned wood, cracked radiators and leaking pipes, frost and rain, the stupidity or idleness of workmen and Martin's own youthful blunders and miscalculations; or how startlingly forgotten extras, lightly ordered, might swell the builder's final statement of account. However, the house was completed, inhabited and paid for; if it did not altogether satisfy its architect or its owner it was not, on the whole, a bad piece of work.

It was during the building of this house and of others which followed it that Martin learnt to appreciate Nicholas Barford for more genuine reasons than his first flattered admiration of prosperity and success. He came to understand the older man's good sense, industry and vigour, to realise the extent of his early, unfailing kindness towards an ignorant beginner, and to enjoy his valiant, vulgar good humour and scorn of difficulties. He found out how much it was possible to depend on Mr. Barford in trouble, how valuable his shrewd practical advice could be, and how profound his knowledge of human nature. It was also impossible for even so innocent a person as Martin not to realise in the end exactly what Mr. Barford's standards of professional honesty were, and at what practices he was accustomed to draw his wavering line of disapproval.

In Martin's assistant days his absent-minded grey eyes had missed much that lay perfectly clearly before them. He did not begin to realise, as a more astute person would early have realised, that there were certain occasions when his dislike of scaffolding did not prevent Mr. Barford from making his own inspection of an unfinished building, that he sometimes kept a blind eye for a contractor who needed it, and that he was not above recommending a builder for other reasons than satisfaction with his work.

There was an odd occasion, before he had been three years in Bedford Row, when Martin was interviewed by a persistent individual who appeared convinced that a dispute between his firm and a building owner, with regard to some defective woodwork, could be adjusted by a payment to Mr. Barford, or to one of his representatives. Martin detailed this interview to his senior with great indignation, but Mr. Barford did not turn a hair. "Of course he was trying to square you," he said, without any of the indignation which Martin had expected. "Stupid of him not to shut up sooner, and I suppose you didn't see what he was driving at, and let him go on. He ought to have guessed you were new to this kind of thing." And he glanced at Martin in an odd, amused, rather furtive manner, laughed for no particular reason, and said, "You should have referred him to me." Martin saw nothing ambiguous in this remark and demanded innocently, "What proceedings can we take against the fellow?"

"You can't take any," Mr. Barford told him, star-

ing. "There's only your word and his in the matter.
He'll deny everything; he'll say you misunderstood
him and he was only proposing a cash settlement: he's
been too clever to put anything in writing. It's all a
regular trick of the trade; no good making a fool of
yourself by taking it seriously. You don't understand
how to handle this kind of thing, my dear boy." And
again, and more urgently, he insisted, "You'd better
send the fellow to me." Martin somehow never heard
the outcome of the whole business. It was not until he
had had ten years' further experience of Mr. Barford
that he recalled the incident in another connection, and
wondered for the first time whether the ingenious
contractor had found his interview with the senior
partner more fruitful than that with the junior; but
for the most part he went his own quiet way, and
developed his own style and mannerisms, and was too
busy to notice anything that went on in the office outside his own work.

2

Martin had thought when he married Letty that
they would have the most glorious holidays together
each year on the Continent, tramping through the
countryside with their knapsacks on their backs, putting up at cheap, clean, simple, country inns, living on
red wine and omelettes, and discovering a cathedral or
a palace in every town they came to; but somehow
things never quite worked out as he expected.

Letty was delighted with his ideas, and used to listen amiably with her sewing in her lap while he got
out his maps and guide-books and planned their tours

through France, Spain, Greece and Italy; however when their first August came round Stacy was a baby and could not be left.

Lady Stapleford, who had taken a furnished house at Worthing, had her daughter and granddaughter down there for two months; and Martin went to stay for a fortnight, and for three week-ends. It was not quite the holiday he had wanted, but funds were low after Letty's doctor and nurse had been paid; and Martin was in so blissful a daze of relief and tenderness that he placidly accepted the long, idle days on the pebbles, the monotonous expanse of wet sand and worm-casts at low-tide, the shimmer of heat above the red-brick villas, tamarisk hedges and distant Downs, the shelterless glare and dazzle of the concrete parade and the bathing which never seemed to be anything more than a painful knee-deep wading over sharp stones towards the receding indigo streak of the horizon. It was enough for him to watch Letty's pinched, sharp face rounding itself again to beauty and the colour returning to her cheeks.

"Next year we'll go abroad," he said to her, and she smiled faintly, and did not contradict him.

Next year, however, it was not so easy to go. Letty was in the sick, early stages of her second pregnancy; Lady Stapleford, who insisted on having her daughter and granddaughter to stay with her at Bournemouth, invited Martin as well, and he was obliged, for economy's sake, to accept. He wanted to save all he could towards the next winter and the move from Gray's Inn which would become inevitable in the spring of 1895; but he was in a far less submissive mood than at Worthing, and the company of an ailing wife, a critical

mother-in-law and a teething baby did little to recon-
cile him to the band in the ornamental gardens, the
crowds at the foot of the pier, and Lady Stapleford's
bright little turreted villa among the sandy roads and
pine-trees on the edge of the golf-course in the Talbot
Woods. He escaped two or three times for a day by
himself. Once he went to Wimborne Minster and once
to the airy ruins of Corfe and its grey, stone-tiled cottages huddled in the gap between the Downs. Once he
spent a day walking over Hengistbury Head, and
sailed back up the shining loops of the river to Christ-
church, where the stringy yellow wallflowers were in
bloom on the long parapet of the Minster, and between
the stones of a little round Norman tower, enriched
with lattice-work and fish-scale carving; and once he
went as far afield as Romsey Abbey, and although he
looked at it with eyes that were two years older he
found it noble and unchanged. He had not told Letty
where he was going that time, but he betrayed himself
on his return.

"You never said you were going all that way. I
expected you back hours ago," said Letty rather
crossly, "I do think you might have told me."

"Well, you couldn't have come so far, could you,
darling, even if you'd wanted to?"

"I suppose not," she admitted petulantly. "Oh! I
am so sick of all this lying about on sofas and feeling
rotten. I do wish it was over. I should have liked to go
there with you again, but we never seem to manage to
do anything together nowadays."

"I'll take you as soon as you feel a bit better,"
promised Martin, playing with her fingers and feeling
utterly miserable, vexed, self-conscious and inadequate.

"I don't suppose I'll be able to manage any long days like that while we're down here," Letty grumbled. "May as well give up the notion."

"I do wish you could have come," sighed Martin, helplessly. "It was looking so lovely, just the same as ever."

"Just the same as it did two years ago," began Letty valiantly. "Do you remember?" and then her courage broke and her soft lips quivered; she began to cry in a helpless sort of way. "Oh, but it's all so different now," he heard her sobbing.

The second baby was a boy. It was born in February 1895 and was christened Martin for official, and Aubrey for daily use, to commemorate Letty's father, the Indian judge. It was a delicate, fretful thing and created much more disturbance than cheerful, healthy little Stacy had done. She was by this time a vigorous, noisy child, beginning to babble unintelligible nonsense, and to crawl and stagger about the small rooms of the flat, clutching at chairs and tables and capsizing them on top of her. Letty had begun to find her daughter troublesome before Aubrey was born, afterwards she neglected her for the sickly baby, and between the two of them was distracted and worn out.

It became evident to Martin that prudence must be disregarded and a move made to larger and more expensive quarters. Fortunately, he was beginning to get on in his profession. He had more work of his own to do than Nick Barford altogether appreciated and he had just been taken into partnership, rather to his own surprise, and promoted to a small back room of his own next to the drawing-office. He took his courage in both hands and moved out of Gray's Inn at last, after

Aubrey was born. They went to a white-washed, six-roomed cottage in Downshire Hill, with a green-trellised verandah smothered in jasmine and a small garden fended off by a low paling from the Bank Holiday crowds, cocoanut-shies and roundabouts of Hampstead Heath.

Martin was very excited over this cottage and bought a good deal more furniture for it than he could really afford. He had lately developed a mild collector's mania, and spent his Saturdays poking about the King's Road, Chelsea, for the old oak which was then coming into fashion. Letty was disappointed by all this, she had wanted the stained green wood furniture, Japanese fans, blue plates, and cosy corners of the middle nineties; but she was still sufficiently devoted to Martin to accept his verdict. For her own part she enlarged her scheme of housekeeping, engaged an elderly, bad-tempered cook and an inexperienced house-parlour-maid, who were rather beyond her management, and ventured timidly on one or two not particularly successful dinners. She was not quite so economical as he had hoped; she had not developed any very definite system in her housekeeping, and she varied between unnecessary extravagances and alarmed parsimony; but he was too inexperienced to check her, he merely paid her bills and hoped for improvement. She spent a good deal of time with her mother, who had settled in a dingy block of red brick and terra-cotta flats near Baker Street. She managed the children herself, and took a great many walks along the Spaniards' Road, or across to Parliament Hill, pushing Aubrey in his pram, and putting Stacy into it when her fat legs were tired on the way home.

Now that Martin was a partner he was no longer
kept late at the office by Mr. Barford's work and could
bring his own home if he chose; he had a drawing-
table at a window in the attic, with sloping roofs on
each side and an unexpected view of smoky-grey London between two chestnut-trees. Here he could draw
at night after Letty had gone to bed, if necessary, and
on Saturdays and Sundays, while she sewed in the garden with the children on a rug beside her. It was all
very simple and unexciting and pleasant, and at this
stage of their existence it was all that the Lovells
wanted; a gardener might have said that they were
striking their roots.

3

Martin had been married six years before he took
his first holiday away from England and without his
wife. Letty had always seemed willing enough to fall
in with his plans up to a point, but she hated leaving
the children, even after Martin had become prosperous enough to afford her a stout, bearded, reliable old
Nanny who allowed very little interference in the
nursery.

Lady Stapleford always offered to take the children
and nurse with her to the seaside, but she never failed
to point out the pleasures and economies of a joint
holiday. Martin could not deny that his family was
expensive and that Letty was never so happy as with
her mother; he was becoming more and more busy
and he was glad to know that his wife and children
could be out of London for a couple of months while
he was working. He did not actually admit that he

could get much more done when he had his time to himself, and draw and plan all day and half the night
without interruption from the drawing-room or the
nursery.

He used to run down for week-ends to the seaside
lodgings of those days, where he would be greeted by
a sunburnt, smiling, compassionate wife and a riotous
sandy pair of children, and could get through a couple
of days' bathing, and picnicking, and sleeping in the
sun without too many quarrels with his mother-in-law.
In this way he survived the two summers at Bournemouth, one at Littlestone and one at Broadstairs before he protested.

In 1898, however, there was a change of plan. It so
happened that the lease of Downshire Hill came to an
end that year, and that the house in Maida Vale, to
which the Lovells were moving, would not be ready
for them until the middle of September. Lady Stapleford had arranged to spend the summer holidays at
Felixstowe, a healthy but, to Martin's mind, uninteresting neighbourhood which had been recommended
for Aubrey's convalescence after whooping-cough.
Letty was to take the two children down there from
the middle of June; the furniture was to be stored, and
Martin was to stay in London in lodgings, amuse himself in his spare time by watching over the structural
alterations in the new house, and take a fortnight's
holiday in September with his family. It was only the
last part of the programme which somehow had for
him a faintly depressing flavour. He listened obediently, however, while Letty and her mother discussed
it, and made so little comment that they both supposed
the matter settled: Letty was perplexed and even re-

sentful when he told her later, "I don't know that I'm
so very keen on Felixstowe."

"But it's all settled," she protested, "Granny's taken
the lodgings, and everything, weeks ago." They always
called Lady Stapleford "Granny" nowadays, in imitation of the children. "We couldn't possibly ask her to
go anywhere else."

"I don't want her to go anywhere else," said Martin, almost crossly. "She can take the kids down there
for as long as she likes, and you too, if you can stand
the place, and want to get out of London while it's
hot; but I don't see that I need go there myself." He
was rather astonished at hearing himself say such a
thing; he had not known that it was in his head when
he began talking, but it seemed as if he had worked a
whole plan out subconsciously already when he begged,
"Let's go abroad together for a fortnight, and leave
them to it. We couldn't get very far in so short a time,
but we might run over to Holland or Belgium. There
are things there I want to see."

Letty seemed incapable of taking this in. "It would
be awfully extravagant to do that," she objected, without apparently even considering the plan. "We're
spending a great deal on the new house as it is. And
there were all the doctor's bills for the children's illness, and Aubrey isn't really right yet; I couldn't possibly go away and leave him. Besides, Granny would be
so hurt if she didn't have both of us; and travelling on
the Continent is always so uncomfortable and tiring,
and Holland and Belgium would be very smelly and
stuffy, and hot and tripperish in September. And I
should have to sit about in hotels all day while you
were sketching." Her voice had insensibly taken on

the peevish and complaining note which had recently
disfigured it, Martin cut her short with sudden irritation: "And in fact you'd rather not be bothered to
come with me."

He had never said such a thing to her before, and
he was curiously disturbed when he realised it. Letty
herself looked taken aback, but not so shaken as he
was; she murmured, in a confused, but still petulant
tone, "You know I don't care about architectural
sightseeing."

"You liked it well enough in Rome," said Martin
bitterly. That fairly startled her; she looked at him
with her flower-blue eyes wide awake and staring; he
thought unkindly, "That's made her notice me. She
hasn't much lately"; then reproached himself for the
thought.

"Martin, what's the matter?" she asked him, coming up close, and putting a gentle hand on his arm. He
hardly knew, he certainly could not tell her.

"You're always with the children and your mother,"
he grumbled, "we don't do things together. You never
have any time for me nowadays. It isn't what I expected." There was no more to say than that; he had
wanted a perfect, uninterrupted companionship, but
life did not work out such a simple answer to their
multiplication of duties and responsibilities and emotions and years. Letty was a placid, stupid, affectionate
creature, who had been very little developed by six
years of marriage and motherhood; her head and
heart were satisfied, while his were still hungry and
craving.

"Don't come if you don't want to," he muttered,
turning away. If he meant to hurt her he was disap-

pointed. She took her own accustomed way of composing their differences; she would not argue a point when she could put her arms round his neck, press her small, slender body against him, and stop his mouth with kisses which still kept their old power to trouble and satisfy.

"Stupid Martin," she called him, "stupid boy. You're like the children; you want me to play with you all the time even when I've got things to do." He thought that she was laughing and was not sure that she was not crying; but when he pushed her away from him to look into her face, the blue eyes were dry and bright. She had a new expression in them, of astonishing wisdom and sweetness, it made him feel peculiarly young and foolish and unkind.

"I will come with you if you like," she said, "but I think you'd much better go by yourself."

He felt sulky and ill-used; he wanted to kick at the legs of the table to express his irritation.

"Listen, darling," said Letty, looking at him in this new, unexplained way as if he were a very stupid small boy and she were his mother and were sorry for him: "You haven't had a change from me for six years, and I should think you must be getting sick of the sight of me by this time, because I'm very stupid, and I don't understand your old bricks and mortar, and I'm not," she declared, valiantly mastering a quiver in her lip, "much use to you except at home. So you'd better leave me there, and go away and have a good time by yourself, and come back again and tell me all about it; because really," said Letty, giving in to the quiver after all, "you have been too horrible to live with lately, and I think a holiday might do you good."

It was as if the children's tamest kitten had scratched him to the heart unexpectedly with its thorny little claws. He had thought that he had been particularly patient and devoted, and that he had entirely concealed his feelings of discontent and vexation; indeed, he had been priding himself on a certain nobility of attitude which now seemed completely to have broken down. With Letty in his arms, crying and laughing by turns, he could only reproach her weakly: "I don't want a holiday without you, I shan't enjoy a minute of it unless you come too." He believed himself as he said it, but his wife knew better.

"Oh! yes, you will," she insisted, assuming her own particular pose of slightly spiteful, affectionate, teasing martyrdom. "You'll have a perfectly lovely time all by yourself, poking round those dirty old towns in the hot sun, and drawing and measuring, and eating indigestible meals and getting bitten by mosquitoes out of smelly canals. You'll be very glad you left me behind, and you'll come back in quite a good temper and have heaps to tell me. I think it's a splendid plan. I can't imagine why we never did it before." She stuck to her point, and he was left to make his own plans, to feel a sense of guilt in his own enjoyment of maps and time-tables, and to wonder whether he had won his victory or whether she had.

Letty and the children went to the seaside at the end of June, leaving him to spend his August in lodgings. The last few weeks had been filled with all the discomforts of a move; sorting and packing, irregular meals, the disappearance of favourite objects and the discovery of unexpected hoards of rubbish. Martin felt as forlorn and restless as the children's cat; and, although he tried to laugh at Letty for her sentimental regrets over leaving Downshire Hill, he could not but share a melancholy feeling that their time for happy discovery was over. They had learnt each other's limitations, and for him, at any rate, the chief variety and excitement of his future life would lie in his profession and outside his home.

For Letty, he supposed, it was different: a woman planned and hoped for her children, and he told himself that that would content her; but he had a guilty feeling that she was being shut up by her own consent in the narrow limits of her home, while he began to look and move beyond it. He thought of her a great deal as the hot month of August went by, and wondered what more he could have done to help her. He planned the arrangements of their new home, read her most inadequate letters from the seaside lodgings, and wondered whether she would be happy there. He even, during his single farewell visit, made a shame-faced suggestion that she should go with him after all. He was ashamed of his own relief when she would not even consider the idea.

4

The expedition started badly. He had a rough crossing, and arrived at Ostend in the evening feeling unhappy, sulky and cold. Travelling through unseen country at night was not interesting; and at Bruges he drove through a street of shops and trams to his hotel, feeling that the pleasures of travel were overrated. An insistent music which wove itself into his sleep throughout the night merely irritated him; he thought feverishly, "I suppose it's that confounded carillon of theirs. It must be exactly opposite, it sounds as if it were in this room. To-morrow I shall get myself shifted to the back."

Towards dawn, however, he slept; a smell of coffee woke him, and a bright sun outlining his shutters; he rose and opened them, then leant, entranced, upon the sill above the bustle of the market, its coloured stalls of fruit and flowers and butter, its squawking poultry and barking dogs, shouting men and chattering women.

The Belfry was exactly opposite, as he had supposed, rising in three stages above the brown roofs, and rearing its octagon lantern against clouds that were bright with morning. An airy flourish of notes dropped down from it to his ear above the noises of the square. He sat sideways on the window-sill, breaking up the crust of a fresh roll and sipping *café-au-lait* from a thick bowl; he felt a very long way from home.

After breakfast he went out into the autumn morning, and turned himself loose into the maze of narrow, cobbled streets. He leant above secret waters, gliding under hump-backed bridges, lapping at grated doors in ancient stone foundations, reflecting russet brickwork, trailing willows and sleeping swans; he lingered upon sun-warm quays where the leaves of the green-and-gold lime-trees rustled underfoot. He came back to the Panier d'Or, and sat outside at an iron table spread with a chequered table-cloth, enjoying an *omelette aux champignons, ris de veau* with *petits pois,* a big triangle of open tart with cherries in it, and more crusty bread and some powerful local cheese. It was all very different from Hampstead and much more pleasant, though he felt guilty as he made the reflection.

Bruges was his first and clearest recollection; the towns that he visited later were never quite so brightly illuminated in his mind, but this may have been due to changes in the autumn weather. He persistently recollected Ghent as a mediæval and lowering collection of black towers and spires, a grimy castle, a stagnant river belching myriad black bubbles and a ring of factory chimneys pouring out smoke under a heavy sky; the moulded brick front of the Byloke Abbey, then unreclaimed and difficult to discover, became as irrelevant in his memory of the town as a red rose dropped into an ash-cart. Brussels, on a wet day, was only a square paved with glistening cobbles, some pigeon-grey houses whose gilt ornamentation blinked through the sluicing rain, a flutter of pigeons' wings, and an autumnal blaze of brown and gold in the transept windows of Ste. Gudule. Antwerp was a wilderness of sea-fog, haunted by ships' sirens. He recollected a superb, indigestible picture-gallery, another smaller and somehow rather endearing little castle, which he would have liked to take home to his children, a fantastically ornamented, seven-aisled cathedral, of a type which had already fatigued him, and some more of the sixteenth-century guild-houses, which pleased him better than any church.

Standing under the light Renaissance arcade in the vine-wreathed courtyard of the Plantin-Moretius house, he decided, finally and obstinately, that he did not care for Flemish Gothic. There was something sinister, high-shouldered and constricted about the steeply-pitched roofs with their peering suspicious rows

of dormer windows, the crowded, intricate tracery of
the canopied windows and niches, the florid, soaring
multiplicity of pierced belfries and arrowy slender
spires. It all seemed as angular and ascetic as the tor-
tured, lean-ribbed saints and prudish, shrinking virgin
martyrs in the jewel-coloured primitives of the museums. He took much greater delight in this warm
sixteenth-century brickwork, these light round arches
and tall mullioned windows; they satisfied his domestic
and balanced mind.

He bought a photograph for his daughter in Antwerp, of the Van Eyck Saint Barbara, the patroness of
architects, sitting in her jewelled cloak with her em-
blematic spire flowering in all its crockets behind her;
he bought some lace for Letty and a carved wooden
dog-cart for his son; he went back by the night-boat,
and was exceedingly sea-sick.

The journey from Harwich to Felixstowe seemed
full of unnecessary complications. He arrived at Sea-
view Terrace, and found his family at breakfast, Letty
as fresh as the morning sea, in a blue frock the colour
of her eyes, the children babbling excitedly over his return, and Lady Stapleford in office behind the lodging-
house tea-pot.

"You look awfully well," said Letty, scanning his
face with anxious devotion, and perhaps the unac-
knowledged wish to find him a little the worse for his
absence from her.

"So do you," said he, with a light, dancing smile
which made her colour, and glance away.

"Did you have good weather?" asked Lady Stapleford, repressing him. He told her, irritably, "Yes,
lovely; no, dreadful; I mean, heavenly in Bruges to be-

gin with, miserable everywhere else. It broke up with
the equinox; I spent my time sheltering in cathedrals
and galleries out of the rain."

"Oh! you poor darling." Letty forgot Belgium.
"And I don't suppose you got anything to eat on that
dreadful train. Would you rather have fish or buttered
eggs? They're both here. Have fish first and then
buttered eggs." She helped him largely.

"Daddy, what did you have for breakfast in Belgium?" This was six-year-old Stacy, always interested
in food, and pausing with uplifted spoon in her daily
attempt to write her name in treacle across her porridge.

"Just coffee and rolls," said her father, swallowing
a mouthful of Lady Stapleford's astringent Indian tea,
and regretting the hot frothing milky brew of the last
fortnight.

"How horrid!"

"No, it wasn't; it was nice. I used to have it at a
table out in the street in Bruges."

"Was that the place where the dog drew the cart on
my post-card?"

"Yes, it was." He laughed at Letty over his
daughter's brown head, deciding to postpone any serious account of his travels.

"Oh! how funny." Stacy exploded in a shout of
laughter, and splashed her spoon back into the milk.
"Can I go too next time, and see the dog in the cart?
Can I, Daddy?"

"You can't go anywhere with Daddy until you learn
to eat up your porridge like a good girl," said Lady
Stapleford, with an annoying air of reproof. "Aubrey, finish yours quickly, too."

"I do not wish to be asturbed," said Aubrey, with majestic dignity, laying down his spoon.

"I'll take you all there the very next time I go," Martin rashly promised, wishing that his mother-in-law would leave his children and his wife alone. He wanted to talk to Letty, and tell her all about his adventures; he wanted to kiss her much more satisfactorily than had been possible on the doorstep; he wanted to ask her in the right tone of voice whether she had missed him, and tease her into the right kind of answer. But Lady Stapleford went on sitting at the head of the table, helping herself to marmalade, and correcting Stacy's table-manners; and Letty herself was chiefly anxious to talk about the improvement in Aubrey's colour since he had been at the seaside, and the untrustworthiness of the landlady in the matter of the weekly bills.

The Lovells did get an hour or so together on the beach after breakfast, while Lady Stapleford took the reluctant children bathing; but Letty, though she listened politely enough, had half an eye all the time for Aubrey crying and protesting as his grandmother dipped him in the creamy shallows, and Stacy prancing in a scarlet tunic on the edge of a green and threatening wave.

"It must have been lovely, darling," she said vaguely at intervals, "and you do look much better for it; but I wish you could have had a week here as well. The bathing would do you all the good in the world." He knew that she had developed the maternal, medicinal outlook on holidays, and her only really interested queries were about the Belgian food and drains. Martin sighed unconsciously, and gave it up.

Her kisses were as fondly satisfying as ever, and her soft, familiar company was like an enveloping cloud, blotting out the bright recollections of his fortnight's freedom. By the end of the morning he felt as if he had never been away.

They went back to London next day, and in a week were settled in the new house, which was a yellow plaster villa in the neighbourhood of the Regent's Park canal, adorned by a pair of semi-circular bays on either side of a pillared portico, a chubby balustrade along the roof cornice, and curved triangular pediments set like helmet-visors above the windows, which bulged like eyes in a fat man's face.

The situation was damply depressing in the November fogs, and did not suit either Aubrey or Letty, who caught perpetual colds there; but Stacy loved the reflected swans and barges of the canal. Martin used to take his small daughter out to sail toy-boats there on Sunday afternoons, and tell her stories about Bruges and Stockholm and Venice, where all the streets were paved with water, and promise to take her abroad with him when she was old enough. And in the spring of 1899 he betrayed his unspoken fancies by building for a submissive client a hopelessly Flemish little blue-and-red chess-board house, with a crow-stepped gable, a high-pitched roof, attic-dormers, green shutters to mullioned windows, and a quantity of moulded brick ornamentation: all very satisfactory to him and quite inappropriate to its neighbourhood, which happened to be Redhill.

IV

IN THE SPRING of 1903 the Lovells had their first real
piece of domestic misfortune: Letty had a third unexpected child, which was stillborn. She had perhaps
been too active on a summer holiday or overworked
herself in the move from Maida Vale to Old Brompton which had followed it; or else a certain delicate,
feeble element in her, which she had already trans-
mitted to Aubrey, came out too strongly eight years
afterwards in this child. She had been unusually sick
and ailing during the earlier months of her pregnancy,
but had fretfully refused to take life quietly, and had
made a martyr of herself over her household and nursery responsibilities; her doctor ordered her to bed too
late, and at six months the child was born dead, a son,
a little doll-like thing, not looking worth all that trouble. She had not seemed to wish for its existence, and
had told Martin repeatedly that Stacy and Aubrey
wore her out; but she fretted miserably about her disappointment, and was slow to recover from it.

Lady Stapleford took her away to Torquay for six
weeks at Easter, and she came back restored and pretty
and cheerful; but there was a change in her, which her
husband was slow to realise at the time, but could date

definitely afterwards; it was like a crystallisation into maturity. She was as gentle and tender to him as ever, but their young love was over; some vital current had ceased to flow between them. She seemed unconscious of any barrier, but there was no quickening flutter in her look and colour when she met him again: she treated him with placid, calm affection, but she made no movement that could stir a sleeping impulse; she had ceased to look for romance in him, she no longer responded to his love-making, and was quietly content with her daily life. She hardly spoke of their trouble; she seemed to have put it out of her mind, and Martin did not speak of it to her, or of the change in their relationship, which gradually subsided from that date into a passionless affection. He was left with a sense of strange, irreparable loss; the dear, dull, familiar woman who now shared his domestic life was not the Letty he had married; his heart ached for the loss of that bright foolish creature.

Letty had no more children; she subsided into a plump, cheerful, satisfied young matron, innocently boastful about her pretty, noisy daughter, her clever, delicate son, and her husband's growing success. She appeared completely occupied with her unpretentious, conventional, muddled and rather extravagant house-keeping, her mild round of calls, tea-parties and dinners given and returned. She was not the type of woman who diversifies the monotony of existence by more or less serious love-affairs; she had contentedly resigned all that side of life, which indeed had never meant very much to her.

She loved Martin dearly and probably deeply, but he imagined that she thought of him as the eldest of

her children and the most unaccountably difficult to
please. He used to hear her talking about him to the
other women at her parties, and making the most
touching, ignorant, inaccurate statements about his professional life; and he had long ceased to communicate
his disappointments and successes to her, just as she
had given up her early attempts to understand his
work. Her life was centred nowadays on her children;
she had transferred all her hopes and thoughts to
them, or rather to Aubrey, a delicate, intelligent boy
whom she spoilt and petted. She was curiously unsuccessful with her daughter, whom she treated with an
unexpected harshness, injustice and lack of compre-
hension which were the surface signs of an obscure
jealousy. She seemed to realise that Martin might
transfer to the daughter who so much resembled him
an intellectual sympathy which she had been unable to
retain. Martin could not help feeling guilty sometimes
about his wife, thinking helplessly that he had failed
to teach her what he needed from her, but he could not
re-discover that lost key to her thoughts; he was
obliged to acquiesce in a certain mutual disappointment and short-coming. Letty was still the only woman
in his heart, he never loved any other; but his deepest
interest was in his work.

From his first beginnings as a kind, shy, polite enthusiastic youth he had matured into an apparently
competent and serious partner in the Bedford Row
office. Letty had groomed his untidiness, and he was
moustached and bearded in the fashion of a somewhat
earlier time, and enabled thereby to seem older and
more authoritative than his years. He had discarded
his first conscientious anxieties, his youthful diffidence

and fear of responsibility; he had acquired tact, self-confidence and humour, and the power of composing difficult situations. He had ceased to commit himself to rash estimates, to apologise for his own taste or to admit his own mistakes. He had accustomed himself to the confused and vacillating minds of clients, their incalculable meanness or generosity, their uncertain patronage, their ignorance of technicalities, their haggling over fees and payments, their touching aspirations for comfort, beauty, economy or ostentation, their astonishing capacity for misunderstanding his enthusiasms, defeating his ambitions and wasting his time. He had come, more slowly, to appreciate the native shrewdness and humour, the obstinate conservatism and kindly tolerance of working men, their infinite resource and cunning, the kindly, shameless mendacity with which they protected each other, and their still surviving pride in the details of their craft. He had learnt from them a working knowledge of the trades he employed. He had experienced the malice of nature, the heartrending damage that can be done by frost and the penetrating power of driving rain and water springing from underground; he had suffered from the refractory stubbornness of inanimate matter, the warping of unseasoned timber, the bending of metal, cracking of stone, scaling of brick and the infection of dry rot running through damp places like a hidden fire. He had acquired, through much tribulation, an eye for good and bad material; he had learnt to be constantly watchful against small inaccuracies on the part of struggling, careless, or untrustworthy firms; he had become wise in the vexatious technicalities of local by-laws, in disputes over loosely-worded correspondence, in strikes and labour-troubles and the adjustment of accounts. He had discovered how little of his time could be given to drawing and planning, and how much was swallowed up by interviews and correspondence and office-routine. He had learnt the relative unimportance of design to anyone but himself, compared with the multiplicity of detailed information daily required from him about the prices and properties of building material, the latest improvements in systems of drainage, lighting and heating, ventilation and water-supply, the strains and stresses of steel construction and the most recent decorative fashions and fads.

He sometimes thought that no one but himself cared what his houses looked like, and that no one but the owner cared whether they stood up or fell down. He was earning a quiet living in the way that amused him, but he had never been good at self-advertisement, and he seemed incapable of making a name by his work. He found himself declining more and more into domestic architecture; his passing, fantastic dreams of churches and cathedrals had been replaced by ambitions which were more easily put into practice: he wanted most of all, as he had told Letty in Rome, to build good houses. He went on with his work for the next ten years, recording the architectural developments of his tastes up and down the country in the conscientiously picturesque houses of the period, with their tall Tudor chimneys, roughcast walls, gabled roofs of green Cumberland slates, rows of leaded casements grouped between rounded brick mullions, and stout shutters pierced with open hearts. He spent much time and trouble on fitting his rooms into the deliberately irregular ground-plans which came into fashion at the beginning of the twentieth century: the L-shaped or H-shaped groups of buildings, embracing octagonal forecourts, loggias, cloisters and paved sun-traps between their projecting wings and bays. He caught the prevalent style of architectural gardening, and overloaded a site or two for submissive clients with pillared Amalfi pergolas, balustraded stairways, lily-pools, wall-fountains, sundials and cold marble seats before he learnt to discard these youthful affec-tations, and sobered down into mature simplicity.

He had been rather more than ten years with the firm in Bedford Row when it first occurred to him that Nicholas Barford was losing his work. The senior partner was now in his late sixties, and while he might seem to a casual client as vigorous and overbearing as ever, Martin realised that he was becoming at once more irritable and less effective. His kind of work had gone completely out of fashion with the new century, and he was too old and set in his ways to change. He had no more houses to build, and no more banks or offices. It was an obvious delight and relief to him when, in the autumn of 1904, the councillors decided to add a wing to his beloved Town Hall in Wales.

Nick had always considered this Town Hall to be the crown and flower of his professional work, and was accustomed to point it out to his decreasingly numer-ous clients and visitors, taking them into the drawing-office to look at the framed perspective, and creating when possible an impression that the pupils and draughtsmen there were carrying out his designs rather than Martin's. He said with a rather pathetic, ostentatiously irritating triumph to Martin, when the

commission came in, "You see my style's good enough
for 'em even after all these years."

Martin said dubiously and unwisely, "I suppose you
can't very well get away from the original design." It
hung on the wall above them, considerably faded and
fly-blown with years but still recognisable in all its
grim Venetian ugliness; he was thankful that he had
never been obliged to go and see the building itself.

Nick stared, scowled, gnawed his ragged yellow
tobacco-stained moustache and said testily, "I'd like
to see any of you young fools improve on it. Good
thing you haven't got your hands on the job. I suppose
you'd turn it into an imitation of that railway station
with the Roman candle that Bentley has stuck up for
the R. C.'s in the place where the prison used to be at
Westminster." This was an old matter for dispute
between the partners. It was true that Martin had a
great admiration for the building in question, and had
spent much time prowling round it and watching its
development. He had been down to look at it first in a
very early stage, when the walls were going up in a
mass of scaffolding; he had not made much of it and
had hastily decided that the published design, with its
striped, staring walls and saucer domes, would turn out
as fantastic and displeasing as his partner thought it.
Then one Sunday afternoon in the spring of 1902 he
had been flying a kite with Stacy, the eight-year-old,
and Aubrey, somewhere in the windy middle of Hyde
Park, and had noticed what looked like a new factory
chimney pushing up into the sky beyond the Achilles
statue, and had suddenly realised with astonishment,
"That must be the new campanile." Something about
the slender, unexpected shaft had pricked and dis-

turbed his imagination; the next day he had made time
to go and look at the work.

This time he had been fascinated and alarmed by
the way the thing had grown in four years. There was
still a mass of scaffolding round the head of the tower,
and he could not then appreciate what later became his
chief pleasure, the crown of arched buttresses and the
domed cupola set upon them; but the scaffolding was
all struck from the red-and-white building, he could
walk round and wonder his fill at the strange, parti-
coloured walls, with the delicate herringbone and
diapered detail in their brickwork, at the honeycomb
lattices of the great clerestory windows, at the whole
confusion of pentagon and hexagon turrets, of leaden
domes and concrete pyramids, of arcaded loggias and
airy balconies and bridges, of twin and triple groups
of segmental and semicircular arches and flying buttresses and colonnades. It had looked to him like the
skyline of a hilltop town, clinging to a great red cliff.

He had found his way in by an unguarded doorway,
and wandered about in the empty, echoing, unfinished
nave, still encumbered by builders' rubbish; he had
stared up at the sevenfold system of arches in the bays
of the nave arcade, at the dim brown vaults and galleries of rough naked brickwork, at the pale marbles
of the one completed chapel, and Nicholas Barford's
criticisms had come into his head as he stumbled on a
forgotten plank. "The place is just a collection of railway arches," and then he had thought, "No, it's more
impressive than that. It's like stables for the horses of
the Apocalypse." He had treasured the phrase in secret ever since, as if he were proud of it. There had
been nothing in London he liked so well as Bentley's

cathedral at that stage of his development, but he despaired of explaining his affection for it to his senior partner. So now he merely smiled at the old man's irritability, and made one of the soothing answers which were becoming more and more necessary in handling Nicholas Barford. The old man was not appeased, he knit his white eyebrows, and muttered and walked off to his own room; he had no longer any sense of humour where his last piece of work was concerned.

Martin found him more and more changed as the burden of it settled on him. He became intolerably fussy and troublesome about the office work connected with it, expected everything else to be set aside for his designs and specifications, and behaved as if he were a student just out of his articles and confronted with his first house to build. He was always interviewing people from the Welsh place in his front room and taking them out to lunch afterwards. Martin learnt to recognise a stout, noisy, competent man who apparently hoped to become one of the contractors; there were two mean and rather shabby men who were local tradesmen and had seats and influence on the Town Council, and there was a little ferrety, red-nosed Town Clerk who was apparently more important than might have been expected. Nick used to stay out at his lunches until three or later, come back a little vague and irritable, to find fault with something that had been done in the drawing-office, and then shut himself up in his own room, and sleep his lunch off.

Decidedly, he was not the man he had been; he would have taken all this kind of thing in his stride when Martin first came to the office, and thought as little of it as it deserved. He was a great trial to his

subordinates during the four or five months in which
the designs, contracts, bills of quantities and tenders
were being prepared for what was, after all, not a very
large addition to the original design. He was a little
less troublesome once the actual building had started.
He spent a good deal of his time paying more or less
necessary visits to the site and coming back and telling
Martin, or anyone else who would listen to him, how
well the new wing was going up and what an improvement to the building it would be.

Then, after a few months, there was a queer, indefinite, inexplicable change in him. He turned more
strange and sulky than Martin had ever known him, he
sat about in his room, apparently doing nothing; he
stayed after everyone else had gone, became more
irregular than usual in his hours and ways, and seemed
always to be in a bad temper. Nothing was done in
the office to his satisfaction, and no one could please
him; the men in the drawing-office nodded and winked
to each other behind his back, and scarcely concealed
their impatience with his perpetual peering and fault-
finding.

Martin supposed that something had gone seriously
wrong down in Wales, it seemed the only explanation
of Nick's behaviour; but Nick denied anything of the
kind. "What should go wrong when I'm down there
myself twice a month?" he growled, turning his back
on Martin and walking out of the room, a trifle un-
steadily, Martin thought.

It was not the first time, however, that he had
thought his principal a little uncertain about doors and
corners and the shallow steps of the Queen Anne staircase, with the uneven winders at the turn. Nick did not

carry off those convivial business lunches of his as well
as he used to do: he did not steer a very straight course
into the office after them, and if he had to answer any
question he was very queer and dazed in his manner,
and would blink and scowl and stammer as if he did
not quite know where he was. The clerks noticed it
and had their own gossip and jokes about it, which
Martin suspected but could not check.

And then, one winter evening about half-past eight,
Martin had occasion to call in at the office on his way
back from a long day at a job in the country. He had
expected to find the place deserted, and had actually
got out his own key to open the black outer door with
the names painted above it; but to his surprise it was
ajar, and he heard voices within. He wondered whose
they could be: there was no rush of work on hand, as
he very well knew, and no reason for anyone to have
stayed late; but as he crossed the lamplit landing the
door swung wide and Nicholas Barford came out,
staggering and talking to himself. He felt with his
hand along the panelling as if for support, then swayed
and walked right into Martin, as if he had not seen
him, recoiled, and cursed viciously. The outer door
swung to behind him, then was pushed open again; the
small, sharp, scared office-boy, with his red head and
his sly, furtive face, came blinking out into the light of
the landing and opened his mouth to gape when he saw
Martin. Nick pushed by his junior partner, still swearing and muttering, and went off down the stairs, holding very tightly to the carved and twisted banisters.
The boy made an attempt to slip by Martin and follow
him; but Martin put out his arm across the top stair
and demanded, "Where are you off to?"

"Oh! please, I must go to 'im, I must go to Mr. Barford," the boy protested.

"Must go? What do you mean? What the devil are you here for at this time of night anyhow?" Martin was angry because he was afraid of what he might hear; there was something gravely wrong, he could tell that from the boy's scared and twitching face. He did not, however, move his arm, and the boy, unable to pass him, twisted his dirty hands together, and gulped and whimpered: " 'E made me stop. 'E made me swear I wouldn't tell none of you. 'E daren't go 'ome to Mecklenburgh Square nowadays, without I walk 'im back by the arm. 'E's going blind." Martin's arm dropped to his side. In the well of the staircase below him he heard the stumbling noises of the old man's descent. He muttered, "How long have you been doing this?"

"Since before Christmas. 'E gimme ten bob a week to stop be'ind and see 'im 'ome. 'E said 'e'd arf kill me if I told! Oh! please, can I go?" Martin nodded and stood aside; the boy flung himself down the staircase, and Martin heard Nick cursing him down below.

It all came out next morning; Nick must have remembered enough of the evening to realise that Martin knew what had happened. He did not come to the office, but he sent for his junior partner to go round to Mecklenburgh Square, and admitted with a return of his old vigour and irony that the game was up. "You were a set of damned fools not to spot it before," he declared, and seemed to find some consolation in the thought, "letting me poke about there all these weeks without seeing what was up. If I hadn't known the office like the back of my hand I couldn't have done it.

Well, I've had enough of it now. I shall just throw in my hand and leave you to straighten up the muddle. You'll find things in a bit of a mess down in Wales, I shouldn't wonder." And he laughed his old, loud, coarse, defiant laugh. "That'll keep you busy for a bit," he said. He would not talk very much about his eyesight. "Cataract, the doctor says. Told me to knock off and rest some time ago, but I didn't pay any attention to him. What's the use of paying any attention to doctors? Says I've got to wait till I'm quite blind before he can do anything. Tells me I'll be all right again when he's finished messing about with me. Talks about six months or eight months or a year. I don't remember all he said. What's the use of telling me that sort of nonsense at my time of life? Take an old horse like me out of harness; he falls down and dies. Better to have let me go on till I dropped." He gave Martin a number of contradictory directions about the Welsh job and sent him away, grumbling, "Of course you'll make a mess of everything, but I can't help it. I shan't be there. I don't suppose I shall ever come back." It did not seem likely that he ever would. Martin succeeded to the direction of the office, and to the front room where Nick had interviewed his clients, and was obliged to go down to Wales and arrange for the finishing up of the new wing to the Town Hall as best he could.

It was a very unsatisfactory business: there were a great many local interests to consider, and he found himself considerably at sea between them. He never quite got to the bottom of the mysterious understanding which had evidently existed between Nicholas Barford and the contractor and the members of the building committee, an understanding into which he himself was never admitted. But he did detect and condemn some very slipshod and defective work at the back of the new wing just as it was about to be covered up, and made himself very unpopular in consequence. Mr. Barford, he was informed, had passed all that as satisfactory on his last visit. Martin had to persist that his senior partner had been in no fit state to judge what was or was not up to standard on his last visit; he had not been able to see. It was a good thing for the reputation of the firm that Martin had that excuse to offer; there might have been trouble otherwise when he persisted in his objections; but it would have been difficult for anyone to prove that Nick had been as deliberately blind on this occasion as he might have been on others.

The Town Hall was completed after a series of irritating delays and complications, as nearly as possible to Mr. Barford's designs, though Martin had had to deal with certain mistakes and oversights in the plans. He could not say that he felt any pleasure in contemplating the finished work; it was as hideous, inconvenient and debased a building as the original, and it would always be associated for him with the miseries and suspicions surrounding the close of Nicholas Barford's career.

However, the natives were apparently satisfied with their Town Hall and proud of it. They gave a public dinner to celebrate the opening of the new wing. Martin had to take Nicholas Barford down for this function, and see him through it. The old man was more or less blind by this time, he had not more than a faint perception of light, and had to be led by the arm and given his food. However, he was given a place of honour near the top of the table between two of his friends; and when the Town Council had finished congratulating each other they brought his name into the tail of the speeches, which apparently pleased him. Martin, who sat somewhere down at the foot of the table, was not mentioned and found it a relief. Mr. Barford got very drunk and maudlin at the end of the evening, and cried a good deal in the hotel bedroom; but that was no more than Martin had expected, it had been a trying occasion for the old man. It was, after all, the end of his career. The operation for cataract was performed a few weeks later, first in the one eye and then in the other, and was from the surgeon's point of view completely successful; but although Nicholas Barford recovered his sight after an interval of some months, he never returned to the practice to which Martin had succeeded him. The operations had made an old man of him. He came down once or twice and hung about the office in Bedford Row, blinking through his convex lenses, getting in everyone's way, and resenting Martin's presence in his old room and Martin's work in the drawing-office; then he gave up even these infrequent visits, and retired to live in the country town where he had been brought up, and where his father, the builder, had carried on business. Martin went down there, two years later, to attend his funeral. Apparently he had died for no particular reason, except the old irremediable one, which obtains in such cases, that he had nothing left to live for. Martin stared down into the wet winter clay of the open grave and felt more than sober. He had learnt a great many things from Mr. Barford. "A successful man, sir,"

said the driver of the cab who took him back to the
station, "very much respected, a credit to the town."
Martin remembered other things than those about his
partner, but he could not speak of them, even to Letty,
who had said, without much sympathy: "You've done
much better since you had the office to yourself. I never
did like old Mr. Barford. I don't see why you need
a partner at all."

Martin thought himself that he would wait for a
year or two until he could pick some young and promising man. There was a nephew of Nick's who was in
the middle of his training and had possibilities; but he
need not settle that question for the present, and he did
not speak of it to his wife. He seldom took her advice
nowadays.

V

STACY was about twelve years old before Martin discovered what kind of a daughter he had. He was shy
of his children in their earlier stages, and afterwards
Stacy had a little escaped his notice, owing to the un-
deniable fact that Letty preferred boys to girls, had
three stories about Aubrey to one about Stacy, and had
fallen into the habit of blaming her daughter for every
nursery mishap. In the Maida Vale period Stacy was
practically always in disgrace, especially in the holidays.

She had grown into a skinny, active little girl, with
long sunburnt legs, cropped brown hair, holland pina-
fores, and a nose and forehead freckled like a plover's
egg; and Aubrey had become a fair, timid, affectionate
little boy, who followed his sister in everything that
she did but usually came to grief in the process. It was
Stacy who got up donkey-races on the sands at Swan-
age and Aubrey who fell off and broke his collar-bone,
Stacy who suggested mackerel-fishing in Cornwall and
Aubrey who was sick in the bottom of the boat, Stacy
who climbed the crumbling cliffs at Overstrand and
Aubrey who brought down an avalanche of sand which
half-buried him.

On these occasions Letty wept over Aubrey's mishaps; Lady Stapleford punished Stacy, but got no tears or promises of repentance out of her. "Aubrey is a little silly," his sister maintained, with obstinately dry eyes. Martin had an uncomfortable feeling that his daughter was being mismanaged, but he did not know how to defend her; when he had finally forbidden her grandmother's whippings he had nothing to put in their place, and he could not check Letty's tears and reproaches as easily, though he felt that there was something obscurely harmful in their effect on the child. There seemed to be a family rivalry growing up between his son and his daughter, and he did not know how to prevent it, since any display of his own affection for Stacy seemed to accentuate Letty's jealous preference for the boy.

At school their positions were reversed, Stacy failed and Aubrey succeeded. She became a headstrong, impatient, incalculable little girl, always in and out of trouble, capable of passionate friendships and aversions, a born leader, astonishingly fertile in amusing and upsetting suggestions, and a great trial to the authorities. She said that the mistresses were "silly," a favourite word of hers at this time; she found her lessons dull, and would not work. She never won any prizes, except an apparently accidental one for drawing when she first took it up. Her father was immensely proud of this incident, but Stacy refused to go on with the subject, saying that the mistress was "silly" and the regulation cubes and cones and vanishing-points a waste of time. Martin was inclined to agree with her and to fancy that he could teach her drawing better himself. He made the experiment dur-

ing one summer holiday, and found that she had inherited his own peculiar neatness, delicacy and patience; she had no eye for colour, but she had an adult
regard for detail which pleased him.

They were in Norfolk again that year, 1906 it was,
at Mundesley; and for the first time he began to take
his fourteen-year-old daughter with him on the long
bicycling expeditions which had become his refuge from
Letty and Lady Stapleford, who preferred sitting
comfortably on the sands, with their backs against a
breakwater, making or mending the children's clothes,
eating biscuits and occasionally telling Aubrey to keep
away from the sea.

From all this domesticity Martin and his daughter
escaped, at first only to explore the Norfolk villages,
later, as he discovered her inherited thirst for the information, to begin the study of mediæval church architecture. For Stacy Martin traced the branches of his
subject, at first diffidently, then with growing confidence and enthusiasm. It was all mixed up for Stacy
afterwards with the clear East-country light, the salt
airs blowing from the sandy North Sea, the blackberry
and honeysuckle flowers in the hedges, and her father's
kind voice saying, "Never pass a village church without going inside; that's a good motto. There's nearly
always something to see. Always prowl round the outside first, to get the hang of the building and look at
the masonry. Don't just wander round in a sloppy
way, make yourself date the different parts properly.
Try to see what the original plan was, and where the
later additions came; spot where they've put in a
chantry, or an aisle or a chapel. Take a good look at
the tower and the windows and the porch. When you

get inside, don't be content with ticking off the pulpit, and choir-stalls and pew-ends; look under the matting for inscriptions and brasses; keep your eyes open for bits of mural painting, blocked-up windows and arches, and look for squints and aumbries in odd corners. There's generally something hidden away in the vestry if you can get there. Go round the woodwork carefully and take a good look at the roof. Most people never look higher than their own heads. You can miss a lot that way. Never overlook a bit of coloured glass. If you learn a little heraldry it'll make windows and tombs more interesting to you, and I hope you'll keep up enough Latin to read a monumental inscription. And always try and get the key of the tower." He usually succeeded in this himself, and Stacy loved climbing after him round winding stone staircases, up unsteady ladders, and past the furry ropes and silent shadows of the bells to some windy parapet overlooking the pattern of the cornfields.

After they came back to London that autumn Stacy's education was continued on Saturdays and Sundays, as her father could best fit it in. He was just then in an antiquarian stage, and it amused him immensely to work out a systematic course of architectural examples for his young daughter among the public buildings of London. Letty was much occupied that winter with Aubrey, who had had a touch of bronchitis, probably resulting from the fogs of the Regent's Park canal, and needed careful nursing. So it became the custom for Martin and his daughter to prowl together about London in the bright winter afternoons, and Stacy's unformed, enquiring mind received the stamp of her father's enthusiasms in a fashion which was to influence her whole life. Much of what he said, of course, went in at one ear and out at the other; but she retained innumerable half-heard, half-understood scraps of historical fact and architectural criticism, caught from her father's running commentary as they wandered in and out of little, lost City churches or paced the red cloisters at Hampton Court, stared up at the rose-window in the tall transept of Westminster Abbey or watched the ladders of sunshine shift across the dome of St. Paul's. It was all pure childish amusement to Stacy, for Martin it was something better; he began to realise that his daughter might some day give him the intellectual companionship which he had failed to find in her mother. There came a fine spring Saturday when Martin and his daughter, after staring together at the glossy black roof-timbers and screen-caryatides in Middle Temple Hall, walked up past the little grey hall of Clifford's Inn, and came through the arch under the projecting black-and-white houses of Staple Inn. They crossed Holborn and walked under the crow-stepped west gable of Gray's Inn Hall, but the door beneath was locked. "Pity," said Martin, "it's the best of the lot and the oldest. We ought to have done this business the other way round. However, you can see the oriel from outside if we go round the corner, and I'll show you my drawings of the roof and screen when we get home."

Gray's Inn Square was empty and sedate, and the afternoon sun slept upon the worn red fronts of the seventeenth-century buildings. Stacy looked round her with appreciation, and said, "Didn't you and Mother live somewhere near here once?"

"Pretty close," agreed her father with a passing

look of disturbance; his face changed as she watched it to his familiar, puzzled smile of indulgence for himself and all the world. "If you turn round, my child," said he, "you can inspect the house where you were born."

She turned and stared obediently at the corner where he pointed. Neither of them spoke again for the moment: she because she was absorbing the unfamiliar with her usual quiet deliberation, he because his thoughts were busy with something that had happened more than fourteen years earlier. At last he said, as if he were answering a question, "Yes, we were very happy there."

"Were they nice rooms?"

"Very nice, we thought," said Martin wryly, then seemed to correct himself and maintained, "I still think so."

They walked by common consent along the west pavement of the square and came to the little archway, with its spider-web fanlight, that leads into the gardens.

"Can't we go up and have a look?" Stacy demanded.

Martin laughed and said, "If you like. I don't suppose the people will mind." He thought that he would rather like to see the flat again. However, when they reached the deserted landing the black-painted outer door, with the unfamiliar name above it, was shut in their faces. Martin rang and waited; standing in the late afternoon sun which came in by the small-paned sash-window, he was oddly reminded of a summer morning, nearly fifteen years earlier, when he had stood there hammering and ringing, to know whether his daughter was yet born. He stole a glance at her

vivid, excited face; he had not guessed in those days
what a pleasure she would prove. Smiling at her disappointment, he turned away. "There's nobody in," he
said, "but we'll come another time. We'll go round to
the office now and fetch some letters I want, and then
we'll go home."

Stacy was content; she loved going to the office and
prowling round like an inquisitive mouse among the
blue prints and drawings on her father's desk; she
never disturbed things, and he was often amused by
the sharp intelligence of her questions. He stayed
longer than he should have done this afternoon, explaining to her the details of a cottage hospital which
he was building in Surrey. They were late for tea, and
Letty was not best pleased with them when they did
arrive. She said, "I think you might remember that it
makes a lot of trouble when meals have to be brought
back, especially when one of the maids is having her
afternoon off"; and she also showed a disposition to
blame them for going to Gray's Inn without her. "You
might have taken me if you were going to show Stacy
the flat. You might have thought I should be interested
to see it again." Stacy, with that dashed and bewildered look which her mother's injustice so often produced, protested, "But we didn't plan to go there.
We just thought of it after we'd seen the Hall. And
we didn't get in." She sounded forlorn, but Martin was
unable to defend her; he said as cheerfully as he could,
"We'll all make an expedition together another time";
but he was not altogether surprised when his wife retorted, "I don't think I should care to go, after all. I
expect it's spoilt."

He knew better than she or Stacy what was the matter with her: she was jealous of their Saturday expeditions though she had no real wish to join them; and she would have kept Stacy permanently at home from them if she could have thought of a good excuse. She did raise obstacles whenever it was possible; she would magnify a cold of Stacy's or arrange an unexpected tea-party without consulting the child; and once she actually fixed a series of music-lessons for Saturday afternoons; but Martin did intervene that time, and, after a great deal of argument, secured his daughter's companionship. "It'll do her much more good to be out of doors with me," he declared, after Stacy had appealed to him. "She's shut up indoors quite long enough in the week. And you'll never make a musician out of the child, Letty, whatever you do." Letty said crossly, "No, she's taken after you there;" for she had had a pretty voice and played a little when Martin first married her; but all her notes had been lost on his untuneful ear, and she had not been sufficiently determined to keep her music up. Aubrey had inherited this taste; but Stacy's ears were deaf to melody and her fingers were all thumbs on the piano, though they were clever enough with a pencil; so Letty, after a fair amount of the rather spiteful mockery which had lately become characteristic of her, gave up her attempt to encroach upon the Saturday afternoons and left Martin and his daughter to amuse each other in their own fashion.

One day, on top of an old horse-bus, jogging down Ludgate Hill, Martin told Stacy, "They used to say that Wren's daughter, Jane, designed the steeple of one of his churches. I'm sure I don't know which." Stacy was pleased, and said, "I wish you did. I'd like to go and look at it."

"Well, you probably have by this time. I'll try and find out which it's supposed to be. But I daresay the whole story's quite untrue."

Stacy set her sixteen-year-old lips in her own obstinate way, and objected, "I don't see why. A woman could be an architect, couldn't she?"

"Not in those days."

"Could she now?"

Martin was struck, not for the first time, by the bright, sparkling intelligence of his daughter's grey eyes. He was considering their limpidity rather than his subject as he answered absently, "Shouldn't think she'd be much use. Design's not everything. You want to be able to bully the builder's foreman."

Stacy said with determination, "I don't see why a woman shouldn't build a house at any rate. We ought to know more about them than men do. After all, we have to manage them." She spoke with an air of experience which made Martin smile.

"Did Wren's daughter design any of his houses?" she enquired.

"I never heard anyone say so. I don't really know much about her, except that she played the organ, and that her father was very fond of her, and that she died young."

2

Martin's holidays abroad had become too expensive for him while he was paying for his children's education, but after his discovery of his daughter he no longer regretted them. He remembered the next three years as "Stacy's holidays" and found them more satis-

fying than any others. There was a Cornish Easter at
Mullion, in 1908, when they walked for miles over
the gorse-scented heaths of the Lizard, and collected
lovely little granite churches, with barrel-roofs and
elaborate pew-ends and strange, pagan names. There
was a bicycling summer in the Cotswolds, the same
year, when they played truant from Letty for ten
days, and rode from one stone-built, stone-tiled village
to another across the high open country, or followed
slow streams through the water-meadows to their
source. They visited Stacy's grandfather's church, a
great empty Perpendicular barn, "more glass than
wall," with a fan-vaulted roof and three Jacobean
tombs in the chancel, all strapwork, and bosses, and
kneeling children in trunk hose and ruffs. It was in the
Cotswolds that Martin gave Stacy her first lessons in
dry-fly fishing, a sport which they were to enjoy together in later years, though Letty had never cared
for it. The roads were white with dust that September,
between the long stone walls; the weather was as
golden as the Flemish glass that Stacy loved in Fair-
ford church, with its fiery furnaces, its lost tormented
souls, its red and blue devils with basilisk eyes.

Then there was the summer of 1909, when Martin
was restoring a farmhouse in the Kentish hopfields.
The Lovells were moving as usual that year, from
Brompton to Westminster this time, and Martin established his wife and family at Rye, between houses. He
came down to visit them at week-ends, and to keep an
eye on the earlier stages of his new job. They had a
weather-tiled, oak-timbered, lattice-windowed cottage
on the uplifted southwest corner of the town, at the
angle of Watchbell Street and Trader's Passage. It

was dark, cramped, and inconvenient in Letty's eyes;
but it had linen-fold panelling in the single sitting-
room and a four-centred stone arch over a Tudor
hearth with a fireback of Sussex ironwork which had
been fatal to Martin on his visit of inspection. The
diamond-paned windows of its projecting upper story
looked out over the sandstone cliff with its winding
stairway, but were high enough to ignore the immediate foreground of timberyard, tarred warehouses,
huddled cottages and tidal stream; they fronted the
brown, sheep-dotted levels of the salt-marsh, the low
hills by Fairlight and the line of the Channel, where
the ships sailed on air. An attic window of Stacy's,
looking north, got the crowded dormers of Mermaid
Street and the gilt weathercock on the church tower.
Martin and Stacy loved the cobbled, grass-grown
streets of Rye, its warm, confused pattern of roof and
gable, its unexpected alleys and slopes and stairs; but
Letty thought it a stuffy, relaxing place and unlikely to
suit her delicate son, just back from his first year at his
public school. When he came down for the holidays he
spent her time with him on the shore at Camber. They
used to take picnic food down every morning by the
tram across the marshes, and bathe and idle all day
on the sandhills; it was the kind of thing that lazy
Aubrey enjoyed. Stacy was more active: she would
condescend to swimming with her brother, and bicycle
races on the hard sands afterwards, but she greatly
preferred the week-ends when Martin was down and
could be coaxed into taking her over to inspect the
week's progress at the farm.

Pennyfarthing was ten miles inland, among the hop-
gardens and hazel copses and patchwork fields of the

Kent and Sussex border; but it stood upon a little hill above the Rother valley, and secured a mild, pastoral outlook with a hint of the distant marsh. It consisted of a tumbledown, half-timbered, fifteenth-century farmhouse, a good deal plastered-over and pulled about, a range of thatched, dilapidated stables and cowsheds, a rickyard with a granary on staddles, and a couple of oast-houses; it had been bought by rich City people who intended to let the fields and use the house as a week-end cottage.

Martin fell in love with each detail of Pennyfarthing, the mullioned windows, ranged light by light, the porch with its nail-studded, oaken door, the heavy turned balusters, moulded handrail and dog-gate of the oak staircase, the projecting upper stories with their crazy, sagging gables and the steep pitch of the lichen-spotted tiles. A hurried first visit had shown him where a couple of floors had been put in between the stone flags of the great hall and its hammer-beam roof, whose black, polished timbers took his breath away when first he put his head through the trap-door into the cobwebbed attics and saw the tie-beams and chamfered king-post above him and was confronted by the blind, expectant gaze of a supporting angel.

Stacy used to bicycle over with him, and sit about the rickyard in the sun during his discussions with the workmen, and listen dutifuly while he lectured her in fits and snatches about the house.

"This place is the descendant of the original old fortified manor, with a great hall in the middle, where everybody ate and slept, and a solar one end for the family, and a kitchen the other end. Pennyfarthing's a bit more complicated than that at present, but you'll be able to see what I mean when I've done with the place. I shall pull out those two floors that have been put into the great hall, and let it go right up to the roof as it did originally; and I shall put back the dais, and they can dine on it. That ought to make them feel mediæval and lordly. There's not much left of the screens at the kitchen end, but there's enough to restore from. I shall have to put in a fireplace for show; an open hearth with a big stone hood will do, though the place obviously never had one. The smoke must have gone out through a louvre in the roof. There's a place in the attics where the cross-braces are missing. Of course, one open fire won't be much good for the Leadbitters in a damp neighbourhood like this, but they're going to have central heating all over the place. I've got to think of a way to disguise the radiators. A sort of wooden lattice work, I think, the kind you get in a village butcher's shop. Mrs. Leadbitter wanted imitation oak chests, with linen-fold carving, but I stopped that firmly. It's a miracle that the oriel's never been pulled down; the two modern floors went right across it, but most of the tracery is complete enough. I'm going to have great fun turning the solar into their bedroom. I shall make them have it painted pale green and spangled with gold stars; that's what Henry the Third had at Westminster. The little room underneath will make them a winter parlour. I shall have to put a good deal of new work into the kitchen quarters: they're hopelessly rambling and tumbled down. Dairies and sculleries and wash-houses are no good to the Leadbitters' servants, they'll want everything very up-to-date; but I shall be able to use up a lot of the old material from the sheds and barns to make the outside of the kitchen wing match the rest of the house. And we're going to run a covered way round all four sides of the stack-yard, through the old cow-sheds, and use them as the garage and the engine-room and so forth; and we're going to make a billiard-room out of the barn. It's got a perfectly magnificent open timbered roof." This was his first opportunity for an antiquarian restoration, and he was drunk with excitement over it.

One Saturday, however, he admitted to his daughter, "What does rather baffle me, is where to get them any spare rooms. I can manage their own rooms and the servants' quarters, but I honestly don't see what I'm to do for all their week-end visitors. Leadbitter now wants to buy up a fourteenth-century cottage that's for sale somewhere over Lewes way and number all the beams and timbers, then pull the place down and transport it here bodily and stick it down at the end of the house; but I don't fancy that somehow. I'd rather just have used the original work. However, I suppose I've got to let the poor man do what he likes with his own house, though it's very difficult to remember that clients have a right to their own ideas. I shall take the train to Robertsbridge on my way home to-morrow, and inspect his cottage and see what can be done with it."

Stacy swung her feet from the sun-warmed coping of the rickyard wall. It was cushioned with house-leeks and stone-crop, and wide enough to make her a comfortable perch.

"I should make the oast-houses into rooms if I were you," she said, as placidly as if she had considered the whole matter for weeks.

Her father was taken aback; he considered the suggestion and did not find it impracticable.

"I hadn't thought they would be much use for anything but storehouses," he said, in the doubtful, abstracted voice which meant that he was struck by her notion.

"Well, I think they'd make ducky little bedrooms," said Stacy. "I've always wanted to live in a round room. You'd have to put a floor across, halfway up, and cut some windows, deep, splayed ones, with window-sills, that would do for dressing-tables. You could keep that winding open staircase; it's all sound oak timbers. I've been up there several times."

"You seem to have thought it all out," said Martin, with reluctant admiration. "Let's go and look at them now."

The result of the inspection was so satisfactory that he passed it on to the Leadbitters when they came down.

"My little daughter wants us to make a guests' wing out of the two oast-houses," he said, and entered into explanations which concluded apologetically, "I really believe we could, and it would be much less expensive than importing that other cottage."

"Well, we might try," said Mr. Leadbitter, blinking at Stacy with his weak, weary eyes. "Suppose we go and look"; and when they returned from their tour of inspection and he had agreed to Stacy's idea, he said, "This young lady ought to go into your office, Mr. Lovell," which made Stacy blush.

The Leadbitters were rich and rather commonplace business people, but almost ideal clients from the material point of view. They were prepared, from different motives, to spend anything in reason on the repair of Pennyfarthing. Mr. Leadbitter was a kindly, intelligent, deceptively meek and quiet little man, with all the Jew's sensitive perception of beauty and rarity. Mrs. Leadbitter was not quite so sensitive, but she understood the value of advertisement, and a restored farmhouse, at a suitable distance between London and the coast, with a convenient golf-course, a swimming-pool in the grounds, and a sufficiency of bathrooms and bedrooms for the week-end parties then coming into fashion, had become a necessity to her in her particular stage of social expansion. It was all in the picture for Mr. Leadbitter to explain the mediæval traditions of Pennyfarthing, to display the old title-deeds and discuss the various families who might have owned or altered the original manor house; it was equally natural that the traces of its later less honourable existence as a farm should be obliterated, that the stack-yard should become a garden and the farm-buildings bedrooms and garages. Pennyfarthing was to become a detached fragment of London where the Leadbitters and their City friends could discuss business and pleasure in as much comfort as if they had stayed at home. Martin recognised this; it made him feel vaguely guilty and unhappy, in spite of his pleasure in renewing the youth of the old house. He could have wished it another fate. He also had his difficulties with Mrs. Leadbitter, over decoration, in which she inclined to florid, tinselled, pseudo-Italian complications of church candlesticks, wrought-iron grilles, painted furniture, and modern brocade; and over the garden, where she

planned a number of the most distressing horticultural
extravagances of the time.

This garden had proved unexpectedly interesting to
Martin. The raised piece of ground on the western
side of the farmhouse had obviously once been part
of a terrace. There were still traces of a retaining
wall, and it was easily restored and flagged to make
a formal walk, where the sun came in the afternoons.
At either end Martin built a semicircular brick seat,
and in the middle of the low brick parapet, opposite
the oriel of the hall, he put a wrought-iron gateway,
between piers with cannon-ball finials, and a flight of
steps leading down into the meadow. On the opposite
side of the house, facing the entrance porch, he took
the old stack-yard, surrounded by farm-buildings, and
turned it into a knot-garden, where formal box-edged
plots of herbs caught the morning sun. At the north
end of the terrace, where a green and stagnant pond,
beneath a yew-tree, with odd mounds and traces of
stonework about it, suggested a bridge and a moat, he
made a rectangular pool with a lead Mercury alighting
upon it. Otherwise he discouraged Mrs. Leadbitter's
yearnings for statuary and rose-covered arches, and
restricted her to the walled kitchen garden with its
pleached alleys, espaliered apple-trees and pleasant
alternations of flowers and fruit.

And in due course the house was finished, and he and
Stacy actually spent a week-end there together during
the following summer, a week-end which they both
found exhausting and singularly depressing, in spite of
the Leadbitters' constant efforts to entertain them.
Stacy said mournfully, as they went back in the train on
Monday morning, "It's a shame that people like the

Leadbitters and their fat friends have got to live in Pennyfarthing, after we've made it so nice. They spoil it. I do wish we could have lived in it ourselves." Martin laughed at her forlorn tone, but he was obliged to admit that he felt like that about most of the houses he built; his clients spoilt them after they were finished.

VI

CURIOUSLY ENOUGH, Martin had never built a house
for his own family, though the Lovells were always
moving in those days, as the children grew older and
noisier and took up more room, and Martin became a
little richer and a little more hopeful in his ideas. Every
three or four years he would discover some derelict
and charming bargain, which cried out to him for res-
cue; and he would dig up his family by the roots, settle them in their new home, add to it and transform
it until its perfection destroyed his interest and he
could find nothing more to do with it except sell it and
start afresh. He used to explain to Letty that an architect's own house was his best advertisement, and inflict
upon her patient ears long calculations to prove the
economy of his method. "After all, darling, I bought
this house for so much and I've only spent so much
on it, so if these people will take it off my hands for
what they say in this letter, we shall really have lived
here for three and a half years rent-free." Letty never
tried to understand these or any other figures; she was
hopelessly unbusinesslike, all she knew was that she
hated moves. She was as miserable on such occasions as
a cat in a strange house; Stacy at fifteen had said, "It's
a pity there's no way of buttering Mother's paws." By

the time her slow affections had attached themselves
to a new home and neighbourhood Martin had usually
lost interest in both, and was wandering about on Sunday afternoons with Stacy, looking for fresh worlds to
conquer.

They had lived in four houses since they left the flat
in Gray's Inn. Their first venture had been the weather-
boarded, white-painted, six-roomed cottage on the edge
of Hampstead Heath. Then had come their villa on
the banks of the Regent's Park canal: and after it the
Old Brompton house, in a then uncivilised region of
late Georgian terraces, small grey houses with minute
back-gardens where fruit-trees survived from lost
orchards and the underground menace of the District
trains came rumbling through unexpected shafts and
air-holes between the garden walls. Then they moved
in 1909 to a small Georgian house in the Westminster
slums, whose red brick front, hooded doorway,
wrought-iron fanlight and extinguishers and formal
fenestration were all as neat as a classical epigram.
Even Letty admitted that the Barton Street house was
beautiful, though she shuddered at the fumigation
which had to be performed before they could live in
it. None of the doors and windows fitted there; the
cracks which opened in the pine-panelling each summer
let through piercing winter draughts and Martin's little basket grates, with wrought-iron hobs and fire-
backs, never seemed to warm the cold air which moved
along the uneven boards. Neither Letty nor Aubrey
were ever well in that house. The boy seemed to need
a more bracing air when he came back from Eton for
the holidays; he was always catching colds and sore
throats in the winter, and flagging in the summer heat,

and Letty worried about him and seemed to lose her
own energy. Perhaps the fogs from the river and the
marshy subsoil depressed her. Martin himself was
obliged to admit that the water ran down the panelling on damp days, that the Chinese wallpaper in
Letty's bedroom peeled off in strips, and that there
was a musty smell about the basement, in spite of all
his improvements. And Stacy, who loved the house,
and had encouraged him to take it, was away abroad
for most of the two years that he owned it. Perhaps it
was not surprising that he accepted the offer of an enthusiastic American who fell in love with it in 1911,
just after a serious illness of Aubrey's, and gave him
his own price for it.

Aubrey had always been delicate; he had taken his
childish illnesses much harder than his sister, and Letty
had been obliged to devote a great deal of her time
to nursing him. For this reason, and perhaps on account of some unexplained affinity, he had always been
her favourite child. She had a devouring, unbalanced
maternal passion for the boy, and she was jealous of
Stacy's intimacy with her father, but still more jealous
of any influence which Martin might have developed
over his son; she definitely, if unconsciously, tried to
keep the boy to herself. She and his grandmother
spoilt him devotedly, favoured him at Stacy's expense,
diverted his punishments to his sister on the score of
her seniority and greater fertility in mischief-making,
and did their best to establish a subterranean rivalry
between the brother and sister, which only did not
flourish because Stacy loved and protected the quiet
affectionate little boy, who admired and imitated her
devoutly.

Aubrey never got any of the whippings on which his indifferent sister flourished; he was much too docile, virtuous and unenterprising to need them. He was intelligent, fanciful, dreamy, shy and easily fatigued; it was perfectly true that he would never have got into mischief unless encouraged by Stacy. Letty considered him too delicate to leave home, she kept him under her own eye and sent him first to a kindergarten in Hampstead, and then to a preparatory in South Kensington, where he behaved in a consistently virtuous manner. He appeared to have a mind as orderly as his unblotted copy-books, his physique was poor and his vitality too low for insubordination. He always did exactly as he was told, rose surely and steadily to the top of each of his forms, was moved up regularly once a year, and brought home three or four books from each prize-giving. Letty and her mother were inordinately proud of him, and Lady Stapleford in particular never failed to point out how much cleverer Aubrey was than his sister. Stacy did not care; she admired his performances and sighed that she could not hope to imitate them. Martin was impressed and a little alarmed by his son's development, he nodded solemnly when the headmaster talked about scholarships, and agreed with Letty that a public school would be a necessary expense in any case.

He had only been to a country grammar school himself; he wanted this queer, shy, unfriendly child of his, with whom he never seemed to become familiar, to have a better chance than his own had been; and he was the more anxious to be just to Aubrey because of his own conscious preference for Stacy's mischievous ways and company. He said nervously to Aubrey,

"Don't you tire yourself out with a lot of scholarship work. I'll manage a public school for you somehow, whether you get a scholarship or not. You're down for Winchester and Charterhouse, your mother made up her mind to that years ago. She actually put you down for Eton, too, but that I'm afraid I can't afford." He smiled apologetically, but Aubrey remained composed. If his father expected a display of excitement or gratitude he did not get it.

"I don't suppose the scholarship papers are awfully difficult," remarked Aubrey, with perfect placidity and independence. "Anyhow, I can have a preliminary shot this year to see what they're like, and then go all out for it next year." Martin felt baffled. Letty never had any doubts of Aubrey's success, and the event justified her; the boy carried off a scholarship to Eton in 1907, a year before he needed it. Martin was a little taken aback; he admitted regretting the worn, delicate stonework, smooth lawns and sliding river at Winchester, which had taken his eye when he visited them on a day of autumn gold and smoking bonfires; but Letty and Lady Stapleford bubbled with delighted satisfaction, Stacy was unaffectedly joyful and even Aubrey's pallid, composed face relaxed into an expression of relief when the news came; he admitted to having been anxious about his Greek prose.

Letty probably derived the most pleasure from Aubrey's first two years at Eton. She fussed over his clothes, treasured his letters, pestered his tutor for information about him, bought new dresses for all the school functions, and counted the days from one holiday to another with an eagerness which was absent when Stacy went abroad that winter to her finishing school.

Lady Stapleford's interest was naturally of a more grandmotherly order, and did not prevent her from an increasingly critical attitude towards Aubrey's appearance and manners. Stacy was occupied with her own affairs, and Martin used to reproach himself for preferring her lively letters to Aubrey's brief, unsatisfying scrawls, and for missing her bright presence more than the slightly supercilious, exhausted courtesy of Aubrey's conversation.

The boy had not done as well as was expected of him. During his first, and part of his second year he had continued to work according to the admirable but rather mechanical method imposed upon him at his preparatory school; then, as the effect of this stimulus waned, he came under the influence of less strenuous ideals, and began to assert his developing personality in various unsatisfactory ways. Martin had poor reports of him in the spring and summer of 1910; he was not working so well, he had been mixed up in one or two stupid bits of insubordination, he seemed idle, and uninterested in work or games, he formed unwise friendships. Letty was distressed by his ungracious ways at home, and a new distaste which he showed for her company; she had tried, foolishly, to reproach him about his school reports, and then had stupidly accepted his violent declaration that people were prejudiced against him, that you couldn't get on if you weren't good at games, that women didn't understand this kind of thing and only made fools of themselves when they interfered. Martin found it equally difficult to get on terms with his son; he was guiltily conscious that the boy had been left too much to an injudicious mother, and was consequently spoilt; he tried to talk to Aubrey and found him sulky and difficult. He was, however, somewhat reassured by an interview with Aubrey's tutor, a casual, efficient individual, not much liked by mothers, who murmured, "It's the ordinary thing. Most of 'em go through it sooner or later. Perfectly natural for a delicate bookish boy to get a fit of shamming the normal healthy brute. Don't suppose it'll last much longer. Hope it won't."

Martin was encouraged by this professional view to hope that Aubrey was being taken a little too seriously by his family, and that his case was not so abnormal as his parents supposed. Unfortunately, an attack of measles, with aural complications and a mastoid abscess, cut two terms out of the boy's schooling at this critical period. When Aubrey returned to Eton at seventeen it was no longer possible even for his adoring mother to reckon on the scholarship which should have taken him to Oxford. She and Aubrey, however, had set their hearts on Trinity, and Martin found it beyond him to disappoint them. He talked to Aubrey about his future but got very little response; Aubrey was limply acquiescent in the idea that he might eventually come into his father's office, but seemed to think that he need make no hurried decision. Letty was definitely hostile. She distressed Martin by revealing a concealed disdain for his profession which he had never suspected in her; he had realised that she did not understand his work, and that she had always been annoyed by Stacy's genuine interest in its details, but he was not prepared to be told that his unsatisfactory son was too good to waste on architecture. Letty was al-

most spiteful about the matter; she astonished and
wounded him by the obstinacy of her attitude. "I don't
want Aubrey to go into the office, just because there's
a place waiting for him. Why shouldn't he do something better? He's really clever, though you won't
admit it, just because he's been kept back by illness,
poor boy, and had one or two bad reports from people
who don't appreciate him. You've always promised
him three years at Oxford, and it won't be fair if he
doesn't get it. He needs a chance to find out what he's
really fit for."

Martin was accustomed by this time to his wife's
habit of improving her own case by inaccurate recollections of past promises; he knew it would be useless
to protest that he had never expected to send Aubrey
to Oxford without a scholarship. He murmured de-
spondingly, "I don't know what the boy is fit for. He
seems thoroughly casual and slack, and he doesn't show
any particular bent."

Letty said, absurdly, "I'd like him to go into the
diplomatic service." It was the silly kind of contribu-
tion she usually made to a serious discussion and she
hardly listened to Martin's reasoning about the lack
of private means and family influence.

"He ought to do well at the Bar," she went on
vaguely. "He's got such delightful manners when he
chooses, and I'm sure he could speak well." Martin
refrained from saying that he did not think Aubrey
had a legal mind. Letty herself had admitted the ab-
surdity of Aubrey as a doctor, or a soldier; and even
agreed that he would not be likely to do well in business. It seemed as if Oxford, after all, would be the
best solution of the difficulty.

"I daresay he'll find his feet there in a year or so, and make up his mind to work. At present his head's full of vague notions about writing or painting that won't amount to anything. The boy might turn out something of a scholar, after all, if he gets his health back, and picks up his old tastes; or he might make a schoolmaster, or a civil servant, if he could only develop a little more method and regularity," thought Martin, unhappily. "Or perhaps he'll change his mind and come to me. I'd have liked a son to follow after me." But that reflection seemed to be wasted on Aubrey and his mother, so he kept it to himself. He did make a reluctant reference to the expense of Oxford, but Aubrey did not seem to take it very seriously and Letty refused to consider it at all. She had always been vague about money, and Martin had never had the heart to pin her down to the economies which were really needed in their lives.

"I do think you ought to make a special effort about it," she said, with a pouting mouth and a childish frown. "It's only for three years, after all, and it's a time that will never come again."

Martin had realised, after twenty years of marriage, that no arguments ever affected Letty's obstinacy. He was helpless under her soft determined shower of reasons, and he still could not bear to disappoint her in anything that she thought important. Also there was the old feeling at the bottom of his heart that Aubrey was not his favourite child, and deserved at least some material compensation for his father's secret indifference towards him. So that, when Letty concluded reproachfully, "You didn't mind the expense when you wanted to send Stacy abroad," he yielded on the question of Oxford, and said, "All right, the boy shall go. He'd better read law; if he finds he has a turn for it he can go on with it, and if he decides to come into my office a little legal knowledge will be a help to him. But I can't run to more than three years, and I can't make him a very big allowance." Letty flung her arms tempestuously round his neck, gave him the kisses which still had their old power to move and delight him, and shelved the question of the allowance, as he very well realised, for a later appeal.

2

It was true that Stacy's foreign education had been an extravagance of her father's own devising. Letty had said, three years earlier, "A boy must go to a Public School, but a girl is all the nicer for being educated at home." So Aubrey had gone to Eton, and Stacy had continued to attend a High School until she was turned sixteen. She had begun to take rather more interest in her work there under her father's encouragement, and in particular had developed an unsuspected faculty for mathematics; and she had turned out, as might have been predicted, extremely good at games. Martin supposed that both qualities must be part of her inheritance from the Staplefords, whom she resembled in many ways. Stacy was as practical, obstinate and quick-tempered as her grandmother had been, and she did not seem in the least anxious to go abroad and finish her education.

"It's a shame to take me away when I've just been made hockey captain," was her attitude to the discussions which took place in the autumn after the Lovells came back from Rye. Her parents, however, became for once united in their plans for her, though from different motives. Letty had opposed Martin at first on the score of extravagance, but had eventually agreed, "Stacy had better go. If she doesn't get away from that awful school she'll grow up into a regular hockey-hoyden, all muddy boots and freckles and a loud voice. She's too much inclined that way as it is. A year in Paris will teach her to put on her clothes properly, and take care of her hands and her complexion." She glanced down regretfully at her own soft, useless fingers as she murmured to herself, "I did hope I should have a pretty daughter."

"Stacy's not going to be so bad-looking," maintained her father obstinately, admitting however, "Of course, she hasn't taken after you." For Letty had remained fragile, dainty and precise, and he admired her as much as ever, while Stacy was going through an ungainly, colt-like stage of graceful, uncontrolled limbs, innocent, awkward movements and blushes, and wild spirits collapsing uncertainly into self-consciousness.

"No, Stacy's her father's daughter," said Letty thoughtfully, and left Martin with an unexpected warmth at his heart. If Stacy were truly his daughter something in her must respond to what he was trying to give her, although her ignorance might resist him at first.

"I'd like her to go to several places, not only Paris," was all he said. Letty yielded to this and Stacy was sent to Paris for the spring and summer of 1910, and to Dresden for the winter that followed it; and before she had been gone three months Martin realised with satisfaction that he had been right, and that her eyes were beginning to open on his world. She still wrote school-girl letters to her mother. "Am rather short of money, as I had to buy new hair-ribbon. Mademoiselle took me to be fitted for my new Sunday frock; it's going to be black, with a green collar. Please send me some more woolly combinations. Mine have all shrunk, and I can't buy them here. French shops don't seem to sell anything but vests." But she began to send Martin queer little messages. "Tell Daddy we went to Notre Dame on Sunday. It was Heavenly. Tell Daddy we saw the fountains playing when we went to Versailles. The gardens were lovely. Tell Daddy I don't think much of the Arc de Triomphe. It's lumpish and vulgar. Are the real ones, in Rome, any better?" And then she took to sending him picture post-cards: "Here is some Architecture for you" on the sky above the Sainte-Chapelle; "Have you ever been here, and didn't you like the blue windows?" across the west front of Chartres cathedral, where she went on a half-term holiday; and more briefly, but confidently in one corner of a salon at the Petit Trianon, "This is a nice room." And after three months she suddenly began to write him occasional, clumsy, stilted letters which he answered religiously, treasured shamefacedly, and read over to himself at odd times.

Letty had at first decided that Stacy was not to come home that summer, for fear of dropping back into English again. "Much better for her to go to Normandy with Mademoiselle Audemer, and stay there until it's time for her to go to Dresden." But for once Martin was both designing and obstinate. He discovered it was necessary for him to go to Germany, and visit a New Art exhibition there at the end of

August. Letty realised his determination, and yielded with a maternal, disconcerting smile which reminded him of his first holiday at Bruges; but he stifled the recollection. He dutifully visited the exhibition, and disapproved of some fantastically gabled houses and a stupid tower topped by an armament like a policeman's hand; and then he played truant with Stacy for a fortnight through the little cathedral-towns of Bavaria. He remembered the South Germany of those days but vaguely afterwards. Its shining plains and rivers, dark forests, and laden orchards were only a picture spread for his daughter's eyes at the window of a railway-carriage. Its high-pitched mediæval roofs, peering wooden gables and crowded dormers leant crazily together to menace her bright head. Its leafy alleys, formal parks, and creamy, florid baroque façades were only backgrounds for Stacy, leaning her elbows on a café table, opening her wide eyes at swaggering grey-cloaked officers, setting her teeth in a triangle of *Zwetchkentorte,* and stirring up the whipped cream in her chocolate to make it melt the sooner. It was the first and perhaps the best of their holidays abroad together.

At the end of September he left her in Dresden, where she was to spend the winter. She had the summer that followed in Paris again, and met her family at St. Briac just before her eighteenth birthday, startling Martin with her hair done on top of her head, an assured manner and some intimidating French clothes. Almost immediately he had his first taste of what was to be expected in the future.

Nicholas Barford, himself unmarried, had had a long-legged, ugly, untidy, intelligent nephew, who had begun his training at the Architectural Association in Bedford Square a few months before his uncle's death, and was now just up for his finals. Martin liked Oliver Barford, found much amusement in his green originalities, had given him holiday-work in the office during the last two years of his training, and was considering employing him as an assistant, for his own sake as well as his uncle's. He had invited the boy home to supper in Westminster on several occasions, and now suggested that he might spend part of his holiday with the Lovells at St. Briac; but here, oddly enough, Letty demurred and when pressed, made the surprising objection, "I don't want Stacy to marry an architect."

"Stacy?" her father gasped. "Good Heavens! they're only a couple of babies. Why on earth should Oliver want to marry Stacy?"

Letty merely persisted, with her own increasing obstinacy, "Stacy's eighteen, and that boy's nearly twenty-three. What do you expect if you throw them together for weeks on end in fine weather on a holiday with nothing else to do?"

Martin grumbled, "I expect them to go rowing and swimming together, and playing tennis together, and sketching and bicycling round churches with me."

"And dancing together in the evenings," Letty took him up, "and getting lost together on expeditions and going out together in the evenings to look at the moon. Oh! Martin, surely you remember what it's like?" She looked for the moment flushed and vexed, and pretty, and like her old self; Martin stared at her in perplexity, he did not see what he had done to annoy her.

"But Stacy," he repeated stupidly, preoccupied with

his daughter rather than with his wife, "Stacy isn't old enough for love-affairs already." Letty looked at him, sighed and shook her head: the light faded out of her eyes. "We're all getting older," she said, with a trifle of regret.

"Well, I call it pure nonsense," grumbled Martin, "you can't keep all the young men you know away from Stacy, for fear they should fall in love with her. She's bound to get married some time, I suppose." He did not sound as if the prospect pleased him. "You don't want to keep her at home all her life, do you?"

"Certainly not," said Letty placidly. "But she needn't throw herself away on the first young man she sees. I should hope she could do better for herself than Oliver Barford. She's going to be very pretty and charming." And she repeated with petulance, "I don't want her to marry an architect."

"Well, why shouldn't she?" Martin was perplexed and huffy. "After all, you married the first young man you met, and he was an architect; but we've been fairly happy, haven't we?" He kissed Letty ruefully, as if it occurred to him for the first time that she might not have had all that she expected out of life. She kissed him back, as kindly as usual, but she did not reassure him; and the subject of Oliver Barford was dropped. The invitation was not given, but some rebellious instinct made Martin take the young man into his office that autumn, and he became a fairly frequent visitor to the Lovells' house.

Stacy was not there, however; she had gone to Italy for the winter.

VII

WHEN STACY came home for good in the spring of
1911, she found her family established in a new house
in Campden Hill Square. Her mother seemed more
favourably disposed towards it than might have been
expected, considering that she had only been in it six
weeks. She approved of the garden and the neighbourhood of the Campden Hill Lawn-tennis Club, and she
liked the double drawing-room on the first floor, which
was large enough for the simple dances of those days.
"We can have a violin and a piano," said Letty eagerly,
"and a trestle-table for the refreshments in the dining-
room, and the garden will do for sitting-out. People
can go in and out by the French-window in the study,
and we can put coloured lights round the flower-beds
and along the top of the wall."

Martin was, thought Stacy, a little depressed by the
house, and she discovered that he had only taken it in
despair because, as usual, he had left his family without a roof over their heads. He had really wanted to
go and live in a delightful, dilapidated, rat-haunted
William-and-Mary house on Ham Common, with a
classical façade of rusticated Ionic columns, modelled
plaster ceilings, heavy with fruit and flowers, a stair-

case with a carved balustrade, lit by a domed cupola, and wet lawns sloping to the Thames. It was curious that his fancy always led him to these unhealthy and unfashionable situations. Letty had absolutely refused even to go and look at the Ham Common house, and had protested, "How can you talk such nonsense? We can't bury Stacy in the suburbs just when she's growing up, and expecting to go to parties. How is she to get back all that way after dances? It's perfectly absurd." She had been so unusually determined that Martin had yielded, but in comparison with his romantic ruin the house on Campden Hill could not but seem dull. It was of a simple, flat-fronted late Georgian type, with large rooms whose chief merit was that they gave plenty of room for the old furniture which Martin collected; it stood in a row with twenty others, looking on a soot-bitten square garden, and gave him no scope for any structural alteration unless it were the enlargement of his study, and the provision of a second bathroom over it; this Letty had forbidden on the ground that he would interefere with the drawing-room balcony, and the garden under it.

However, there was a sufficiency of bedrooms for Stacy and Aubrey and their friends, and there was a blue and astonishing view from the flat roof westwards over the Thames valley, which reminded Martin of the Hampstead cottage and afforded him some consolation when he discovered it.

"I daresay we shall move before very long," he said hopefully to Stacy, who thought this probable.

Meanwhile, Letty embarked with determination on the task of bringing her daughter out according to the fashions of 1911. Stacy was excited by the prospect and ready enough to wear new clothes; but inclined to disagree with her mother over their choice and anxious to make her own plans for the disposal of the sixty-five pounds' dress-allowance with which Martin had recently endowed her.

"I don't suppose she'll ever keep to it," said Letty, who was incapable of keeping to her own housekeeping allowance. "Girls never do. But I shall pay her shoe-mending and her cleaners' bills, and give her an extra frock when she needs one, so she ought to do fairly well. It'll be good for her to learn to manage her own money. Of course, she'll make a lot of mistakes. At present she's in the stage of buying things that are much too old for her. She wanted a black satin harem-skirt the other day at Marshall and Snelgrove's, but of course I couldn't let her wear that in her first season."

Martin, in turn, was amused to get Stacy's protest, "Mother never buys me anything that suits me. She thinks young girls ought to look pink-and-white like daisies. That may have been all very well for her, with her golden hair and blue eyes, but I'm not that type." In the matter of dress she and her mother belonged to different schools. Letty inclined to the picturesque rather than the fashionable, spent too much on her hats, and too little on her shoes and gloves; Stacy was good at tailored clothes, and particularly neat about the feet and hands, but her boyish, brown-skinned, swaggering youth looked best in country clothes, she never quite carried off the fluffy evening dresses of the period. As far as managing her allowance went, however, she could do that already a good deal better than her mother. Letty had always been unsystematic, and as years went on she had less and less to show for her extravagances. She ran Martin into a long bill for Stacy's coming-out dance, with waiters, refreshments, champagne, the green-and-white striped awnings in the garden, the pink roses and smilax of the decorations, and the two new frocks for the occasion, white and silver for the débutante, pink-and-silver for her mother. They were able to dance in the drawing-room, after Martin had superintended the erection of a baize-swathed pillar in the middle of the dining-room, to hold up the floor. It was difficult to collect enough young men, especially as Aubrey was not going to Oxford for another year, but with the brothers of Stacy's school-friends, the immature sons of relations and clients, a contingent of elderly bachelors provided by Martin, and various long-haired, untidy students, contemporaries of Oliver Barford, they managed to make up their numbers. "Of course it'll be much easier another time, when Stacy has made some friends," said Letty, checking her final list with satisfaction, and evidently looking forward to a repetition of a performance which was vaguely depressing her husband.

Stacy seemed to enjoy the occasion; she danced every dance, and would have looked delightful to less prejudiced eyes than her father's; though she vexed her mother by going down to supper with Oliver Barford, who became rather drunk and riotous towards the end of the evening, and insisting on collecting enough people to dance an eightsome reel. The dance went on until after two; Stacy disappeared into the square garden with Oliver and was missing for twenty minutes or so, just when the band had refused to play any longer, and people were beginning to say good-bye.

She got scolded for that by her mother next day, while the gilt chairs, the red carpet, the ice-buckets and the potted palms were being loaded into the caterer's van, looking very dissipated in the May morning sunshine. Letty and Stacy yawned a good deal and were rather cross with each other for a day or two after this festivity, and Martin received a number of unexpectedly large bills: "To hire of six dozen glasses—of two dozen rout-seats—to eight dozen Pol Roger 1900," and so forth, all of which gave him a new light on the expenses of a grown-up daughter's amusements, and made him thankful that he had just received a commission to add a new wing to a boys' preparatory school at Eastbourne. However, he was given to understand that Stacy's coming-out dance had been at once a triumph and an investment. "We had to give a good dance for her at the beginning of the season," declared Letty firmly. "Otherwise she wouldn't have had any invitations. But the Helstons are sure to ask her to their dance now, and the Merryweathers, and the Vaughans." Martin gathered that the principle of reciprocity was firmly established.

And a week or two later he had to come home in the middle of his working afternoon to play host at a tea-party where Letty and Stacy posed solemnly in Court trains and feathers on dust-sheets spread over the drawing-room carpet. Martin protested nervously against this function, but he found that everything was settled; Lady Stapleford had made all the arrangements. She was to present her daughter, and Letty Stacy; it was a very important occasion, and the old lady was there in full Anglo-Indian splendour, with a gown of amber satin and a topaz necklace, clutching a bouquet of tea-roses, and lecturing Stacy about her curtsey. Letty looked like a Chelsea China shepherdess in rose and lilac panniers; Stacy was bright-eyed and a little frightened above her lilies of the valley. Martin, who had evaded accompanying the party, felt a little ashamed of himself, as he watched them drive away in the hired car; and tried dutifully to believe that all these matters were as important and amusing as Letty thought them.

There seemed to be a new, temporary, feminine alliance between Stacy and her mother over clothes and parties and young men, from which he himself was excluded; he tried to hope that it might become permanent, for he had worried over the lack of sympathy between them. He wanted, more than anything in the world, at that moment, to give his daughter a happy life, but he had no particular notion how to set about it. He was obliged to leave her to Letty, who did not, he suspected, for all her maternal enthusiasm, understand what her daughter wanted; but parents, he was beginning to suspect, very seldom knew what was best to do with their children.

At any rate, the parties continued, and Stacy had some more new frocks, and was often not down to breakfast. She and Letty began to talk about Lord's, and Henley, and making up a party next year for Commem.; she and Aubrey joined the Campden Hill Lawn-tennis Club, and spoilt a great many shoes and balls on its dirty asphalt courts; and strange young men in flannels began to appear at supper on Sunday evenings when play was over. Most of them seemed to Martin immature and uninteresting; he even found some difficulty in distinguishing between them, though he realised that this was a sign of advancing years and conscientiously struggled against it. He observed that Oliver Barford was usually among them, and was welcomed more cheerfully by Stacy than by her mother; he spent a great deal of time with the Lovells, in spite of Letty's discouraging politeness.

There was no holiday abroad in 1911 for Martin; the summer had been too expensive for that, and Stacy and Aubrey, rather to his disappointment, petitioned for a seaside holiday with tennis and bathing and golf. He took a house for them at Frinton, but he did not spend much time there himself. He disliked the place on sight, and was relieved to find that an unusual amount of office work enabled him to stay in Campden Hill Square by himself and earn a little more money towards his family's amusement. On the two or three occasions when he did visit them he found them enjoying themselves immensely with a collection of young people who did not particularly interest him. He described them on his return to Oliver, overworking himself in Bedford Row, as a noisy crowd. Oliver laughed in his usual sardonic fashion, and commented, "That's Stacy's taste." Letty had not invited him to Frinton, and he was perhaps a little sore about it.

The winter was not quite so gay and expensive as the summer had been, but it was expensive enough. Stacy played some hard-court tennis, and took up badminton, and went to football matches on Saturday afternoons with various admirers, a proceeding of which her mother did not altogether approve; and there were parties of six or eight made up for the subscription dances of those days. Letty apparently greatly enjoyed rattling down to the Chelsea Town

Hall and similar places of entertainment, in a station
bus hired for the evening, and going in to supper with
some polite partner neglected by her daughter, and
sitting all evening by the wall with the other chaperons,
counting Stacy's dances. She would discuss every incident of the evening next day with much greater enthusiasm than her daughter, who was becoming, Martin
noticed, distinctly critical with the passage of time,
and inclined to make such remarks as, "I thought it
was rather a rotten dance. There weren't enough men,
and what there were wouldn't come out of the smoking-
room"; or "The floor there is fearfully heavy"; or,
"I'm sick of all Joyce's tunes." Martin's simple pride
in his daughter's successes became complicated by a
misgiving that she was not so perfectly happy as her
parents had expected. He wondered whether she could
be in love with any of the young men who hung about
the house. He really did not see why she should dis-
tinguish one more than another, they all seemed to
him so very callow, and dull, and unworthy of a girl's
notice. All, that is, except Oliver Barford who undoubtedly had a curious, original flavour which prevented him from being confused with anyone else. He
certainly spent a great deal of time in the Lovells'
drawing-room, but Martin, disagreeing with Letty on
this point, did not think it probable that Stacy could
fall in love with anyone so familiar to her and so disagreeable. He watched them both with a growing discomfort, which was the fruit of his wife's perpetual
insinuations, but all he could make out was that they
quarrelled on every possible occasion; and he could
hardly blame a quick-tempered girl like Stacy for flying out at anyone who criticised and contradicted her

with such persistent, brotherly unkindness. By Christmas Martin had decided, with a mixture of relief and
regret, that it had all been a false alarm, and that
there was nothing between the two young people.
After all, he told himself, Stacy was not yet twenty. It
was natural that she should take life lightly for the
present; and he, for one, did not want her married yet,
whatever her mother said.

2

The Lovells were a typical family of the professional classes in their time, reasonably prosperous, respectably if not brilliantly connected, rather more
cultivated than the average, friendly, interesting and
given to much simple hospitality. Letty was a sweet,
indulgent, rather extravagant hostess, who loved to
have young people about the house, and was never so
happy as when her table was full. She was perhaps a
little openly tactless in her attempts to get Stacy married, but Stacy was a difficult daughter to manage.
However, she was amusing and popular, danced and
played tennis well and was pretty enough for all practical purposes in her own bright-eyed, brown-haired
style. People thought that she might give her mother
a little trouble at first, but would marry satisfactorily
in the end.

Aubrey went up to Oxford in the autumn of 1912
and was supposed, on his mother's fond authority, to
be very clever, and to have an indefinite but distinguished future before him. He was considered lacka-
daisical, affected and disagreeable by Stacy's friends,
and conceited, spoilt and unstable by his parents' con-

temporaries; but he was very well satisfied with himself.

The family followed the usual, quietly cultivated London round, gave three or four large dinners and one dance a year, kept open house on Sunday afternoons and evenings to their children's friends, enjoyed serious plays but did not care for musical comedy, liked an occasional concert, went the round of Art Exhibitions and spent their holidays on the Continent. Martin had developed into the typical father of such a family. He was indulgently devoted to his wife and children, was taken perhaps a little too much for granted by them, and cheerfully overworked himself on their account, without questioning their expenses. He did not grudge Letty her lavish housekeeping, Stacy her frocks and parties, or Aubrey his Oxford debts; it never occurred to him that their demands on him were excessive, and he took an indulgent, vicarious interest in Letty's enthusiastic accounts of his children's performances. His own pleasures were simple, and were becoming more and more his own concern; music meant little to him, and he left that to Letty and her son, but he liked a theatre when he could get Stacy to go to one with him, and he enjoyed a picture-gallery even if he had to visit it by himself. He had always been a great reader, and with advancing life he had come to prefer the library to the drawing-room: he was not of an unfriendly nature, but he had always been shy, contemplative and easily fatigued; it was his own fault that his family had begun to leave him out of their calculations when they were planning any festivity. "Dad would rather stop at home and have the house to himself," Stacy would murmur, amiably rub-

bing her head against his shoulder like a kitten; and
Martin would smile and honestly agree with her.

Apart from foreign travel, his pleasures and interests were now almost entirely professional, sympathised with by his daughter but unshared by either his
wife or his son. He discovered a deep sense of fulfilment in his work which was curiously lacking in the
personal side of his life. Bricks and mortar had come
of late years to satisfy him better than human relation-
ships. He found an odd, passionless delight in turning
back from his daily life to the blind stone memorials
of the past. Letty had said to him once in their young
days with childish resentment, when they were closer
together, "You don't care about people, you only care
about houses," and he had been alarmed by the suggestion; he had forgotten that, but it was true; he
had grown out of touch with actual life. He had become increasingly bound by a need for some daily portion of solitude; people and conversation fatigued him.
He liked to finish off his letters and interviews, and
shut himself up in the office when the draughtsmen had
gone, for a satisfactory lonely hour or two with his
plans; he grudged the necessary human side of his profession more and more, and suffered accordingly.
Oliver Barford confided to Stacy, "Your father's not
nearly so good with clients as he used to be." And he
had developed a habit of solitary walks, which was not
new to him, but was unsuspected by his family. When
he was supposed to be working late, or when they had
left him alone at home, he liked to go out and explore
London as if it were one of his beloved foreign cities,
to walk home by unfamiliar routes, to go out and collect little lost houses and architectural remains in slums

and suburbs, and to chew the cud of recollected beauty afterwards. Stacy, who had been the companion of such expeditions at an earlier date, had now become temporarily uninterested in them; she preferred the company of her various young men. Martin found it only natural that she should do so. He subsided year by year into the quiet, shy, simple father of a family, dreamy, artistic and unpractical, turning back from life to find his consolations in himself, a gentle, untidy, silent, hardworked man, with an awkward manner and a tired face, who had lately taken to glasses to rest his overstrained eyes.

In his own work his tastes were becoming simpler and much more urban. He had become ashamed of his earlier extravagances in plan and detail. He had grown to dislike his own asymmetrical irregularities, the wings, bays and gables, loggias and balconies, porches and suntrap courts of the last fifteen years. Planning interested him more than it had done in the days of his youthful inexperience; he found that nowadays he thought of an unbuilt house as a solid thing, and could play with it in three dimensions inside his head. On the other hand he was less interested in a façade than he had been, and was best satisfied by plain symmetry and a lack of ornament.

A client in Sussex, who had commissioned a small holiday house, and had expected, after seeing examples of Martin's earlier work, quaint nooks and corners, was somewhat taken aback when confronted with the elevations of an austere and simple block with a pedimented doorway, two plain rows of sash-windows and an attic-story in a hipped and dormered roof, behind a classic cornice crowned with urns. And when he had reluctantly accepted the plans he was perplexed by the enthusiastic way in which his little architect fussed over material. "You must have the proper bricks," said Martin, peering up earnestly over the spectacles to which he had recently taken. "The thin, plum-coloured handmade kind, set with wide joints. I know where you can get them." And, "You can't possibly have crazy paving for that terrace on the garden front. The blocks must be plain paving-stones or you'll spoil the whole effect."

And in the spring of 1914, before the War stopped his building for a time, he completed a pure Queen Anne house, the best he ever designed. It was of red brick with stone quoins, heavy white sash-windows and green jalousies; it had a central block set slightly forward and a semicircular flight of steps rising to the garlanded, hooded doorway. He sent a little model of it to the Royal Academy; it was the year he was elected an A. R. A.

3

Aubrey went up to Trinity College, Oxford, in the autumn of 1912 at the conclusion of a last unsatisfactory year at Eton, during which Martin had tried to hope that the boy's apathy and idleness were only convalescent symptoms and would be cured by a change of life and scene.

At first it appeared that this might really come about; the languid Aubrey was surprised into approval, almost into enthusiasm by the domestic, classic charm of his college, the dark panelling of the hall, the fat plaster swags and garlands on its pale green ceiling, the carved Grinling Gibbons foliage and painted ceiling of the chapel, and his own dark friendly comfortable rooms. He worked virtuously for his preliminary law examination during his first term, then subsided into more congenial occupations, with the comfortable knowledge that his honour schools were three years ahead. He found friends of his own type; he had a small part in an O. U. D. S. production; he played tennis and discovered the pleasures of the Cherwell, the buttercup fringe of the meadows, the trailing willow branches, the chestnut blossom dropping into the bottom of a moored punt. His mother was delighted by the change in him; she boasted to Martin and to anyone else who would listen to her, that Aubrey had found his feet at last and would do great things. She and Stacy appreciated the gaieties of his first summer term enormously; Martin, mildly beaming on their enjoyment of Eights Week, found his own secret satisfactions in the half-hours when he escaped from the rooms of their crowded, uncomfortable hotel to wander in a contented solitude through cobbled lanes, between overhanging, timbered houses, or blind walls shaded by orchard boughs. He paced the clipped lime and chestnut walks of bird-haunted gardens, where mouldering fortifications were tangled with flowers. He explored brown halls and chapels, dim with painted windows, and little quadrangles of peeling, scaling, intricately ornamented, blackened masonry, each enclosing its own echoes and its own sunlit square of grass. He came back always in the end to his own favourite ground for meditation, the flagged space in the rear of St. Mary's, with the flowering stonework of the church behind him, the attenuated cardboard towers and little fish-scale cupola of All Souls on his right, on his left the satisfying brown dome and colonnade of the Radcliffe Camera, and his beloved, blind stone Cæsars just round the corner, where he could visit them on his way home.

Aubrey's second year was not nearly so satisfactory as his first. He had collected a disappointing set of friends; Martin struggled not to find them irritatingly decadent, they were of a type with which he had never yet become acquainted. Stacy declared their green-sickness to be a familiar symptom. "There's plenty of that kind of thing about," she said disdainfully, "and Aubrey was sure to pick it up." Her own tastes were more straightforward. Aubrey declared that she liked the obtuse, athletic brand of partner, but these were the natural exchanges of a brother and sister who had lately become a little jealous of each other. Martin thought Stacy's criticisms more just than Aubrey's.

"Heaven help the man who marries Stacy," said Aubrey, unkindly. "She'll always want to boss every show she's in"; but Stacy in her turn could say with a precision which shocked and startled her father, "Aubrey's turning out a rotten slacker; he'll never be any good." She did not, however, say it in the hearing of her mother, who was still pathetically convinced that Aubrey had some great future before him. She encouraged his extravagances, teased Martin for an increase in his allowance, and when this could not be afforded, paid, according to Stacy, the most urgent of his debts. Martin relieved his own vexation on hearing this, by a rare explosion of temper towards his daughter, which she received meekly enough. "Of course, I thought you knew, or I wouldn't have said anything," she admitted with cheerful unconcern. "I didn't mean to give poor Mother away. But you know she always does look after Aubrey." And she added still more cheerfully, "Don't you worry. Aubrey is the kind that some woman will always look after. He won't come to grief. It's people like me who have to fend for ourselves." She did not look as if she dreaded the prospect. She was at this time touchingly certain of her ability to manage her own affairs; and her father was not one of the many who found this attitude irritating and snubbed her for it. He thought her crude and youthful self-satisfaction endearing; it was a quality which he himself had lost many years earlier, and he reflected with some melancholy that life would rob his daughter all too soon of her innocent, ignorant confidence.

In the middle of Aubrey's second year at Oxford there was an uncomfortable family discussion about his future. It began in the garden of the Campden Hill house, after tea, on one of those hot spring days which occasionally converted a late Easter into a seeming summer. Stacy had insisted on a somewhat unseasonable tennis-party, before going off with her father for a fortnight's holiday. She had invited a young married couple named Prestwick, who lived across the square, two of Aubrey's more vigorous undergraduate acquaintances, and a couple of girls to match them; and she had paired herself off as usual with Oliver Barford, who was an effective, if ungraceful left-handed player, so that there was no need for Aubrey to exert himself unless he chose. He lay back in the lowest deck-chair beside the remains of Letty's tea, after the two other fours had gone back to the club courts; and in response to some awkward attempt of his father's to question him about the term's progress he had stated, in his faint, exhausted voice, that he didn't think he cared much about the law, after all.

"It's hopelessly dull stuff," he declared, "and I don't seem to be doing much good at it." Letty began a string of plaintive protests; Martin, just back from the office, and tired by the work of clearing his desk before a holiday, felt his heart sink at the prospect of a family discussion; it appeared to him that Aubrey was enjoying the sensation he had produced.

"It's a pity you didn't think of that before," he said, in what was for him an irritable tone, which made Letty glance at him reproachfully.

"Well, I had to try it to see how I liked it," Aubrey pointed out in a martyred fashion, which he had inherited or copied from his mother. Letty lamented, "Oh! Aubrey, how dreadfully disappointing! I thought you were enjoying it all so much; and I wanted you to make a great success of your time at Oxford, and then get called to the Bar. I never thought you'd give all that up just to come into your father's office." She was too much hurt herself to care whether or not she hurt Martin; he, however, said displeasedly, "I don't know that Aubrey particularly wants to come into the office."

"I don't know that I do," fenced Aubrey, lying back in his chair and seeming more unconcerned than he probably was. "I don't suppose I'd be much use at figuring strains and stresses, or working out a specification, or hobnobbing with a builder's foreman. That kind of thing might appeal to Stacy, but I'm afraid it wouldn't suit me. I should think you'd do better without me." He sounded so fatigued, convinced and rea-

sonable that his father could only look at him in despair; it was his mother who cried out, "But, darling,
what do you want to do?"

"Oh! I don't know," murmured Aubrey. "Couldn't
I be an interior decorator, or something of that sort?
or design stage-scenery, or open an antique shop? I
think that would be more amusing than bricks and
mortar. I know a good deal about china and furniture
already; that's the kind of thing I like. Or I might go
on the stage. Plenty of people think I've a turn for act-
ing. I've got quite keen on it since I've been in the
O. U. D. S. Or I might see whether any of the stuff
I've written is bad enough to find a market. There's
plenty of rubbish printed that's worse than mine. It's
just a question of hitting the fashion of the moment."
He was so particularly casual about this last suggestion
that Martin wondered for a moment whether it were
a deep, cherished ambition, so serious that the boy
was hiding it in veils of mockery. But Aubrey's yawn
was so realistically well-timed that he decided he had
been mistaken; literature was only another of Aubrey's
innumerable poses. "I'm afraid none of those plans
would be very profitable," he hesitated.

"Oh! profitable; perhaps not," murmured Aubrey
disdainfully. "Do we have to put that first?" Martin
said, vexedly for him—"I'm not a rich man, though
you all of you seem to think so." It was rare for him to
utter such a complaint, but he was cut to the heart by
his son's arched eyebrows and pale, indifferent look.
"I can't afford to go on giving you one chance after
another," he muttered, then finished with a sharp sigh,
"I only wish I could."

4

The conversation did not end there, but it came to
no satisfactory conclusion. It merely extended itself
into an uncomfortable family argument which went
on all evening, and left Martin in no cheerful mood
to begin his holiday. However, his spirits began to rise
as soon as he and Stacy had driven off from the house
next morning; and the happy accidents of a good crossing and a quiet back-room in their favourite hotel
in Paris disposed him to enjoy the long journey south
next day.

The fortnight in Provence was a great success. Stacy
was as interested as her father in all the minor pleasures of foreign travel, and at her best when she was
alone with him. He found her quieter, happier and less
aggressive than she had been at home, and was willing
to believe her contented and happy. He postponed his
perplexities about Aubrey and gave himself up to the
enjoyment of the holiday. The father and daughter
stared up at the sky through the arches of the aqueduct
at Pont-du-gard; they strolled up and down the stairways and terraces in the garden at Nîmes, and leant
on its formal balustrade to trace the lines of Roman
brickwork submerged in the fountain-waters. They
attended an absurd Provençal cow-fight in the elliptical
arena which infuriated Martin, and went out by moonlight to look at the Maison Carée, sunk in its unexpected hole. They stayed in a dirty hotel at Arles, with
three columns of a Roman temple built into the staircase, and climbed about the ruins of the theatre and
the circus, and loitered among the sarcophagi and

cypresses of the Aliscamps, and sketched the capitals
in the cloister of St. Trophime. They walked round the
stunted white walls of Avignon, and the yellow ramparts of Beaucaire; they went to Orange to see the
ochre-coloured triumphal arch and the monstrous
brown theatre wall; they drove up into the pale lime-
stone mountains of St. Remy, and saw the barren ruins
of Les Baux, and the arch and the toy memorial in
their lonely meadow.

It was not until that morning at Les Baux, the last
before they went home, when they were sitting on the
top of a wall together at the edge of the cliff, that
Stacy said to Martin, "Father, I can't stand being at
home any longer."

Martin's mind seemed to open and shut again, but
it did not take in what she said. He looked at her,
perched on the broken yellow stones; her legs were
curled under her, she leant back on her hands. There
was nothing behind her except the sheer drop from
the parapet, and the faint Mediterranean sparkle on
the horizon, and the brown empty levels of the plain
shining in the midday sun. There was a hawk balanc-
ing in the stream of heat that rose from it; he saw the
bird tilt and slide away down some invisible plane of
air. His old unconquerable fear of heights came back
upon him and he muttered stupidly to his daughter,
"Don't sit there; you might fall."

"I shouldn't care if I did," returned Stacy, under
her breath, but she moved unconsciously a little
further from the edge, then turned and clasped her
thin sunburnt hands round her knees, and attacked him
fairly. "I must get away from it all. I must have something to do outside."

He thought, "This is what it means to be a parent," and enquired, with a careful, forced lightness which surprised himself, "Anything particular?"

She flung back, "Nothing—anything will do that will keep me out of the house all day. You don't know what it's like, trailing round after Mother, having invitations arranged and reluctant young men collected for me, getting nagged the whole time about marriage. Oh! I know she doesn't mean it," as Martin gave a smothered exclamation, "half the time she doesn't realise she's doing it. She means to be kind; she doesn't know it hurts, but she can't help the way she's made. And she interferes with everything I do. She runs after me all day long, wants to know where I spend every minute of my time, thinks every man who speaks to me twice is in love with me, tries to live my life as well as her own. And I can't stand it; I shall go off my head," said Stacy, with her voice breaking suddenly. Her father saw her as a slender shadow against the light and dazzle of the plain below; he pleaded "Stacy, I'd no idea of this."

"Well, you don't see, you aren't there; we pull ourselves together when you come home. It wouldn't be so bad if I were away working in the daytime, but now it's more than I can manage. And so," said Stacy, quite humbly, like the little girl that he still thought her, "I said to myself that if Aubrey didn't really want to come into the office you might let me do it instead of him. Couldn't I come and work with you?"

Martin was puzzled and distressed; he said, "But, my dear, surely you'd find that very dull. It isn't all design and archæology, you know, as it used to be when we went round London together. It's a very stupid life really, planning drains, and dictating letters, and fitting garages and bathrooms into ugly old houses, and building banks and schools." He sighed; he had not realised that he was beginning to think of his profession so drearily.

"You wouldn't find it as amusing from inside as it looks from outside," he told her, hating to extinguish the light of innocent, youthful enthusiasm in her grey eyes, wishing helplessly that her brother had been like her. He longed to give her the promise she tried to coax out of him, but he was afraid of tying her down to what he fancied was only a passing, discontented impulse, though he realised the comfort she might be to him. But there was all the trouble which he foresaw with Letty; and this in fact descended upon him as soon as they got back to London, and Stacy insisted on discussing her plan.

"How could you let her get such a thing into her head?" his wife protested; and, "Stacy, you're too disappointing! I've so loved choosing your clothes, and arranging your parties, and we've taken so much trouble to give you a good time. You can't want to stop dancing, and playing tennis, and meeting people, just for the sake of burying yourself in a dirty drawing-office." She would not consider any of Stacy's arguments, though she said to Martin, with more reasonable kindness than he had expected from her, "It's only some passing fancy or disappointment, I can't let her spoil her life and chances at twenty-one, my pretty, silly Stacy." She cried a good deal over the whole business, and over the attendant uncertainties about Aubrey's future; she had always cried easily, and felt the better for it, and in these anxieties her blue eyes

brimmed over as readily as ever. Stacy did not cry,
it was not her way; but her face looked pinched and
defiant; something bright, bold and defenceless about
her tore at her father's heart. He spoilt the whole
effect of Letty's tears by relenting weakly and saying,
"You might try for a year and see how you like it."
This revived the arguments and appeals. Lady Stapleford, taking her daughter's part against her granddaughter, as usual, said, "Stacy is an obstinate little
fool. What she needs is a good whipping, and I should
like to give it her. She ought to have been taken in
hand years ago, but you've always spoilt her, and even
Letty has been far too gentle with her." She added
contemptuously, "Of course, there's a man behind all
this," and swung Martin round into a defiant alliance
with his daughter.

Curiously enough, it was Oliver Barford who settled
the matter when everyone else had failed. Martin had
invited him in to Sunday supper, to relieve the
domestic strain, but repented it because his wife and
daughter revived their argument, and carried it on
throughout the uncomfortable meal. Oliver did not
interrupt them, but continued to feed himself methodi-
cally; Letty had once declared in a sympathetic inter-
lude that he was starved at his lodgings. When
appealed to, however, by Stacy herself, whose bright
eyes and ruffled hair betrayed her increasing agitation,
he helped himself largely to cheese, and said, as one
unable to avoid admitting his considered opinion,
"Shouldn't come to the office, if I were you."

Letty said, with what seemed a malicious significance, "There, darling, you see even Oliver agrees
with me."

Stacy ignored her mother and protested to Oliver, "I did think you'd back me up." Her resentment and astonishment were unconcealed.

Martin thought that the young man avoided looking at her. He replied sulkily, slicing at his cheese, "You women are no good at our job. You plan very nicely, and all that, but you don't understand managing labour or keeping a proper hand on the accounts, or controlling the practical details of a big job. Interior decoration is about all you're fit for. Besides, you aren't serious about wanting to work. You'll play about for a year or two and take up room in the office and keep somebody else out of a job, and then you'll go off and get married."

"I do call that unfair," Stacy burst out. "But I might have expected it." And she raced on, "It's people like you who put obstacles in a girl's way, simply out of jealousy. The older men who've made their own way don't try to keep us out of the profession: they can afford to be generous and give us our chance of a fair field and no favour. It's the young men who try to edge us out, and talk about play-work, and pretend we're not serious rivals, just because they're afraid of us."

Oliver retorted, "Well, if you girls are going to cheat us out of our jobs, how can we afford to marry and have homes of our own?"

A lovely, deep, protesting colour rose to the girl's forehead; she looked at Oliver with shocked and piteous astonishment, as if he had boxed her ears before her family. Martin saw with intense distress that her eyelashes were wet with tears. Letty, rather unkindly, broke an awkward silence with, "I told you it was a silly plan," and Oliver, seeking to justify his position, muttered harshly, "Nobody wants you hanging about Bedford Row. You wouldn't be the least use."

The girl pushed her chair back, jumped up and ran out of the room, banging the door behind her. Letty began to encourage herself and her ally: "What you said was very helpful, Oliver. I hope Stacy will take some notice of it. She's more likely to listen to you than she is to us." Oliver scowled and looked ashamed of himself, and Martin was glad of it; he guessed that Oliver had settled their business for them, but he was angry with the young man, for all that, and wished, illogically, that Stacy had carried her point. However, he heard no more of the architectural plan, that night or any other night. Stacy was not in the drawing-room when they went up: she had rushed away to her own room and did not reappear. She was very subdued and silent next day, but she had apparently accepted her failure, and did not speak of it again. Letty, however, was cheerful, and assured Martin that Stacy would get over the disappointment sooner than he expected. "It wasn't architecture the child wanted in Bedford Row," she said, with an air of having received new light on a perplexing subject. "She was running after Oliver, and that's just what I've been trying to stop. Granny said so from the first, and now I agree with her." Martin was vexed and incredulous, but his wife stuck to her opinion and he gave up the argument. He had learnt by this time that Letty yielded a point quicker if you left her alone. As for Oliver Barford, he certainly kept away from the house in Campden Hill Square all that summer, and whenever Martin invited him to tennis he made excuses and said that he

was too busy. It was true that he was beginning to
make his way and that lately he had managed to
salvage a few pickings from his uncle's municipal
affairs. He seemed to be heading away from Martin's
mild domesticities in the direction of public work. It
was true that no one would be likely to want to live
in so ugly a house as. Oliver Barford would design for
them; but he had, Martin considered, some useful if
grandiose ideas about shops and offices and banks.
He seemed to spend all his time in Bedford Row, and
to become more and more unapproachable in temper
as the heat of the summer wore on.

Aubrey had gone back for what was to be his last
term at Oxford, with his future still unsettled. Stacy
went dutifully to dances with her mother, and played
tennis and made herself dresses, and even flirted with
a stray young man from time to time. Her mother and
grandmother nodded their heads approvingly over her
recovery. She seemed to talk and smile much less than
usual, but perhaps that was only her father's fancy.
And June and July burnt themselves out, the last and
loveliest months of quiet; and by the beginning of
August it no longer mattered to anyone that Stacy
had been disappointed of a profession, or Martin of
his son's help, or that Stacy and Oliver had quarrelled,
because the year was 1914 and the world had other
things to think about.

VIII

THE LOVELLS had been going to Austria, that August,
to look at the baroque palaces down the Danube; but
fortunately they had not started. They remained in
London through the long, anxious autumn months.
Letty and her mother spent most of their time in the
little panelled Queen Anne rooms of the Hospital
Supply Depot in Kensington Square, with their heads
tied up in white veils, making swabs and pneumonia
jackets, padding splints, and lightening their labours,
Martin gathered, by an active exchange of rumours
and gossip. Stacy accompanied them for a week or
two, then tired of indoor work and the company of
her elders, and found herself employment as the driver
of a station ambulance. She had learnt to drive that
summer, and had been pestering her father continually
for a car. Letty was very much upset by this move of
her daughter's. She imagined all kinds of accidents and
mishaps; and Lady Stapleford disapproved of the uniform, and told Stacy that she ought to have her ears
boxed for wearing it. Martin, however, found an un-
confessed amusement in his daughter's swagger over
her breeches and gauntlets and badged overcoat; he
did not even share the women's distress when Stacy
cut off the long brown·hair which had been her one

real beauty, and appeared with a bobbed, sleek head which reminded him of her childhood.

Aubrey had finished with Oxford and was waiting about quite patiently at home to see how things would turn out before taking any further steps. Letty thought him sensible and Martin supposed that he ought to agree with her. He was very much confused by the change in his own world; he wanted to do something helpful, but he did not know where to begin. Everything was at sixes and sevens in Bedford Row and work was at a standstill. Martin had not had so much time to himself for years. It did not seem to matter that two of his young draughtsmen had gone off to the Army; and the third, who had been rejected on account of his eyesight, spent his time smoking cigarettes, and grumbling about his medical examination to the brisk typist recently installed by Oliver Barford. She had plenty of time to listen to him in those days, until she went off to one of the new Ministries, and there was hardly anything for the two of them to do or for Martin either. Work had been stopped for the time being on two houses which he had begun building in the country; a client for whom he had drawn the plans of a house at Hampstead postponed the building indefinitely, and an office building in the City, for which Oliver Barford had just got out the scale-plans and specifications, had to be countermanded altogether.

Oliver turned very sulky and silent after that, and disappeared from the office for three days. On the fourth he walked into Martin's room in khaki with the helmeted profiles of Mars and Minerva on his collar, and explained that he had joined the Artists' Rifles and was going off that night to camp. He only stayed a few minutes and was very excited and wild in his manner. Martin tried not to think that he had been drinking. He had a feeling that Oliver had yielded to some unsteady, unconsidered impulse, and the thought worried him all that afternoon. He said to Stacy and her mother, over dinner, "I had no idea the boy had anything of that kind in his head."

"You might have guessed," observed Stacy. It was the first comment she had made; her tone, and the look which accompanied it, startled her father a little; but Letty distracted his attention by her usual soft, plaintive, resentful flow of comment.

"Whatever made him rush off in such a hurry? It really must have been quite unnecessary. But I suppose he wanted to be in the fashion." She had never liked Oliver, and she was always more spiteful about him when Stacy was listening. "He might have thought twice before leaving you in the lurch like that, Martin. Who's to do his work for him, I should like to know?"

"I'm afraid there isn't likely to be much work in the office for some time to come," admitted Martin soberly, and for the first time. Stacy glanced up quickly, and seemed to follow the implications of this speech; but Letty, who as obviously did not, returned, "Nonsense. People are in a panic just now, cutting down expenses right and left; it's all so very silly. The War can't last beyond Christmas, everybody says so; and even if it did people have still got to have houses to live in. I don't think he ought to have done it."

"I suppose he thinks he'll be more use where he's going," observed Stacy drily; and added, "The office will be all right. Father is certain to get one of those Belgian refugees planted on him."

This prophecy turned out singularly accurate, for by Christmas, when the office wheels were grinding again, though very slowly and rustily, there had appeared behind Oliver's desk the neat head, gold-rimmed glasses, pointed grey beard and tight frock-coat of the enthusiastic M. Nicole, late of Antwerp, a gentleman who would gladly have done much more work than the office at that time provided in return for the meagre salary which it was able to offer him. He had a stout, silent Flemish wife and three frightened children, who were all camping out in a back bedroom in Battersea. Martin used to go and see them every now and then, and practise his rusty foreign languages upon them without getting much response; and Letty once invited them to an uncomfortable tea-party in Campden Hill Square, where the only real conversation was between Stacy and the children over her Siamese cat. But M. Nicole was a great talker, and enlivened the emptiness of Martin's unoccupied days with long histories of the invasion and the bombardment of Antwerp, and laments over the destruction of Ypres and Louvain. He was really keen on his profession and had evidently had a flourishing practice of his own. He told Martin a great deal about recent developments in Continental architecture, and spoke with an incurable hopefulness of plans for the reconstruction of Belgium, which were destined to be delayed for many years. He was a confirmed optimist and a great comfort to Martin, who was very much depressed by the events of that black autumn, and tried in vain to persuade himself that his own committees and intermittent war-work were of value to anyone. Stacy was still exhausting herself with long hours of

driving in all weathers; Aubrey had taken up an
obstinately pacifist attitude which troubled his father,
who did not think it altogether genuine. He was very
little at home, and after Christmas went off into rooms
by himself, saying that he had secured a post on some
obscure, socialistic, revolutionary paper. Letty was
very much upset by his departure, and as one result
made no objection when Martin found himself obliged
by the financial uncertainties of the times to accept an
unexpected chance of selling the house in Campden
Hill Square. Stacy found a top-floor flat in Brunswick
Square and moved her parents into it in the spring
of 1915, and they remained there throughout the War.

2

Oliver Barford got out to France in the spring of
1915, but was wounded almost at once, fortunately for
him in the right arm, since he was left-handed. The
Lovells saw his name in the casualty-lists, but through
some official confusion could get no more news about
him for a week. The young man's nearest relative was
an old aunt, a sister of Nicholas Barford's, living in
the Midlands; and it was through a letter from her,
asking them to visit him, that the Lovells first heard
of Oliver being in an Officers' Hospital in London.
Martin went off to see him that afternoon. He was
lying in a back-attic bedroom at the top of an immensely tall, white plaster house in South Kensington.
Martin arrived breathless, since the lift did not go
above the third floor, and the two men passed an
awkward ten minutes in professional condemnation of
the architecture of the sixties.

"Nice place to choose for a hospital," said Oliver, with his eyes shut. "These wretched nurses spend their time running up and down stairs. There isn't a tap above the third floor or a bathroom except on the first landing, and the whole place is heated by coal-fires. I hope the man who designed it is frying in hell."

"I daresay he is by this time," observed Martin, accepting the topic, since Oliver evidently did not intend to talk about the War, or any of his own experiences. He was sitting up against a heap of pillows, with his bandaged hand crucified upon an extension splint. The pale fingers were spread as if they were playing a tune. He was evidently in considerable pain. His face twitched nervously at any movement towards him; he kept on shutting his eyes as if the light hurt them. Martin did not know what to say to him. He delivered messages from Letty and Stacy, they were coming to see Oliver as soon as possible. They would no doubt have come with Martin that afternoon, but Stacy had gone off to Victoria to meet a hospital train before the news arrived, and her mother was at the supply depot, rolling bandages. "But Letty's free two afternoons a week, and Stacy any day after five, if that's allowed," said Martin. He added, more doubtfully, since Oliver did not at once reply, "Or she could come on a Sunday."

Still with closed eyes, Oliver said faintly, "Tell 'em I'm not up to visitors yet."

Martin took the hint and got up to go. The young man's eyes opened fully then for the first time, and his eyebrows twisted into a frown of apprehension.

"Don't—shake the bed," he whispered. Martin did not dare to take his free hand, or touch him; he got himself out of the room with some kind of farewell, but afterwards he could not remember what it had been.

There was a nurse writing at a table outside in the passage, not a V.A.D. but a regular Army sister in a wide veil and a grey cape with a red edge. To her he said, wiping his damp forehead, "I'm afraid I ought not to have seen him."

"Oh! this is just one of Mr. Barford's bad days," said she in a mild, soft, professional, but not indifferent voice. "I hope he'll be better next time you come. He particularly asked for you; but he really isn't up to much talking yet." And she concluded kindly enough, "Of course, it's a serious wound, but Mr. Jennings hopes to save the elbow."

Martin found her slow smile reassuring. She was a tall, dark, handsome, rather heavy girl, with a rich colour and maternal movements; she looked inert but very strong. He thought that she would be soothing and kind, and was glad to think that Oliver was in her hands.

Stacy was unexpectedly angry with him that night at dinner, for visiting the hospital by himself.

"You might have told me you were going," she fumed. "I do think you're unkind."

Martin was perplexed. "But, my dear, I only heard where he was after you'd gone out. I rang the place up and they said I might look in for a few minutes on my way home. I didn't know you could get away this afternoon." He did not add, "You always say you can't when your mother wants you to do things with her."

"Well, you could have rung me up and asked me.

You might have known I should want to go and see
Oliver." Her voice was a little unsteady on the name.
Her father was astonished by the light sparkle in her
eyes, it hinted at suppressed tears. He thought that
something in her day's work must have upset or over-
tired her, and this made him speak quite gently and
apologetically as he said, "I never thought of your
wanting to go to-day, but you shall come with me on
Sunday." Then he reflected, and concluded, "No, better
not, he said he'd rather be left alone. We'll wait a few
days. After all, he'll be there some time, poor chap;
and the sister said she'd rather he didn't have too many
visitors at present."

"Oh! that's the way these damned nurses always
talk," said Stacy, with resentment. "They love to treat
relations as if they were some kind of small unpleasant
vermin, and had to be kept out of the wards at all
costs."

"But we aren't Oliver's relations, darling," her
mother pointed out.

Stacy said hotly, "Well, who else has he got?" then
sat scowling at her plate, while Martin soothed her
obtusely.

"This nurse was a very pleasant, motherly young
woman. I liked the look of her. She seemed as if she
would be kind to Oliver."

"Oh! I daresay she'll make an idiotic fuss of him,"
said Stacy. "That kind always does. He's fatal to
them. It's his rudeness does it, apparently. They lap
it up. I can't see why. I've no use for a man who tries
to bully me." Martin decided that she was offended
with Oliver for refusing an early visit from her, and he
said in apology, "I'm afraid the boy's badly hurt."

Stacy turned white, but said nothing; it was her mother who exclaimed, questioned, and asked for details. Stacy got up in the middle of the conversation and went out, leaving her father with the uncomfortable suspicion that she was more upset about Oliver than he had supposed.

He and Stacy did not go to the hospital that Sunday, because they heard, when they telephoned in the morning, that Oliver had just had another anæsthetic and was not fit for visitors. But they went on the Thursday after, which happened to be Stacy's half-day off. She had persuaded Martin to go with her, but surprised him by being very silent and awkward when they got there. She hardly spoke to Oliver, and sat with her grey eyes cast down as if they were afraid of everything they saw. Martin found the whole business mysterious, especially on their way back, when Stacy said to him abruptly, through the rattle of the District train, "Oliver is in love with that nurse of his."

"Nurse? What nurse?" echoed Martin, thinking that he must have misunderstood her.

"The fat one with the red cheeks," said Stacy viciously. "The one who came mooing in like a cow and put her hand on his forehead and said we weren't to stay any longer."

Martin recognised this prejudiced description, and agreed absently, "Yes, the one who was there before"; then recollected himself, and said "Nonsense"; but Stacy persisted, "It isn't nonsense. It's perfectly true. You wait."

She said, "I saw it," and seemed unable to get any further, then recovered herself, and concluded in a

voice which forbade him to recognise her trouble, "I
saw it when they looked at each other."

To this Martin had no reply; he glanced sideways
at his daughter, and found her with compressed lips
and frowning eyebrows. She did not speak of Oliver
again, and they returned to the Brunswick Square flat.

Martin refrained by a considerable effort from
reporting this exchange to his wife, for fear that she
might tease Stacy on the point; but he was all the more
upset when Letty made the same suggestion after her
own visit to the nursing home.

"Well, we needn't worry any more about Oliver
Barford," was her maternal version. "I was a little
afraid that he and Stacy might get sentimental about
each other again. She was very much upset when she
heard that he was wounded. But he hadn't any eyes
this afternoon except for that girl who looks after
him." Martin was unexpectedly disappointed even
while he agreed that marriage would be a good thing
for Oliver.

In about a fortnight's time they heard that Oliver
had been transferred to a convalescent home in the
country. Martin felt hurt that the young man had not
told them he was going, but reminded himself that the
move might have been unexpected. He wrote a condol-
ing, encouraging letter, but got no answer of any kind
until three months later, when a letter came to the
office in a green field envelope. It was extremely short
and to the point, like all Oliver's communications, but
it left Martin with a feeling that the ground had been
cut from under his chair as he sat. "Dear Lovell," it
ran, "they have sent me out again, as my arm is supposed to be cured. I thought I could have wangled

another month, but had no luck, as my battalion is getting pretty short of officers. However, I got a week's leave to end up with and married Dorothy Collins. I expect you will remember her, she nursed me in that first hospital. She is down in the Aldershot Command now, and wants to keep on her job at present, so we haven't told anyone. Please keep it dark. Yours. O. B."

The words were scribbled on a flimsy sheet of paper in indelible pencil, and at first Martin overlooked a smudgy postscript in one corner. When he did see it he found that it consisted of three words which disturbed and alarmed him, "Better tell Stacy."

He took the letter home with him, and produced it after dinner when he and Stacy were alone; but, to his vexation, Letty came back at that moment, and when she saw the field envelope, she asked with immediate apprehension, "What's that?" Martin was obliged to say, "It's a letter from Oliver Barford."

He glanced at Stacy involuntarily, and was certain that he saw her lips move, but she said nothing; it was Letty who exclaimed, "I'd no idea he'd gone back to the front. Why didn't he come here to say good-bye to us? He must have been in London."

"He was pretty busy before he left," said Martin grimly, having just discovered that he was angry with Oliver. Then he told himself, "Better get this over."

He said aloud, "You can read it, both of you, if you promise not to say a word about it outside this room," and while he gave Letty the paper to flutter and exclaim over, he looked straight at his tall daughter, and said to her, in a low tone, "Oliver has married that girl after all."

Stacy took it with a widening of the eyes and a parting of the lips, but she found nothing to say. "I suppose," thought her father, a little taken aback, "that she'd made up her mind to it long ago."

But Letty, fluttering with confused vexation, cried, "I never thought he'd do such a thing without letting us know, after all our kindness. We should certainly have gone to the wedding if we'd known in time. Stacy, did Oliver tell you he was going to be married?"

"Why should he tell me?" demanded Stacy, in a tone which silenced her mother. In the pause that followed she got up from her chair and said, with ostentatious carelessness, "If that's all the news in the letter I think I'll go to bed. I've had a pretty long day." She kissed Letty, and afterwards Martin, who had time to notice that her lips were cold.

When the door had shut behind the girl her parents looked at each other, and Martin expressed an enormous sense of disruption and loss, which had suddenly overwhelmed him, when he said slowly, "Do you know, I'm sorry about this. I can't help wishing the boy had waited for someone—something—more permanent."

He felt his wife's impatience and said, apologetically, "I'm being foolish, I expect, but I feel fearfully taken aback. You see, darling, you'd somehow put it into my head that he was rather devoted to Stacy. And this, this is so very different. It might be just a passing fancy—she seemed so unimportant." He stammered as he used to do in his young, anxious days, but Letty did not help him out. She only pursed her lips obstinately, and he was obliged to continue, "Evidently there was nothing in that other business. Perhaps we took them too seriously. I suppose a father thinks his daughter more attractive than she really is. But I can't help wondering how Oliver could look at that girl, after Stacy." He smiled sheepishly, and concluded, "Ah! well, it wouldn't have done, I suppose."

"No, it certainly wouldn't," declared Letty, surveying him in that old manner of hers, as if he were a very stupid little boy and she were his mother and sorry for him. And she, too, kissed him, as coldly as Stacy had done, and went off to bed.

3

It was in the spring of 1916, and not very long after this marriage of Oliver Barford's that Stacy changed her job and gave up ambulance-driving for a post in one of the new Ministries. Letty was pleased and said, "I always thought that driving too much for her. Now the child won't have to work such long, tiring hours and we shall see a little more of her." However, matters did not seem to work out quite like that; Stacy's hours may have been more regular and her work less exhausting, but she took to dancing in the evenings and spent less time at home than ever. Martin only saw her for ten minutes or so at breakfast-time, when she rushed down late, drank a cup of black coffee, shuffled through the pages of his newspaper and left it in confusion, then departed with the almost invariable words, "I shan't be back to dinner. Don't wait up for me, I might be late."

He did not think her looking well although she wore enough artificial colour on cheek and lip to perplex his innocence. She had grown very thin, and

looked heavy about the eyelids; she had a queer, unsettled, impatient manner which disturbed him. However, he put it down to the troubles of the time and
accepted her mother's placid view, "Stacy's probably
finding the new work a little difficult. She misses the
fresh air and feels being shut up all day. But I'm glad
she's beginning to go out again a little and make new
friends. She works so hard; she's entitled to a little
enjoyment." She also hinted, in her old manner, that
Stacy would forget that nonsense about Oliver Barford
all the quicker for meeting plenty of other men. "I was
afraid she might shut herself up and mope," was her
way of putting it. Martin asked her, jealously, who
was entertaining Stacy so frequently, but Letty was
cheerfully vague on the point, and he did not get any
very satisfactory answers. Stacy had said, "Oh! nobody
you'd know," and said the same to her father. "One
meets people working or when they're home on leave."
She became irritable when questioned about her movements.

Then, quite suddenly, she spent three or four evenings running at home, was very strange and unhappy
in her manner, turned sulky and impatient when Letty
fussed over her, and followed Martin about as if she
wanted to tell him something, but could not find
courage to do it. And then, one fine June day, she came
down particularly late in a new green frock, refused
breakfast, kissed her father with a strange, inexplicable violence, went away, and appeared at mid-day
in his office with a complete stranger, of whom she said,
defiantly, "This is Philip Giffard. We were married
this morning."

Martin hated the man at sight. He was a captain in

the Flying Corps, twelve or fifteen years older than Stacy, a big, swaggering, handsome, red-faced fellow, with a hot blue eye, a loud laugh and an easy, aggressive manner. He treated Stacy as if she were a little girl, annoyed Martin by calling her "Kid," instead of using her own name, was demonstratively cheerful and did nearly all the talking. He did not seem to think that anything but a perfunctory explanation or apology to Martin was needed; said, "We wanted to fix things up before I went back to the front, and I told the Kid it was no use wasting time in these days. A short life and a gay one." Stacy was quiet and unlike herself. She had been very nervous when they first came in and when Martin, after his first pause of horror, had recovered himself sufficiently to make some advance she had come forward, flung her arms round his neck and kissed him passionately; otherwise she had hardly taken any part in the interview that followed. She had gone back to her husband in obedience to some imperceptible sign; and he had pulled her down on to the arm of his chair and held her hand in a possessive, victorious manner while he talked to her father.

Yes, they'd known each other quite a long time—three or four months—he called that quite a long time nowadays. Of course, they'd only seen each other on and off, when he could get up to London. He'd exchanged out of the cavalry into the Flying Corps, because he thought he'd see more of the fun that way. Personally, he'd made up his mind to marry the Kid quite early on, but she hadn't been able to make up her mind, and had wasted a lot of his time in fact; however, she'd come round when she heard he was going out to France. No, they hadn't thought   (in answer to a very gentle reproach of Martin's)   that there was much point in his coming round to her place for inspection; Martin would find that there wasn't anything against him. He was a decent, sober, hard-working chap   (with a loud laugh)   and he'd money enough to leave the Kid fairly well-off if the Huns got him. He'd made a will that morning; they'd been to his solicitors in Lincoln's Inn about it after they'd finished with the registrar. And they were pretty well satisfied with each other, weren't they, Kid?   His arm went round his wife. Stacy was flushed with a deep, bridal colour; she seemed only half-conscious of her surroundings. Martin felt utterly sick at heart.

Reproaches seemed useless; the thing was done and could not be undone. He left his office and went round with the young couple to the flat in Brunswick Square. Letty was fortunately there and took the news better than he expected. She was apparently not so distressed as Martin had been over the secrecy of Stacy's proceedings, and her reproaches were changed to excitement and pleasure as soon as Captain Giffard took her in hand. He handled her with great skill and plied her with a certain broad flattery which appealed to her; she laughed at his compliments, told him that he ought to be ashamed of himself and appeared disposed to accept the whole matter as a romantic joke.

The four of them had an uncomfortable, noisy, festive lunch at the Savoy, and afterwards Captain Giffard took Stacy away, "to buy some more of her trousseau," he explained with a cheerful wink to the company. Martin was left to take his wife home, to encourage himself as best he might by listening to her obstinately improbable forecasts of Stacy's happiness, and to put the best face he could on the matter, when Lady Stapleford appeared, in response to a telephone message and demanded details of Stacy's escapade. She detected Martin's misgivings immediately, and said with a kind of savage gusto, "This is exactly what I expected. You should never have let Stacy run about all over London as she has been doing, getting herself mixed up with all sorts of queer people. Of course, she was bound to do something idiotic. I could have told you that long ago; but you always spoilt her thoroughly, both of you. Letty hasn't been quite so silly about the girl as you have, Martin; but she's always let her do much too much as she liked. She ought to have had all her self-willed nonsense whipped out of her when she was little. Well, I hope this man will be able to keep her in order, but I don't expect it's at all likely, Stacy needs a very firm hand." There was a gleam in her eye which suggested a willingness to discipline her granddaughter herself. She seemed to find complete satisfaction in this fulfilment of her gloomy prophecies.

"I always said you'd have trouble with that girl," she told Martin truthfully enough, and added, "If she were here I'd soon show her what I thought of her behaviour. It's time someone pointed out to her what a fool she's making of herself; it would do her good. You neither of you know how to manage her."

"I think I can manage Stacy myself," said Martin coldly, to which his mother-in-law replied, "You haven't made much of a success of it so far. I suppose you'll make a great fuss of her now, and invite the young man here, and behave as if you were thoroughly pleased with the whole business."

"Stacy can certainly bring her husband to this flat whenever she chooses," said Martin, and he got up and walked out of the room to fetch Letty. He thought that for once she might take her mother off his hands.

Stacy, however, did not seem particularly anxious to display her husband; or perhaps he was not very anxious to be wept over by Letty, and snubbed by Lady Stapleford, and entertained by Martin with polite and awkward ceremony. It was, after all, his honeymoon, and he and Stacy spent it in a glittering, noisy, over-heated hotel near Piccadilly Circus, where they had a suite full of gilt furniture and rose brocade, spent their nights dancing and their mornings in bed, and professed to be enjoying themselves immensely.

The Lovells did not see much of them, but were invited to one family dinner, probably rather by Stacy's wish than by Philip's. Letty was prevented from attending this party by a touch of influenza, and was greatly disappointed; she would probably have enjoyed it much more than Martin did. The three of them dined together in the hotel restaurant, went to a revue which bored Martin excessively and did not seem to please the young couple, and returned to supper in the Giffards' sitting-room. The evening was not a success. Captain Giffard irritated Martin by everything that he said or did. He took continual freedoms with Stacy, could not go near her without catching at her hand, jerking her head back by the chin from behind, or running greedy fingers up her arm; he was in no way reticent, and made intimate allusions for the pleasure

of watching Stacy's blushes. What annoyed Martin
even more were his impudent, patronising, verbal
familiarities, which might have suggested to a more
acute and unprejudiced observer that the man had a
sense of inferiority, and chose this method of reassuring himself. He said, for instance, when Stacy ventured
some opinion which differed from his, "Little girls
should be seen and not heard. You'll get packed off to
bed if you talk nonsense"; and when she questioned
one of his sweeping assertions, "You'd better not contradict me if you want me to let you off that spanking
I promised you." Stacy, who had once been of such a
high temper, took this kind of swagger without protest; her defiant glance, if she had one, was for her
father, and warned him that what she chose to accept
was not for him to criticise. She was altogether very
much on the defensive, her bright, hard look avoided
her father's eye, she talked and laughed a good deal
and drank more than her father liked, but not as much
as her husband wished. He was perpetually filling her
glass, and complained of what he chose to consider
an unenterprising reluctance; once he muttered in an
insufferable tone, "What's the use of stopping cold
sober when we're out to enjoy ourselves? By God,
you've got something to learn!"

He was himself far from sober, Martin considered,
when they parted; he had reached the quarrelsome
stage of his intoxication, and Stacy became the object
of his annoyance. "You chose this rotten show," he
grumbled, at the play; and afterwards at their hotel,
"You would come back to this mouldy place for supper,
instead of going on somewhere decent. I think you
might consider me, I've only got three days and I want

to enjoy myself." Martin reminded himself despairingly that it must be the three days which were influencing Stacy; she could not always have let the man behave like this to her. She must have determined to refuse him no gratification, not even that of his temper. She submitted just as calmly, if with a rebellious colour, when he turned demonstrative, put his arm round her waist, caressed her with an air of ownership, and said roughly, "Now then, Kid, get off to bed, can't you? Your father doesn't want you to stop up late for him. He can see you haven't had much beauty-sleep lately. If you don't get some you won't be fit to be seen to-morrow. Don't hang about, now; I shan't be long."

Martin accepted this unvarnished hint and said good-night to the young couple. Stacy's cheek was burning hot when he kissed it; she hid her face on his shoulder for a moment and he felt her whole body shaking; his heart sank when he tried to picture her future.

Captain Giffard went down to the door of the hotel with him, slightly uncertain in his speech and breathing a taint of whiskey.

"C-can't thank you enough for what I've got. Stacy's a g-great girl—a g-great girl," he repeated solemnly once or twice, nodding his head; then added with an intolerable grin, "Doesn't know much yet, but she'll learn." Martin wanted to hit the smiling, shining red face of his son-in-law, as he stood swaying slightly in the entrance of the hotel.

"Got to get back to her now," the Captain concluded, with an owlish stare. "You'll excuse me, I'm sure. Doesn't do to neglect one's wife in these days."

And he gave an idiotic chuckle and turned away, lurch-
ing into a man who stood behind him and swearing
at him with fluent readiness.

Martin was left to make his way home through the
darkened streets, to close his mind in vain against the
images which invaded it, and to mutter unconsciously
as the searchlights crossed above him, "Oh! God, I
hope he gets killed! I hope he gets killed!"

4

In the spring of 1916 Aubrey was called up. He did
not, in this final test, adhere to his pacifist principles;
and his parents exchanged one anxiety for another
when he was sent to a camp near Aldershot, from
which he wrote his mother depressed, short, pitiable
letters, complaining of fatigue and discomfort. They
were strikingly petulant and childish in tone, there was
none of the boy's usual careless self-sufficiency in them;
Martin could see how much they distressed Letty. The
summer and early autumn were wet and miserable.
Aubrey hated his training; he could not get on with
the other men, his officers had a down on him. It was
all like the letters of a homesick schoolboy, like his
own letters when he first left home. Martin thought
despondently, "The boy hasn't grown up; he doesn't
know how to face things"; and, with still more
anxiety, "Is this all the courage we've given him?" He
was profoundly disturbed about his son, but did not
know how to help him. Letty clamoured to go down
and see him, but Martin, to his subsequent and infinite
regret, discouraged her. "Better leave him to find his
own feet," he told her, with a melancholy recollection

of having said the same thing, how few years earlier,
when Aubrey was unhappy at school. "After all, we
shall only unsettle the boy, and we can't do anything
to help him over this part of it. He's got to get used
to the life, and it's bound to do him good in the end."
He did not add, "They've got far worse than this before them."

Letty cried and protested, but was obliged to submit
to Stacy's less tactful verdict, "You'll only make
Aubrey look a fool if you go rushing down there after
him." And Aubrey himself wrote, "I expect we shall
be out of this soon. I hope we get a move anyhow, they
talk about sending us to Africa. I daresay it's only a
rumour, but I'd like to go somewhere warm. I'm sick
of this place," but his escape came in another fashion.

His mother had had one last letter from him, more
miserable than any other, saying that he felt too ill to
write more than a few lines; and in Martin's absence,
she rushed out with a telegram declaring that she
should come down to Farnham next morning, and wait
there till she could see him. Martin and Stacy persuaded her to wait at home next day for some answer,
but none came; it was not until the following morning
that they had the official notification of Aubrey having
been moved from camp to a military hospital, with
cerebro-spinal meningitis. His parents were to go down
and see him that night. The permission alarmed
Martin, he did not think it would have been given
unless Aubrey's condition were serious; but he would
not hint that to Letty, who was pitiably distressed. She
kept on sobbing and wringing her hands, and accusing
him of having kept her away from Aubrey earlier.
Stacy was very helpful to him and he was thankful

that she had continued to live at home while her husband was in France; she could not leave her work at the Ministry without more definite news of her brother, but she went with her father and mother to Waterloo, consoling and upholding Letty to the last, and saw them off from the darkened platform on a nightmare journey in a slow, stopping train with drawn blinds.

They got to Farnham late in the evening, and with difficulty hired a car to take them out to the hospital. It proved to be a converted country house, somewhere in the dripping woods towards Frensham. They drove up a sighing avenue of fir-trees, passed a row of wooden huts in what must once have been the garden, and waited in a draughty, uncomfortable, pretentious hall, hideously panelled in fumed oak, lit by stained-glass windows which were opaque against the darkness, and smelling of furniture-polish and lysol. A flat-footed, grizzled, kindly orderly in R.A.M.C. khaki returned after an interval and shuffled before them down a dimly-lighted passage. Martin smelt the smell of drugs and ether, and had a glance into a long, white-panelled drawing-room whose mirrored walls reflected a double row of beds; a ghostly Venetian chandelier glimmered in the half-darkness above them.

There was an interview in an office with a rather casual, swaggering young doctor who was handsome and dandified in a very new uniform half-covered by an aggressively clean overall; and a worried, grey-haired nursing-sister with a matron's scarlet cape over her grey and white gown, who seemed chiefly pre-occupied by quarantine regulations.

"Of course, you'll have to take every precaution

against infection if you see your son," she repeated, as if it were vital to establish this point. "You'll have to put on an overall and you mustn't go near the bed. We can't have any infection brought out of the room." Letty, with a strangled, gulping sob, wailed, "But I must see him"; she clung trembling to Martin as if he could protect her from all this misery. The elder woman surveyed her with cold disapproval. "We can't let you go in if you excite yourself like this," her look declared.

Martin appealed to the young doctor, "It won't hurt the boy to see his mother, will it?"

The young man looked awkward and perplexed. "Don't suppose so," he muttered, glancing at the matron as if, under his swagger, he were more than a little in awe of her. "Afraid he may not know you though," he added, as if to justify his hesitation. Martin felt the leap of Letty's heart; he pressed her hand between his arm and his side to quiet and console her. They were taken up a back staircase to what had been the servants' floor of the house. There was a pair of red screens outside an open door, and here a nervous little nurse dressed them in white linen gowns under the awkward eye of the young doctor who had accompanied them.

There was only one bed in the hot, bright, little room, where a masked and overalled nurse was standing beside the patient who must be Aubrey, though his father looked twice before he recognised the boy's features in that strongly retracted head, arched painfully back on the shoulders in its wet turban of ice, those squinting, blinking eyes whose dilated pupils dreaded the light, those contorted lips parched with fever and muttering their inaudible complaints.

Martin heard Letty beside him give a little moan; he kept tight hold of her hand, because he was afraid that she would run across the room and take that restless, tormented head into her arms, but she had enough self-control not to do that; only she clung to him and shivered all over. He heard her saying, "Aubrey—Aubrey——" She had forgotten everything else.

They stayed at the hospital through a long night. The young doctor came back and stared at Aubrey from the foot of the bed as if perplexed to know what to do with him, and would not give any hopeful prognosis. He seemed to want to encourage Martin, but to be paralysed by youth and inexperience. "They sometimes improve on the third day," he said, and added gloomily, "for a time, you know. I gave him a lumbar puncture and an injection of serum to-night and he's to have another in the morning when the specialist comes. There's really nothing else to be done, I'm afraid, except to be generous with the morphia." He was fortunately out of Letty's hearing when he made that admission. She had refused to leave Aubrey's bedside until late in the night, when a friendly nurse persuaded her to go away and lie down. Martin got an armchair in a passage and a mug of syrupy, astringent, lukewarm tea from the fatherly sergeant who had admitted them; he dozed and started through the interminable small hours to wake with stiff limbs at a jangling of basins and crackling of rekindled fires. He wandered out in a cold mist between the rows of hospital huts, and saw the yawning night-nurses scurrying back to breakfast in their gum-boots through the mud.

That day was the longest and weariest of Martin's life. Stacy came down, but Aubrey did not improve as they had hoped; and a grave, bemedalled specialist who saw him during the morning offered Martin no encouragement. Letty sat with wild, dazed eyes, imploring comfort, but he had none to give her; she maintained that Aubrey had looked at her in the early morning and known her; but the nurse glanced behind her at Martin and shook her head. The boy was quite comatose when Martin saw him again. His face was no longer informed by human intelligence, it was merely that of a dying animal; but at least his movements were quiet, he rested in a stupor and sighed away his life. It took many hours to kill him. His mother would not leave him, but at the end she could hardly have known when he died. She had been as quiet as he; never moving, hardly breathing, as if her fixed gaze and clenched hands could hold her son back to life; only when everything was over she abandoned herself to a passion of grief which terrified Martin, sobbing over and over in his arms, "We oughtn't to have let this happen to him. We ought to have kept him safe. He was too young, he hadn't had any life. It wasn't fair, it was all for nothing, my own poor darling; my little, little boy."

They took her away from him and he heard her screaming and crying in some other room: in the end he supposed they gave her something to quiet her, for she became gradually silent and they told him that she was asleep. He could go back then and watch the dead, discarded, useless body of his only son. The lips were still retracted by some ultimate effort, there was a painful furrow between the brows; it was the face of something young, and desperate, and defeated, gone for ever beyond a father's and a mother's help.

5

Letty changed very much after her son's death; indeed it would be just to use that familiar, often misapplied phrase and say that she never recovered from it. She was absolutely broken by her loss. Martin had thought, perhaps even hoped, that after the first bitterness of her lamentations had spent itself she would turn back to him; but she did not do so, instead she subsided into a strange, dazed melancholy stupor. Her husband and her daughter hardly seemed to exist for her; she met them with a vague, remote fretfulness and perplexity as if they were kind but disturbing strangers. From Stacy in particular she turned away, seeming to resent her very presence; she fell into a habit of constant, sour criticism of her daughter's behaviour, clothes, work and way of life, and even reproached her, as she had not done at the time, for the unkind folly of her secret marriage. Stacy took it all with a patience which astonished Martin; she said once to him, with a resignation which was less bitter than he had expected, "Poor Mother can't forgive me for surviving Aubrey." Martin could find no answer. His heart ached for his wife, wandering about like a lost creature, muddling through her days with constant mistakes and repetitions and forgetful omissions in all her words and actions. Her gentle serenity was lost; she treated him as she treated her daughter, with an unjust, unkind irritability. She could not sit still, or keep silent, or continue or finish anything that she began; she could not sleep at night, she sat up late and woke early and wandered about; by day she would fall asleep alarmingly in the middle of something she was doing, then start awake and stare round her, perplexed as to where she was, and Martin would see the recollection of her trouble come back and cloud her bewildered, pretty face. He thought, "This can't go on. She'll go out of her mind." But it did go on for three or four months; the overworked, preoccupied civilian doctors of the time talked to Martin vaguely and not very reassuringly of the effects of a great shock at a critical age. They recommended change and rest, which were not easily obtainable. Stacy could not give up her work to take her mother away, and Letty would probably have refused to go with her, as she did refuse to go with Martin or by herself.

"There's nothing the matter with me," she repeated obstinately. "You just want to get rid of me. I know I'm not very good company nowadays, but I can't help it." Martin could hardly bear to listen to her.

It was Lady Stapleford who ultimately justified herself by taking Letty in hand with her old blend of authority and devotion, marching her off to South Devon, feeding and nursing her with vigorous discipline, and returning her to Brunswick Square two months later a gentle shadow of her old self, but with the wild, desperate fixity gone from her look. She took up her former life with more courage and even showed some interest in Stacy's husband when he came back on leave in the spring of 1917.

Philip Giffard carried his wife off to spend their week together at the same hotel where they had spent their honeymoon; but on this occasion Stacy's recent mourning checked festivity, and her family saw something more of her husband, and were able to make up their minds about him.

Letty continued, inexplicably, to like him; but he took a great deal of trouble to ingratiate himself with her and paid her much attention. She said that Stacy did not look after him properly, and contradicted him too much; she took her son-in-law's side in any disagreement.

Lady Stapleford rather approved of him when she got to know him, and declared that he was the right kind of husband for her wilful granddaughter. At their first meeting she had said to him, "You must keep Stacy in good order, Captain Giffard," and he replied with his loud laugh, "Don't worry. I'll make her toe the line. She knows what she'll get if she doesn't do what I tell her." And he struck the palm of one hand into the hollow of the other with so unexpected and menacing a sound that Stacy, sitting by her mother, started and turned her head; he nodded towards her with satisfaction and boasted to the old lady, "I don't believe in standing any nonsense from women."

Lady Stapleford chuckled and approved; she was not averse to seeing her granddaughter in the hands of a man who was able and willing to humiliate her for his own amusement.

"Stacy's been spoilt," she said, and he replied, with confidence, "Well, I shan't spoil her." They understood each other from the first.

Martin, however, disliked his daughter's husband

even more than he had done a year ago. The man had
an aggressive, bullying manner; he appeared to be
both stupid and opinionated; he had an uncertain,
alarming temper, he was quick with his hands and
rough with his tongue. Martin could not think why
Stacy had ever married him. He was undoubtedly
handsome, and he had an accustomed, experienced,
effective way with women. He was vigorously in love
with Stacy, but he did not conceal the fact that he
thought her childishly inexperienced and absurdly preoccupied with her literary and artistic nonsense. He did
not doubt his own power to obliterate such fancies
from her mind and to put more useful matter into it;
his attitude seemed to be that with time and trouble
he could make her satisfactory to himself, and that she
was just worth the trouble. Apparently he had never
met a girl of her type before, and found her an amusing
novelty. At any ordinary time he might have satisfied
himself by a flirtation with her, in war-time it had
been simpler and more expeditious to remove her hesitations by marrying her; their future, if it ever
materialised, could take care of itself.

Martin was obliged to admit that the man had
absolute courage of the unimaginative order; it was
impossible to picture him as alarmed or even discon-
certed by any danger, he would always be profanely
and harshly adequate to the occasion. He said to
Martin, without either ostentation or melancholy, and
apparently without the least alarm at the prospect,
"You see, sir, I'm pretty sure to be killed; so we may
as well enjoy ourselves while we can." Probably he
had said the same thing to Stacy, when he had persuaded her to the wedding, and with the same cool

indifference had calculated its effect upon her; he had, for his part, accepted the chances of a violent death and saw no reason why he should not make them serve his turn. He seemed aggressively determined to enjoy the whole of his wife's attention. He would not let her out of his sight, and was very jealous of her company; whatever faults might be found with his behaviour, he seemed as much in love with her as ever. Martin would have liked to have been as certain that Stacy was perfectly happy in her marriage. She was outwardly cheerful enough, looked elegant and dandified in her new clothes, skirmished in a lively, perhaps too lively fashion with her husband and submitted to his public and demonstrative love-making with a fair grace, though she sometimes checked him a little sharply and got a fiery blue glance and a harsh word in return. There seemed to be a good deal of friction between them; but Martin reminded himself that they were a hot-tempered couple, and yet unused to each other. He persuaded himself that their quarrels were a slightly morbid form of love-making, in tune with the time. He gathered that Stacy had quite forgotten Oliver Barford, who had gone out to Mesopotamia, been captured at the siege of Kut, and was now a prisoner in a camp in Anatolia; certainly she never spoke of him.

Captain Giffard returned to France in April 1917, but he was not so fortunate on his second occasion; he was shot down and slightly wounded after three months at the front. He had six weeks in hospital, and a little later Stacy informed her family, without showing much pleasure at the prospect, that Philip had wangled an instructor's job and was going to be in

England for a bit; she supposed they'd have to set up housekeeping. Captain Giffard's appointment was to one of the new flying schools on Salisbury Plain, and there were no quarters available immediately for Stacy, but she found a furnished four-roomed cottage in a village near by, and her husband was able to spend a fair amount of his time there. Letty, in her apathetic state, did not take much interest in her daughter's plans, but Martin went down once, and liked the place, in spite of the barbed-wire ugliness of the neighbouring camps and the constant drone of the aeroplanes overhead. The cottage had cob-walls as white as cream, a deep dove-coloured thatch lifting surprised eyebrows over latticed windows, and a garden that in summer would be filled with sweet williams and hollyhocks. It was approached by a narrow footbridge over a brook running in a channel of stone. The village stood among water-meadows in a sheltered winterbourne valley, and all about it rose the soft sides of the naked chalk downs, pitted and dimpled with the rings and mounds and terraces of a prehistoric civilisation. The slopes were cloaked in their brown winter velvet as yet, but they promised coloured crops, wandering sheep, heat and light and a blue lark-thrilled distance when summer should come. Martin, when he first arrived, thought that Stacy ought to be able to be happy in such a cheerful, lonely place, but he was less certain after three days with her. It seemed to him that Philip, when he came, was altogether too off-hand and dictatorial, that the numerous, riotous friends who accompanied him must needs be uninteresting or irritating to Stacy, and that her life was not turning out as successfully as she pretended. He overheard

Philip bullying her pretty sharply once or twice, and once late at night, he thought he heard her cry out from another room as if in stifled protest against some injury; but she put on her bright, cynical look when Martin approached the subject, rebuffed his nervous enquiries and said, "Dear me, yes, Phil and I have a splendid time. Why shouldn't we?" Her father was obliged to suppose himself mistaken that evening when he watched her flirting in her own old determined fashion with a couple of youths imported by Captain Giffard, and being encouraged by him in her audacities with loud laughter and mock scolding. "I'll give you what you deserve when these chaps are gone," declared the Captain, lolling back in his chair, emptying his glass, and striking his knee with his hand. Stacy gave him a sidelong, wicked glance and spurred on the young men to more outrageous remarks than before; his threats did not appear to alarm her and Martin was forced to assume that there was nothing in them. He went back to London next day, reluctant and dissatisfied, but found nothing to report to Letty except that Stacy seemed well and not unhappy, and Letty herself went down later and came back contented with the situation. "The only thing I do wish," said she regretfully, "is that Stacy had a baby to occupy her time, now that Philip has to leave her alone so much." Martin did not reply; he had not the heart to tell her that Captain Giffard, on receiving some such suggestion of his own, had replied with his vigorous laugh, "We're not such damn fools as that."

"But the war can't last much longer," said Letty wistfully, "and then they'll be able to settle down somewhere and be comfortable. I shouldn't think they'd

send Philip out again, should you?" Martin agreed
without enthusiasm that Stacy's husband was probably
safe where he was; but he had failed to reckon with
the chances of experimental aviation. In the spring of
1918 Captain Giffard was killed in trying out a new
machine.

Martin got Stacy's telegram at his office; she had
either calculated that her mother would not be at home
at midday, or else had turned instinctively to her
father. Letty, however, infinitely distressed, insisted
on coming down with him. They found Stacy at the
cottage, as white, cold and silent as Martin had somehow expected; she withstood her mother's lamentations
with a controlled tremor, even to her father she said
very little. She did not speak much of her husband.
"He always thought he'd be killed," she said once
without a change in her frozen look; and after another
burst of Letty's tears and regrets, "He didn't think the
new machine was much good." She seemed dazed by
the whole business. Martin hoped that most of the
details had been kept from her. He had been up to the
camp and seen various people in authority who offered
vague condolences and explanations; and he had
gathered a good deal more from the subsequent nods
and winks and unfinished sentences of three or four
hard-featured, off-hand youths whom he remembered
from Stacy's parties at the cottage.

"The poor chap always said that bus would turn
her tail up in the first stiff breeze," one recollected, and
"Top-heavy, crazy pattern—any fool could see it,"
agreed another. One excited, talkative boy, with less
discretion than the rest, emptied his glass, put it down
with a somewhat unsteady hand, and giggled, "Worst

of it was, he thought he could fly better when he was a bit on." This youth was talked down and shouldered out of the conversation by an affable, temporary, elderly R.A.M.C doctor, who gave Martin an edited account of the accident. "Not a very good flying day; poor Giffard might have come down earlier; but he was a reckless, courageous fellow, as you know, and he was anxious to try out this new type of machine thoroughly." He was a little taken aback, however, when Martin, with a vague feeling of doing the proper thing as Stacy's representative, asked whether he was expected to see Captain Giffard's body. "Afraid there isn't much to see," confessed the doctor, blinking behind the horn-rimmed glasses, which combined so oddly with his mild civilian appearance and ill-fitting uniform. The mess glanced at each other awkwardly; Martin discovered from their guarded references that the machine had been completely smashed and that Philip Giffard's body had been burnt in the wreckage. "He must have been dead before he reached the ground," asserted the doctor without much conviction. One or two officers supported him. They did not appear to have been subdued by the spectacle of a death which might equally overtake any one of them, they spoke of it with a careless bravado which might or might not have been assumed. Martin left the mess and went back to the cottage. After he had turned his back on the asphalt squares, the cinder-paths, and ranged huts of the camp he found himself alone on the enormous shoulder of the down, where five mad hares were racing in a circle on a fallow upland. It was a mild spring evening, very clear and still, from the bottom of the valley he could hear the contented murmur of a lambing-fold. The lambs wrung his heart as he went down by the wattled fence; they were so feeble, and innocent, and unconsciously gay. There were lighted windows in the cottages by the time he reached the village, but Stacy's windows were dark; he found her sitting with her mother, and told her what he dared. Her mother shed her easy tears and was relieved by them, but Stacy was dry-eyed; he could not tell what she felt.

Philip Giffard was buried next day, with all the circumstance and ceremony of war, the flags and drums and music; and afterwards Stacy went home with her father and mother.

IX

THE ARMISTICE was signed that autumn, and Lady
Stapleford died unexpectedly during the influenza
epidemic of the following winter. She was not mourned,
except by her adoring daughter; but Martin found that
the death of the unpleasant old woman shook him. He
could not help reverting in his mind to those first, far-
off, obliterated weeks in Rome when she and her
daughter had seemed to him everything that was sweet
and delightful. He had, of course, long realised that
she had arranged his marriage, and had had an easy
task with two young people who hardly knew what
love was; but he had never borne her any malice for
that. He and Letty had come to love each other in the
end with all their hearts; it had not mattered to them
that they had few tastes in common, or that the old
woman had done her best to spoil and weaken their
mutual pleasure. He had never wanted anyone else
but Letty and he did not believe that she had ever
wanted anyone but him. They had eaten their portion
of disappointment together, and they had shared one
great sorrow; they had become indivisible.

The death of Lady Stapleford was a piece of his
own youth gone for ever. He had disliked and feared

the old woman, but he could not imagine life without her perpetual, critical presence; he kissed and comforted Letty with a maimed feeling, as if he had lost a painful, useless limb. "You never really loved her, you never really understood her," sobbed Letty, childish and petulant as ever; but he was able to assure her with serious candour, "Darling, I did understand, perfectly. You were the only person she cared about, everything she did was for you." Letty sobbed more quietly, and he kissed her and pardoned the old woman for sacrificing everyone and everything to her daughter's happiness.

Stacy made no comment, and no particular pretence of regretting her grandmother; she said with her usual careless kindness to Martin, "The poor old woman had an unsatisfactory life." He answered thoughtfully, "Not so bad as you might suppose. She had one object and she attained it. You can't say as much for everybody." Stacy agreed in an off-hand way, "Yes, she didn't care what happened to anyone but Mother."

Letty was not present at this conversation, but no doubt she understood her daughter's mind. She constantly indulged in reproachful allusions to Stacy's past disagreements with the dead woman; Martin thought that his daughter showed a good deal of self-restraint in not taking them up more frequently than she did.

Philip Giffard's young widow was still living with her parents at this time in the Brunswick Square flat. Her mother had urged her to it, and her father and she enjoyed the little they had of each other's company. She had been left enough money by her dead husband to set up a home of her own but had not thought it worth while so far. She spent her days at the Ministry and was seldom at home even in the evenings. She was growing restless again, however, had tired of her war-work, now that its urgency was over, and had begun to talk about her old plan of an architectural training. Martin did not think that she would stop with him permanently, but he did not encourage Letty to discuss the future with her; he did not wish to disturb a situation which was a comfort to him while it lasted. Stacy Giffard was not so near to him as Stacy Lovell had been; something had happened to her which he did not understand, and she kept her defences closed against him; but he had set all his remaining hopes upon her. If she were not some day to be happy, then life would have no more meaning for him.

Stacy's employment at the Ministry came to an end in the spring of 1919, and just one week later Oliver Barford walked unexpectedly into Bedford Row, as if he had never been away.

Martin had been out to attend one of his increasingly numerous official committee-meetings; and when he came back a new and stupid office-boy put him off the scent by telling him that a Major Wreford had called; so that Martin went into his own room completely unprepared. There was a very tall, thin, shabby man standing at one of the windows against the light, staring out into Bedford Row; and Martin, whose eyesight was not so good as it had been, stopped, and fumbled with his glasses and said, "I'm Martin Lovell. Can I do anything for you?"

"I hope so," said the visitor, turning round, with a short and mirthless laugh, and then Martin saw who he was.

Taking a long look at Oliver, once their greetings were done with, and getting him in fair light, Martin realised that Mesopotamia and his Turkish captivity had put ten years on to the young man's back. He was deeply tanned, but his skin looked sallow and unhealthy beneath its pigmentation. He was pitiably thin and there seemed to be no flesh on his bones; there were two deep, crescentric hunger-lines from his nostrils to his mouth. The most conspicuous changes, however, were the close cropping and bleaching of what had been a dark, untidy head of hair, and the strange wandering tricks of his eyes, which had been bold and staring once, but now slid desperately from floor to ceiling in an attempt to avoid Martin's pity. His long-fingered, sensitive draughtsman's hands had lost their old sure movements; Martin, to whom they had once been as familiar as his own, noticed immediately how they felt about the arms of the chair as the young man sat back in it. He jerked out single sentences that came with an intolerable effort.

"Yes, I've just come back from Constantinople. Of course we all ought to have been let out months ago, but you can't hurry the Turk, and then I was kept in hospital in Malta when I got there. They said my head was queer, I daresay they were right. We were up in the mountains of Anatolia over towards the Black Sea, and got left to the last. No, we weren't very uncomfortable, as camps go. It would have been easy enough to escape, but not worth it, we should never have got as far as the Black Sea. Yes, I got some parcels, daresay I got all that were sent; but it was a long way for the stuff to come, and naturally a good deal of it was stolen. I got some cigarettes once from Stacy, I remember, and another time she sent me some chocolate; I was fearfully thankful for that." He licked his lips in a peculiar fashion, and laughed again, on a note that did not amuse Martin. "I wrote her a letter or two," he confessed, looking sideways under his eyebrows, "but I don't know if she ever got them."

"I never heard of any," said Martin, and the conversation seemed to languish; to revive it he asked hurriedly, "Is your wife in London?"

"She's with her people at Northampton," said Oliver. "I came up from there to-day. We've had six weeks of it. I went there when I landed, hadn't anywhere else to go. We want to get off on our own as soon as we can, of course. Not much fun, having a second honeymoon in somebody else's house, you know. I didn't plan it out like that in camp." His eyes shifted about Martin again as he enquired abruptly, "Everyone all right at Campden Hill Square?"

Martin had foreseen that he would be obliged to answer this question sooner or later. He steadied himself, and began, "We're not in Campden Hill Square any longer. We sold it quite early in 1915. We couldn't afford it in war-time. Letty and I have been in a flat in Brunswick Square for the last four years." He smiled half-heartedly at an old family joke, "In another year it'll be time for the Lovells to move again."

"Stacy not with you?" enquired Oliver, who seemed to have forgotten this mild pleasantry.

"Well, just at present she is. You knew," (Martin felt his way uncertainly here), "that she'd married, and been left a widow?"

"Yes, I'd heard that." He did not explain how. "Airman called Giffard, wasn't he? Killed just before the Armistice, distinguished sort of chap?" Oliver was scowling at his own unsteady hands. "I suppose Stacy was fearfully cut up about it at the time," he muttered.

Martin said slowly, "I don't know." He had never been altogether sure, and he found that he could say to Oliver what he had never yet said, even to Letty: "I sometimes think Stacy felt that she'd made a mistake in marrying him."

"Why, what sort of a chap was he?"

"Rather a brute, a great big, handsome, stupid fellow—not at all her type. He used to bully her a good deal. I don't know how it would have worked out in peace-time. They only had two years of each other, and he was in France most of the time. She was very much taken with him at first, of course, thought him simply wonderful. Letty liked him too; he had a way of getting round women. I never cared for him, as you'll gather," confessed Martin, smiling dubiously at himself. "Fathers are like that, I'm afraid; I didn't think him good enough for Stacy."

"Doesn't sound as if he could have been," muttered Oliver, in his old contemptuous manner. "Why on earth did you let her do it?"

"Couldn't stop her," admitted Martin, though the words stuck in his throat. "They just walked in one morning and said they were married. I'm afraid she knew we shouldn't have approved. But, of course, it must have been his suggestion, and she was ready to do anything he told her at that stage."

Somehow he did not mind telling Oliver these things.

"Good Lord!" said Oliver staring at the floor, "I

should never have expected Stacy to behave like that."

"Well, you know what Stacy's like when she wants a thing. She won't wait," said Martin. "And she was certainly desperately in love with him at the time, whatever she felt afterwards."

"Must have been," agreed Oliver, with his deepest frown. He brooded over the story, while Martin continued, "Giffard left her a fair amount of money. She talks of setting up for herself sometimes, but Letty has persuaded her to stay with us so far. She's been working in one of these new Ministries, but she's just been axed. I don't know what she means to do next, or whether we shall be able to keep her much longer."

"Probably she'll marry again," suggested Oliver, as if he hardly relished the prospect. Martin shook his head, doubtfully. "She's been going out a good deal lately," he admitted. "She's plenty of friends and her mother likes to make plans—always did." Oliver nodded as if he knew something about that. "But I don't think there's anyone in particular. It's too soon to say she'll never marry, but somehow I feel as if she'd been put off it for the present, whatever she may do later. No, what I do think is that she's looking for some permanent job. She was talking the other day about her old plan of an architectural training. Perhaps that's what she has in her mind. After all, it's not much of an existence for her to settle down at home again and wait on her mother and me. Young women aren't content with that kind of thing nowadays; and at twenty-seven Stacy ought to have a life of her own. She's too good to be wasted."

Oliver made a painful, unhappy sound of assent, and then as if to shake off the consideration of Stacy's wasted youth asked the inevitable, dreaded question, "What's become of Aubrey?"

Martin had been waiting for it to come; he took a steadying breath, and said, "Aubrey died in hospital in 1916 of cerebro-spinal meningitis." He saw the young man wince as if from a lifted hand and heard him mutter, "God! I didn't know"; then, to himself, and almost unconsciously, "It must have nearly finished his mother."

Martin admitted gravely, and for the first time, "She's never got over it."

There was a long silence; Oliver, who had seen so many deaths by violence, passed his hand across his forehead, and repeated in bewilderment, "I didn't know. I thought I'd find him here."

Martin, with slow realisation, admitted, "There's no one left here that you know. Markham and Phillips joined up and were both killed. Orchard went off to some Ministry or other, they wouldn't take him for the front because of those eyes of his. I don't know what became of him. I had a Belgian to help me through the worst of it, and now that things are looking up again I've got a couple of new boys in the drawing office. There's a chance of a pupil in the autumn. Things have been fearfully slack, you know, and they're only just beginning to pick up again. All these housing schemes they talk of won't be much help to people like me. Still, I suppose I shall scrape my practice together again in time." And he concluded, as if the words had been put into his mouth by some outside power, "There's no one in your old room if you want to come back." He might have dreaded gratitude; he got what disturbed him much more, an

evasive flicker of eyelids and mouth, and the unexpected mumble, "Better not risk that, had you?"

He found no reply; the young man covered his eyes
with his unsteady hand, and behind that screen got
out his painful words. He said with tolerable firmness,
"I meant to ask you for a job when I came in. I'm
pretty well on my beam-ends. I've got to get something from somebody, but not from you. I've had too
much in the old days. I won't stick you with a broken-
down prisoner-of-war, who can't sleep at night, or do
two hours' steady work, or keep himself sober for a
week together." He took his hand away from his face,
and looked straight at Martin for the first time. The
elder man was too much moved to speak, and Oliver
concluded the silence by saying with his old harsh,
mirthless laugh, "Better give me a testimonial to
somebody you don't know too well."

That made Martin's mind up for him; he found the
only possible words to use.

"You're not going out of here. I can't do without
you, Oliver. I must have you to help me, now that I've
got no son of my own."

2

That was all very well for the moment; but Martin
had to face his own reaction whilst Oliver became
noisy and excited over a prolonged luncheon together,
and during the afternoon when Oliver had rushed away
to tell his news to his wife at Northampton, and in the
evening, when the tale had to be told to Letty, who disapproved. She said immediately, "Oh! Martin, how
could you?" in a tone of reproach and dismay, and had
no patience with his excuses. "Well, I couldn't help it,

really, darling, I had to do something for him. He is in very low water. You know he's got hardly any money of his own. His uncle was to have left him everything, and then there was nothing to leave. The old man had speculated it all away. Oliver only got his finals two or three years before the war began; he was promising well enough, but he hadn't collected any practice to speak of. He's right back at the beginning again, to all intents and purposes."

It would have been useless to tell Letty what had been the conviction at the root of his own offer: "If I don't take the boy nobody else will. I shall have to see him through." He said instead, and mildly enough, "Oliver's got his wife to support."

"He had no business to marry her if he couldn't support her," declared Letty, who was sulky. Martin tried to reason with her, "Come now, darling, you were pleased enough at the time. You said it would keep him out of Stacy's way." He tried to smile at her misgivings as well as his own, which seemed to him much more serious; he could not think that there was any chance of that old mischief between Stacy and Oliver being revived. Stacy had changed from a romantic girl to a disillusioned woman, and Oliver was evidently as dependent on that stout, dark, efficient, commonplace young wife down at Northampton as a sick child is on its mother. Letty, however, disagreed with his anxious optimism.

"So it would have been if you had left things alone. Now they'll start seeing each other, and Stacy will begin to feel sorry for him, and we shall have the same trouble over again. Stacy is in a very queer mood just now."

"Well, Oliver's entirely devoted to his wife. He couldn't talk about anything else. I wish you wouldn't get such nonsense into your head, Letty. It can't matter to Stacy who works at the office."

"Stacy's always running in and out of the office, and you encourage her to do it," objected Letty jealously. "Besides, you'll start inviting the two of them here. I know your ways, Martin, you can't help being kind to people. This is absolutely typical of you. You could easily have passed Oliver on to someone else."

"He told me to," admitted Martin ruefully.

"Then why on earth didn't you?"

Martin despaired of gaining his wife's sympathy. "Don't you see how that was just why I couldn't do it?" he began. "It would have been like turning a dog out into the street." But he gave up the explanation very quickly. Letty was kindness itself in many cases, but when she suspected that the interests of her own family were being threatened she displayed a blind and ruthless maternal prejudice which no argument could affect. Martin was prepared for her opposition, but he was a little surprised that his daughter, when she came in after her dinner-party, did not show more enthusiasm over Oliver's return.

"Yes, I suppose you had to take him back into the office," was all she said. "You couldn't help yourself."

"Well, I've only taken him on at a salary for the present," pleaded Martin, aggrieved, and justifying himself as best he could. "That was all he wanted. I used to think I'd take him into partnership; but it'll be time enough to talk about all that when we see how he does. Perhaps he'll prefer to go somewhere else." He felt disappointed with his womenkind.

Oliver took a long time to settle down in Bedford Row. Martin never admitted in Brunswick Square how often he had reconsidered that first generous impulse or how little work he got out of the young man for the first few months after his return. Oliver was helplessly restless, he could not sit or stand at his drawing for half an hour without stopping to smoke and talk and grumble; he infected the whole staff with his irritable discontents and gave little help or gratitude in return for his principal's encouragement. He seemed bent on wearing Martin's patience out.

His wife had left her parents' house in Northampton and come up to a cheap Bloomsbury boarding-house to be with her husband. Martin went there to an uncomfortable tea in a room full of red plush chairs, fly-blown mantel-mirrors, immovable old ladies, starched antimacassars and potted ferns. He did his conscientious best to make friends with her, but could not find her particularly interesting. After he had reminded her of their first meeting, and talked to her as encouragingly as he dared about Oliver's prospects, he found it quite difficult to keep the conversation going. He could not help wondering what the brilliant, intolerant Oliver had seen in such a stout, silent, unhappy creature; but he reminded himself of the circumstances of their meeting, and hoped that her inert placidity would quiet Oliver's tormented, impatient nerves. It was difficult, however, to feel very sanguine about the relationship of the young couple. Mrs. Barford seemed too stupid to manage her husband and sensitive enough to realise her failure; she was constantly making pathetic bids for his notice, and got one or two answers which brought tears to her eyes. Oliver was in one of his worst moods that afternoon; nothing that his wife could do or say appeared to satisfy him; yet all his peevish and disappointed complaints were brought to her as a child brings its troubles to its mother. Martin wondered whether she was wise enough to realise the dependence implied. She was very unskilful in her treatment of her sulky husband: she was nervous and uncertain, lamented what she should have ignored, was humble when she should have been angry, and gave Oliver pity when a laugh was what he needed. He would have fared better at the hands of some cool, firm, lightly humorous young woman with a sense of her own dignity; he needed, thought Martin, before he could check the thought, someone more like Stacy. But that chance was lost and gone; Oliver had chosen another bed to lie in, and must find what comfort he could in it. Martin sighed and said goodbye and went home; the world did not look too cheerful a place to him in those days. He did not tell Letty much about his visit, for fear of her satisfaction, but he did say to her that he thought the young Barfords were uncomfortable and unhappy in their boarding-house, and that he hoped they would soon be able to afford some place of their own.

Letty went dutifully to call, though Stacy refused to accompany her, and on her return agreed that they must have Oliver and his wife to dinner.

"The poor creatures must be very uncomfortable in that dreadful boarding-house," she declared. "They'll be glad of a good meal." Martin noticed, however, that she only invited them to a Sunday supper, the occasion on which she entertained people whom she thought uninteresting or deserving of pity. It was always an uninspiring, economical, and indigestible meal:

it began with hot bovril, but went on drearily to cold
beef, ham, salad and the drumsticks of the chickens
which had been carved hot at lunch-time, and finished
with tinned fruit and blancmange, and the kind of
cheese which produces bad dreams.

Stacy had lately taken to motoring into the country
on Sundays, with one friend or another, and supper
usually waited until she came home; but the Barfords
had been asked for half-past seven, and at eight o'clock
Letty, whose conversation had been running short, decided that they had better not wait any longer. The
Lovells and their guests sat down at the dining-room
table, leaving gaps and feeling all the awkwardness and
suspended interest of an uncompleted party. Martin
did his best to talk to Mrs. Barford, but found her
heavy in hand; her abstracted, adoring gaze was all for
her husband. Oliver was keeping a firm hold on himself, or so it seemed to Martin; he was subdued, silent
and fatigued, very attentive to his dull wife and rather
touching in his solicitous endeavours to draw her into
the conversation. He seemed very devoted to her and
rather worried about her, he was evidently anxious to
show her at her best. Letty did not help the conversation much; as always when Stacy was late on Sundays,
she was imagining accidents and listening for nothing
but the sound of the front-door bell of the flat.

It did not come until almost nine; then there was a
slamming and a commotion, and Stacy burst into the
room, with cheeks like roses and her bright hair loose
under a leather helmet. She seemed to have a great
many coats and scarves hanging about her, and she
brought a waft of cold night air with her; she looked
amazingly wild, lovely and strange. She glanced from

one to another of the dull quartette as if she hardly
saw them, she tossed them fragments of a long, gay,
involved story about a breakdown near Arundel and
pushing a motorcycle and side-car two miles to a
garage and coming home by a stopping train. There
was a reluctant and irrelevant young man in the background, barely known to Martin, who kept on trying
to apologise to Letty for Mrs. Giffard's delay; Stacy
treated him as if he had been her oldest friend, standing between him and her mother, and laughing and
chattering with her arm through his; she scarcely
looked at the Barfords. Letty was only interested in
the details of the adventure and the chances that Stacy
might have been hurt; when she was reassured she devoted herself entirely to feeding the young couple and
lamenting their rashness. The Barfords were quite forgotten by everybody but Martin; Mrs. Barford sat
silent, with her mouth a little open, staring at Stacy
as if she were fascinated; Oliver stared too, rather
sulkily, but did not say anything. Martin watched his
daughter with disapproval; it struck him that she was
flirting rather excessively with her young man, whose
name he could not even remember. He had not seen
her behave like this since the days when she was married to Philip Giffard. He wondered whether she was
engaged to the unknown escort, and then it occurred to
his simple mind, a little later than it should have done,
that, although she never looked at Oliver, she might
possibly be doing all this for his benefit. He made a
move, then, taking the Barfords across the flat to the
drawing-room, and leaving the travellers to finish their
meal with Letty.

He and Oliver fell with unconscious relief into professional talk about post-war housing schemes; Letty, appearing a little later, maintained a discussion on domestic economy for some time with the neglected Mrs. Barford; but the young people did not reappear until some time later, though they were to be heard laughing in the dining-room, and about half-past ten the Barfords went away.

The hospitable Martin could not think that they had enjoyed themselves, and he said so to Letty and Stacy after the young man had departed, but got little sympathy. Letty merely said vaguely, "Oh! I'm sure they quite understood. Oliver's such an old friend you couldn't expect me to stand on ceremony with him or his wife. He'd think it only natural for me to be anxious about Stacy. And, you see, I was perfectly right, there had been an accident. I was quite certain something had happened." Stacy, however, disdaining to evade attack, said frankly and crossly, "I wasn't going to come in and have to talk for hours to that stupid wife of Oliver's. She's even worse than I expected. She's got a face like a sheep and she never opens her mouth. She just sits there the whole time making eyes at Oliver. I can't stand young married couples."

Letty said with a certain spitefulness which had been growing upon her lately, "Well, I think she's a very suitable sort of wife for Oliver. After all, he's nobody in particular, and I daresay she'll make him very comfortable. They won't be rich, but you can see she hasn't been used to very good society. Anyhow, they seem devoted to each other." Stacy made no comment; she pitched the end of an unfinished cigarette into the fire as if she had determined to smoke no more, and then changed her mind and lit another with a vicious spirt of the match.

"I suppose I shall have to toil all the way down to Sydenham to call when they're settled," said Letty mournfully. "You'd better come with me and see what the house is like. After all, he was your friend." Stacy scowled and muttered, "I'm not going near them," and went off to bed, she would not discuss the Barfords any longer.

3

The young Barfords took some time to settle. Economy and the housing shortage obliged them to spend several months in their Bloomsbury boarding-house, which was at least convenient for Oliver's temporary office-work in Bedford Row. "And I expect," said Stacy, who kept up her original spite against Oliver's wife, "that Mrs. Barford loves the place. It's full of women just like her, all playing patience, and gossiping and lending each other patterns for knitted silk jumpers"; but Letty, more charitable and more discerning, professed to be sorry for young Mrs. Barford, and maintained that she was longing for a home of her own. ("Sets of crochet-edged teacloths and a fumed oak suite, and pink eiderdowns," said Stacy pettishly.)

Oliver, who had always been singularly careless of his surroundings, was down at the office the whole day and half the night, appeared entirely indifferent to his own comfort, and would have accepted the boarding-house for an indefinite period; it was Mrs. Barford who insisted on living in the lower half of a Victorian house near the Crystal Palace. Letty and Martin, when they went down to see it on a hot Sunday afternoon in

July, 1919, were confirmed in their impression that
Oliver had not really been interested in the move.
There was nothing of the proud owner about him. He
left his wife to conduct Letty over her domestic arrangements after tea, and took Martin away down
a flight of iron steps, to smoke and talk in the back-
garden. It was overshadowed by neglected trees and
given up to a rank lawn, a bed of lilies-of-the-valley,
a border of grimy flag-flowers and a clinkered rockery
hidden by discouraged ferns.

"You've got a cedar-tree at any rate," said Martin,
doing his best. "I've always wanted to live in a house
with a cedar of Lebanon in the garden, but somehow
I've never managed it in spite of all our moves."

Oliver stretched himself perilously in his deck-chair
and gave his short, singularly mirthless laugh, tilting
back his head and staring up into the dark and secret
branches above him. "Afraid these details are rather
wasted on me," he said; and then grudgingly, "One
gets them in gardens of this date; but cedar or no cedar
it's a pretty damnable house."

Martin studied the building with a professional eye,
and put it at 1830, or thereabouts; it was of a sober,
sand-coloured brick in three stories, and had round-
headed sash-windows in plaster settings. There had
been a not undignified plaster portico over the front
door, as he remembered; and there was a flat roof behind a plaster balustrade. The house answered in all
respects to its semi-detached companion. He had
thought that the two of them presented a fairly satisfactory front to the road; but he now had leisure to
observe, and to remark to Oliver, that the proportions
of the garden-front had been considerably upset by the

addition of a conservatory of coloured glass to one house, a hanging cistern, and a makeshift corrugated-iron bathroom to the other. The interior had been clumsily adapted by an economical and unimaginative landlord to the requirements of two servantless households. The Barfords were occupying a tall, draughty sitting-room on the ground floor, separated by folding doors from a back-bedroom looking on the garden. They had a dining-room, a kitchen and a bathroom somewhere in the basement, which Martin had not seen; and he had heard Mrs. Barford complaining to Letty at tea-time about the mud on the linoleum in the hall when the other tenants had visitors on wet days. "Dorothy's always having rows with the upstairs people," Oliver told Martin vexedly. "However, she gets her own back over the garden. They're not allowed in the garden. That's our preserve. They can only look down on us from above." And he pointed out to Martin a balcony, ornamented with boxes of trailing geraniums, and sheltered by a striped yellow awning. "That's post-war domesticity; not very dignified, is it?" He scoffed as if he were thoroughly out of temper.

When Martin replied gently, "It must be pleasant sitting out here together in the evenings," the young man shrugged his shoulders, and returned, "Afraid we don't do much of that. I spend most of my evenings at the office nowadays. I go out and get something to eat in Holborn, and then I go back and work till the last train. Fortunately I can get down here in thirty minutes from door to door. I wouldn't have left Torrington Square otherwise."

Martin was taken aback, and said, "I'm afraid that makes a lonely life for Mrs. Barford."

"Well, it's her own choice," retorted Oliver, still looking at the cedar-tree. "I told her what it would be if we came to live down here. But we couldn't afford anything in town at present, and Dorothy's one of those women who must have a house to fuss over or they get miserable." He gave Martin a brief, apologetic, and unexpectedly youthful glance which the older man found touching.

"Don't suppose you'll stay here very long," he muttered, not knowing what to say.

"Hope not," Oliver concluded. "It's just the sort of place I can't stand. I don't know why she likes it."

Martin went back to London rather depressed about the young couple, but Letty was encouraging, "Of course, it's really a dreadful house," she told Stacy, who had submitted reluctantly to an account of the afternoon's expedition, "and it must be very trying to have to put up with strangers in the other half, but plenty of people are having to do that nowadays, and it ought to suit them very well for the present." She continued, with the slight snobbishness which always reminded Martin of Lady Stapleford, "Of course, they won't go on living there if Oliver begins to make his way, but just for the next year or two, while they're short of money and until he gets a practice together, it's very wise of them to live quietly."

Stacy glanced at her father, who shook his head. "I found the house very depressing," he admitted. "It seemed to me to have no dignity and no privacy, and I'm afraid Mrs. Barford finds life rather dull there." He had been sorry for Oliver's wife, and was disappointed that his women did not support him.

"I don't see why she should be dull," objected Letty, quite resentfully. "She's got her home and her husband to look after. That ought to be enough for her. I've no patience with young brides who want to be out amusing themselves all the time." She then softened a little, gave Martin one of her pretty looks, and said, "I didn't find life dull when I first married."

Martin smiled back at her; Stacy, impatient of this exchange between them, put in crossly, "I should think it's Oliver who's going to be dull. Mrs. Barford is just the sort of woman who hasn't a thought outside her own home. She'll bore him to death in a year or two. I expect he'll end by beating her."

Letty gave a shocked exclamation; her daughter persisted with astonishing violence, "It would do the woman good. Why should Oliver be tied up for life to a fat lump like that? If she doesn't make him utterly miserable it'll only be because she's turned him into a dull stupid idiot like herself."

Martin could not understand what was making his wife and his daughter turn on each other like enemies.

"Stacy, you think that nothing matters except bookwork and brains. That's the mistake you've always made. You despise everyone who doesn't talk clever nonsense about art and literature. I should have thought Philip would have taught you that a man wants something more than that from his wife." Letty's voice was shrill and unsteady, her cheeks were flushed with angry colour; but Stacy's face was perfectly white, she neither moved nor spoke to avert her mother's attack.

"They'll have their life together, they'll have their

children," stammered Letty, as if it were her own defence. "Why should you think you've the right to look
down on that?"

Martin tried to interrupt her, but he could not find
any words. He saw his daughter put out her hand with
a gesture of defeat; she turned and went uncertainly
out of the room. He was left absolutely bewildered, he
said to his wife, "Why are you always so hard on
Stacy?" She did not reply, although she gave him an
inexplicable look. He struggled on, "You don't mean
it, I suppose. You love her and you want to do what's
best for her, but you don't know how cruel you sound.
This business, now, about Oliver, you're treating her
so harshly over it."

Letty dabbed at her eyes and said with unexpected
firmness, "She'd better realise the true situation. She
won't get over it till she does."

They looked at each other, and Martin yielded before the significance of his wife's expression. "I suppose you were right," he admitted, "I suppose she was
in love with him in the old days."

"Of course she was," said Letty tartly, "head over
ears. I always told you so, but you wouldn't believe me.
If he'd been allowed to run in and out of the house as
you wanted he'd have proposed to her the year she
came out, and she'd have taken him. She was quite silly
about him then. But I wasn't going to have my only
daughter tying herself up to a disagreeable young man
with no money before she'd seen anyone else. I thought
they were too strong-willed ever to pull together, and
I discouraged the whole business. It's easy enough for
a mother to turn a girl against a young man if she
chooses."

"I suppose it is," Martin admitted, with a passing chill, remembering Lady Stapleford and thinking that it was perhaps equally easy for a mother to marry a girl to a defenceless young man.

"That part wasn't difficult," Letty told him triumphantly. "And once he was safely married to that nurse of his I never thought of Stacy seeing him again. I was horrified when you told me he'd come back, and you'd taken him into the office, where Stacy can make an excuse for seeing him any day she chooses."

Martin stared at his wife; he was amazed by this revelation of the sustained, obstinate, subterranean warfare which existed between her and her daughter. Letty continued sourly, "If Philip had lived things would have been all right. He understood how to manage Stacy. He wouldn't have let her turn romantic over Oliver Barford. He'd have given her a good shaking, and told her to mind her own business, and she'd have been too busy with her home and her children to care what happened to Oliver. Just now she's at a loose end and ready to make a fool of herself. She feels sentimental and upset and jealous, she's got to have an outlet for her feelings, and she thinks she can find it in Oliver. We shall have trouble with her if we aren't careful. We've got to find some young man of her own age who'll put both Oliver and Philip out of her head."

"I don't know," returned Martin soberly, "that there are many of those left." He stared at Letty with astonishment, almost with dislike; her cool assumptions baffled him.

"I think you made a mistake when you interfered with them at first," he said, after a troubled pause.

It was a rare thing for him to criticise his wife directly. He awaited an indignant defence, and probably a burst of tears, but, as once or twice before, she surprised him. Her blue eyes were dark with the strangest wisdom.

"I see that now myself," she told him, with a bewildering, resentful composure. "I was unjust to her. I'd have done better to let them marry, but I thought it was only a girl's first love-affair; I thought he was harsh and unkind and would never make her a good husband. I fancied I knew their business better than they did. I was wrong to interfere, but then I've never understood Stacy."

Martin was amazed by her humility; he had not thought her capable of it. Her voice was tremulous with unaccustomed effort; she said, "I've never known how to make Stacy happy. She's your daughter, not mine. You and she have always done everything together, and left me out. I wasn't clever enough for the two of you; I understood that and I tried to accept it, but I've always been jealous. That's why I've treated her so unfairly. She came between me and you." She began to shed her accustomed, helpless tears; she was afraid of her own admissions, and Martin was appalled by them, he had never thought that she was conscious of her own injustice. He had no words for the feelings that oppressed him, the dull, heavy resentment and aching pity, the sense of disappointment and loss. He heard her sobbing, "If Aubrey had lived—if I'd had Aubrey——"

He whispered with his arms round her and her forehead against his shoulder, "Letty, don't; you'll break my heart"; but he did not know how to comfort her. He could only think of her as younger and more defenceless than her daughter; she did not know what she wanted, except to make time and the growth of her world stand still, and that he could not do for her. The nest was empty, the young birds were flown, and she had nothing left.

He said to her, "We can't live Stacy's life for her. She'll have to make her own mistakes"; and then he said, "I sometimes think we made our own biggest mistake about her when we wouldn't let her work. She ought to have gone in for that architectural training of hers or something like it years ago at the very beginning of things. She's always been a restless person; she's never had quite enough to occupy her energies. She needs something to take her outside herself. She was happier driving that ambulance than I've ever seen her before or since."

Letty drew herself away from him, and sighed, and said resignedly, "Well, let her start her training now. You and she have been planning it for weeks, and hinting it to me, and threatening all sorts of trouble if I don't give in. What's it got to do with me? I'm only Stacy's mother; she doesn't need to ask my permission nowadays, if she wants to make a fool of herself. She's an independent married woman with her own money. Let her go away and live in a flat by herself, and pretend she's studying architecture, and invite Oliver round to tell her his domestic troubles; I don't care what happens to her. I've given you my advice, but you won't take it, and you'll only have yourself to blame if there's trouble."

Martin did not pay very much attention to her peevish, exaggerated, mock-tragic complaints; he recognised them as her own individual method of putting

herself in the right after a difference of opinion and a
defeat. He understood that she meant to make such
amends as she could to her daughter for past unkindness, and he translated her verdict next day to a subdued and bitter Stacy in terms of surrender.

"Mother's given in about your architectural notion,"
was the way he put it.

"I suppose she thinks it's the next best substitute for
a husband," said Stacy, who was in a bad humour. She
was, however, as relieved as her father to escape the
necessity for a series of family arguments. When Martin, rather ruefully, protested, "We want you to do
whatever will make you happy," she kissed him with
a certain repentant vigour, and although she declared,
"I should have done it anyhow," he could see that she
was not ungrateful.

Oliver Barford heard of the plan a few days later,
but did not, to Martin's secret relief, manifest any
particular interest in it.

"I daresay Stacy won't be too bad," he said
gloomily. "But all women architects are pretty hopeless, I think. Still, she probably won't stay the course.
Five years is a long time for her to stick to one
notion."

Martin did not altogether agree with this estimate
of his daughter's character, but he did not repeat it to
her. It struck him that the misogynistic Oliver was trying to reassure himself against the possibility of Stacy
or any other woman appearing in the office.

X

STACY began her five years' training at the Architectural Association in the autumn of 1919. Martin was relieved to find that she did not want to be articled to him, and spend her days in Bedford Row, as Letty had hinted; and he fell in love with the tall rooms, the dignified staircase and delicate Georgian ornament of the old students' house in Bedford Square. He was deeply interested in the details of her training, the purchase of her text-books and instruments, her lectures on history, theory and method, her six- and twelve-hour sketches, the analysis, design, construction and decoration of her set problems. He told her with envy, "You're going to get a better chance than I ever had. People talk a lot of nonsense about the value of the old articled system, but the opportunities varied tremendously; I practically had to train myself. My first chief never taught me anything in the office, except how to rub up Indian ink and use a T-square. He did that the first morning just to make an impression on me; but I had to pick up everything else. I wasted years of my time, and learnt most of my practical work from builders' foremen."

Stacy laughed, she did not intend to waste any of her

time. He was amused by her new airs and graces, and her delightful readiness to instruct him in the modern developments of the profession. She was immensely pleased with her new departure, and her father congratulated himself on having encouraged her to win her point.   -

She had left Brunswick Square and set herself up in a couple of rooms in a tumbledown Adam house on the farther side of the Tottenham Court Road, at a corner of Fitzroy Square. She was on a top story again, with three floors of offices beneath her, but declared that her chimney-pot view and the oval glass dome and classic plaster medallions of the staircase compensated her for the seventy-five stairs to her landing, the sloping ceilings of her attic rooms, and the desertion of the building at night, which so much alarmed her mother. She had made herself very comfortable in the ramshackle student fashion which was characteristic of her, with a good deal of peasant pottery, a great many bright cushions, two comfortable arm-chairs and a litter of books and drawings which were seldom disturbed. Letty declared that the flat was dirty and neglected, and seldom went there; she was growing heavier and less energetic, and she professed to find the stairs too trying. She insisted on a Sunday evening visit, otherwise she left her daughter much more alone than might have been expected from her lamentations over the girl's departure.

Martin, however, saw quite as much of Stacy as he had done when she was living in Brunswick Square; he was always making an excuse to himself for going over to lunch with her in the students' dining-room in Bedford Square, or spending an hour at the flat between

tea and dinner to discuss her latest problem and taste
her latest discovery in food or drink. Stacy, though
she was badly served, according to her mother's con-
ventions, was something of an epicure, and she liked to
have her father's opinion on the queer foreign deli-
cacies which she produced from the hidden cupboard
under the window-seat. She dropped in, also, once or
twice a week, at Bedford Row, without any particular
warning, to take her father out to lunch or walk home
with him; and he could not resist the old pleasure of
letting her browse among his plans and papers. Her
comments had always been intelligent, now they were
becoming better informed. It amused and delighted
him to see her lean her elbows on his tall, flat desk,
and shake her short hair out of her eyes as she planted
a brown finger on his curling tracings and made some
absurd, unexpected, yet somehow stimulating suggestion which might or might not solve a problem.

He did his best to keep her out of Oliver Barford's
way, partly because Letty's talk had made him self-
conscious, partly because he had a notion that Oliver
did not much care for her company. There had certainly been a contraction of the young man's eyebrows
when he first found Stacy smoking a cigarette on the
hearthrug in Martin's room, although it was after six
and he could have had no professional objection to her
presence. There had been a hostile exchange too on
that occasion, much as in the old days.

"Hullo, Oliver, how are you liking living in the
suburbs?" from the girl, and "Suppose you know more
about bricks and mortar than any of us by this time,"
from the young man; but after a few minutes they had
dropped back into their cool, baffling, accustomed im-

pertinence to each other, as if they were boy and girl again, and Martin thought that he had fancied the spark of real enmity between them. He could not keep Oliver out of the front room if the young man chose to make himself an errand there, and there were a hundred natural, professional reasons for consultations between a principal and his assistant. It was extremely difficult for Martin to decide whether Oliver did or did not seek Stacy out; and she, for her part, made no obvious attempt to meet him, never commented on his absence if he failed to appear, contradicted him and quarrelled with him when he came in a perfectly casual and unembarrassed fashion. There was no evidence that she entertained him in Fitzroy Square, though it would have been perfectly easy for her to do so, and she certainly never went down to see his wife at Sydenham. She seemed contented, cheerful and absorbed in her work, and she appeared to be enjoying her first taste of student life. Martin heard her talk of sitting on committees and designing costumes for a play, and of taking up tennis again when the summer came round; though she was less enthusiastic about such matters than she would have been at an earlier stage, and counted up her twenty-seven years with a seriousness which made her father smile regretfully. He would have liked her to waste a little more time than she did; he thought that, like most women-students, she was inclined to overwork, though he was proud of her successes, and enjoyed teasing her about them.

"Examinations are neither here nor there," said he, "you wait till you get on to the practical side; that's where you'll find the real difficulties"; and Oliver, less kindly, growled out, "Women can always reel off bookwork like parrots, but they can't design, they've no originality."

Stacy did not care, she laughed in his face as she could never have done in the old days. Oliver seemed mysteriously to be losing his power of annoying her though he treated her more rudely than ever. Martin decided that Stacy was getting over her sentimental fit, and told Letty so with a good deal of triumph. Letty was unwilling to relinquish her theory, but even she admitted that Stacy's first year of work had done her no harm.

"It's given her something new to think about," she allowed grudgingly; "but of course that may not last. Just at present she talks of nothing but the school, and we can only hope that she won't get tired of it." She added, characteristically, "What I should really like would be for her to meet a nice young man there who'd persuade her to give up all this nonsense, and settle down and marry him." Martin grumbled, but nothing would cure her of regarding Stacy's training-school as a matrimonial agency. Privately he guessed that Stacy's fellow-students were all too young for her, but that she was not troubled with thoughts of marriage at present.

During her second year in Bedford Square he indulged himself by taking her abroad. Travelling in France was still uncomfortable, but not impossible, and they both longed to revive their old custom of a holiday together. Letty would not uproot herself; she betrayed a touch of her former jealousy but admitted her disinclination to move; and her husband and daughter were able to make a duet of their Easter fortnight in Touraine. Martin had excused it by saying, "You really ought to do the French Renaissance properly. It'll be good for your education," but they took anything that came in their way. They explored the winding alleys of Tours; they stared at the brown fish-scale towers of St. Gatien in its ring of chapels, and walked under the striding buttress which plants down its foot in the grass-grown cloister of La Psalette. They made expeditions by rattling, shaking, cindery, local trains; they saw Judas trees, wine-purple under the ramparts of Chinon, and cowslips powdering the meadows beside the brimming Loire. They saw the black towers of Langeais blocking the village street, and the pale turrets of Azay-le-Rideau and the arched gallery of Chenonceau reflected in their gliding streams. They looked down from the airy terrace at Amboise and the hanging gardens and bastions at Loches upon orchards white with blossom and thin lines of poplars shivering in the bright spring weather. They visited the solemn stupidities of Chambord and returned for contrast to the château at Blois, with its birdcage dormers, its plum-coloured brickwork and painted ceilings, its double nautilus-shell staircase, its fantastic ornamentation of porcupine, salamander and ermine-and-cord. Martin came back looking ten years younger, and Stacy won a prize for the portfolio of sketches and measured drawings she brought home with her; there could be no doubt that the holiday had been a success.

2

That was in 1921, a year in which Martin first dared to feel a sense of returning prosperity. People had begun to build again after the war, and though he

had lost most of his old clients he found a few new
ones; his investments had revived and there was no
longer any necessity for him to lay up for the future;
he had no son to provide for and his daughter had her
own money and might earn more. He was talking about
leaving the Brunswick Square flat for something better,
and, though Letty was making her usual difficulties,
and worrying over the difficulties of post-war housekeeping and the deficiencies of modern servants, he did
not despair of uprooting her when he had finally decided between the various little houses, in Chelsea,
Westminster or Tyburn, which he had begun to discover with Stacy on Saturday afternoons.

There was a fair amount of business coming into the
office in Bedford Row, though not all of it was Martin's, for Oliver was still there, and likely to remain.
He had acted as Martin's assistant for a year after he
came back; for six months after that he had paid Martin rent for his room and his share of the drawing-
office and had carried out a couple of commissions of
his own; then, just after the Touraine expedition, he
secured two really profitable pieces of work within six
weeks of each other, an office for a provincial newspaper, and a large factory near London. It became
obvious to Martin that the young man was going to
succeed, though on lines which were rather different
from his own, and he said to Stacy one evening, rather
doubtfully, "I suppose Oliver will want to go and set
up for himself somewhere else now."

He was in her blue-and-yellow sitting-room in Fitzroy Square when he said it, and he had been amusing
himself with her latest solution of a problem design,
an island church, whose bare walls rose in a continua-

tion of its own granite cliffs. "You've only put three Norman windows in the apse, and a few slits in the nave," he had pointed out. "The place will be as dark as a cellar, even at midday."

"So it ought to be," Stacy had persisted. "Candles are the proper light for a church, reflected from gold mosaic." Her father had laughed, and advised her, "Don't say that to your professor"; and then he had mused, "It's a funny thing, I've never built a church, though I've always coveted the chance. The first competition I ever went in for was a village church, but of course I didn't win it. A violently Byzantine design it was, I remember; most unsuitable to the site. When I was a beginner I dreamt in terms of cathedrals, but I suppose none of you moderns have the least wish to try one. You're all for banks and cinemas and jam-factories, like Oliver Barford," and after that, he had said, in a discouraged voice, "I'm afraid he's getting too successful to stay with me much longer."

Stacy was leaning against the wall, in a favourite, familiar pose of hers, with her arms folded and her head thrown back; she had an odd way of standing and smoking like that when another woman would have been resting. Her father looked at her and thought how like a bad-tempered boy she seemed; in a cool, detached voice she dropped the words, "Better keep hold of him, hadn't you? He's your only chance of any new blood in the office."

He was startled and taken aback; she had put a feeling of his own into words, but he did not wish to give way to it. "All this domestic business is very pretty," said Stacy, with a certain resentful disdain. "You do it very nicely, and I daresay I shall be fit to carry on with it some day, but Oliver is going to be better than that. If you just want to go pottering gently on with week-end cottages, and golf-clubs, and conversions and additions for country-houses, well and good; let Oliver set up for himself somewhere else. He can afford it now, and I daresay it would be his own best chance; but if he's fool enough to want to stay on in Bedford Row, make him a partner, it'll be worth your while."

Martin was not offended by her tone; he guessed at some irritation behind it which was not directed at him.

"We were discussing something of the kind yesterday," he admitted. "But we were interrupted. I'm not so sure that I want him; it would mean a good deal of change in the office, and I don't know that I care for his kind of work."

He was aware that his reasons did not sound convincing; he glanced at his daughter, and found her clear, direct eyes fixed upon him; she said unflinchingly, "I know perfectly well what you've got in your head. You've been thinking that Oliver and I were in love with each other once, and you're wondering whether we've really got over it."

He had not thought that she would say it, and he did not know how to answer her; but she did not wait for his defence. She gave a short, contemptuous laugh, directed more at herself than at him, "I'm not such a fool as that," she declared, "I don't go on crying for years over spilt milk."

He stammered uncertainly, "We wanted to do our best for you. I didn't understand." His daughter paid little attention to him.

"It wasn't anything to do with you," she said, al-

most carelessly, "it was Mother's show. She had determined not to let me marry him, and she got her way.
She always does, you know: she's the most determined
woman on earth. Arguing with her is like hitting your
head against the walls of a padded room; you exhaust
yourself, but never change her. I suppose she's still got
her fixed idea about Oliver and me. A little thing like
Oliver's marriage wouldn't stand in her way once she'd
made up her mind about us, and it wouldn't occur to
her that it might stand in mine. I suppose she thinks I
shall try and break up Oliver's home." She laughed
again, but her father could see no amusement in her
face. "I daresay I could work up an affair with him if
I chose," she said disdainfully. "Oliver's easy enough
to make a fool of, if any woman cares to try, but I'm
not going to take advantage of our old feeling about
each other to get six months' excitement from him with
nothing but misery to follow. That game isn't worth
the candle. He's too decent; he'd never forgive me for
it. No, Father, you can trust your precious Oliver with
me."

He groaned, "I'm not thinking of him, I'm thinking
of you."

"Don't worry about me; I've got more sense than
you two give me credit for. I don't belong to Mother's
generation; I've one or two other subjects to think
about besides love-making. I shan't spend the rest of my
life moping over Oliver. I've got my work to do.
Mother would tell you I took it up to put Oliver out
of my head; and so I did, in a way; and so it has. I
shan't waste my time thinking about him. It won't
make the least difference to me whether he's in your
office or whether he isn't. All that's over."

She did not speak in the least vehemently, but her detachment was far more convincing than any protestations; her father might pity her but he was forced to believe her; he contented himself with the gentle suggestion, "You're only twenty-nine. You may meet someone else."

"Mother tells me that fairly constantly," his daughter remarked, lighting a fresh cigarette with a steady hand. "It doesn't seem to occur to her that my generation of young men were all pretty well disposed of by 1918. Besides, I've had enough of marrying to forget Oliver. That's how I fell into Philip's hands."

Martin almost held his breath, for fear of scaring her away from a revelation which he had hoped for since Philip Giffard's death.

"I never understood why you married him," he ventured.

"I didn't dream of marrying him at first," said Stacy indifferently. "I just thought he was the most amusing man I'd met. He was great fun to go about with, you know; and I couldn't help enjoying the way he made love to me. He did it so well. I was frightened at first when he wanted to marry me; I even told him I was in love with another man, but he only laughed and said he could make me forget Oliver in three weeks. I remember just how he looked when he said it; you know that sort of wicked grin he had. I believed him, of course, I wanted to believe him; he knew just how to get round an inexperienced idiot like me, and I didn't care what became of me just then. He managed me very cleverly; in the end he drove me quite off my head about him. That stage wasn't a long one, but I'd have done anything he told me while it lasted;

I didn't much care whether he actually married me or not, but I wanted him to go on making love to me, and put Oliver out of my mind. I had just enough sense left to know that you wouldn't like him, so when he suggested that registry office business I agreed at once. I think I wanted to tie myself up so that I couldn't have any second thoughts. I should never have got through an engagement. When I saw your face, that day we came to tell you, I realised what I'd done, but somehow I couldn't admit it. Do you remember that awful evening when you came to the theatre with us? I knew by then what a mistake I'd made in marrying him, but I tried to put a good face on it. We'd nothing in the world in common, and I suppose I was as much of a disappointment to him as he was to me.

"Of course, he used to beat me when he was drunk. Didn't you guess that?" (as Martin made an inarticulate sound of dismay) "Oh! dear me, yes, he got a lot of amusement out of it. He was queer on the point; always had been, I daresay, but the war brought it out. Granny knew all right, but she pretended to think it was all a joke; they used to laugh together about it. She told him once that it served me right for being such an idiot as to marry him, and he said he quite agreed with her. I don't suppose she cared particularly, she always took the line that I hadn't had enough discipline and I daresay she thought it would do me good. Of course, Mother never realised anything that didn't happen exactly under her nose, and she was too much upset about poor Aubrey to care what became of me. She saw we weren't getting on too well that first time Phil came back; but he was very clever at getting round her. She used to take his side when she came to

stay with us and tell me I was quarrelsome and didn't
manage him properly. I wasn't going to let her know
what went on behind the scenes or you either. I'd married him without consulting any of you, and I wasn't
going to admit that I'd made a fool of myself. I
wouldn't give in to him either; I used to keep my end
up with him in public, even if it did make it worse for
me afterwards. Oh! well, the whole business only
lasted two years. Luckily for me," said Stacy, with a
face of iron, "he was killed before the war came to an
end. But I'm not likely to marry again in a hurry. I've
had enough of it for the present, thanks." She
shrugged her shoulders, and added, "I haven't been
very clever with my love-affairs, have I? I must be the
kind of woman who always muddles them. I think I'd
better stick to bricks and mortar instead," and she concluded in the tone he had always respected, "Don't
make Mother's mistake; don't mix up business and
emotion. I've grown up now; I shan't make an ass of
myself in that way again. Oliver's worth keeping from
every point of view. He's grateful to you, he remem-
bers that you gave him his first and his second chance.
You'll be a fool if you let him go."

3

That was how the partnership came about and the
names of Lovell and Barford were again associated
above the door of the office in Bedford Row. Letty
disapproved, of course, but not so violently as Martin had expected; she said grudgingly, "I don't suppose
it'll make much difference." Martin hardly liked to
admit even to himself how much difference it actually

made, or how the character of the work in the office
changed during the years which followed his junior
partner's admission. Oliver became an extremely busy
man, but he did not design convenient little houses as
his uncle and Martin had done; he came to build an
increasing number of factories, and warehouses, and
blocks of offices, and shops. His plans and drawings
overflowed his own room and his usual desks in the
drawing-office, the draughtsmen were always busy on
some detail of his work. Martin constantly found himself staring at plans whose complexities were strange
to him, and elevations which struck him as wantonly
massive and ugly. He did not think Oliver's buildings
were eccentric or unbalanced; but he could not easily
accustom his tradition-blinded eyes to their plain, un-
compromising air of utility, their packing-case outlines,
blank, unornamented concrete surfaces and gridiron
fenestration, and the monotonous run of vertical panels
from foundation to roof which was so constant a feature in Oliver's exterior treatments. He disliked the
graceless interiors where slender ferro-concrete shafts
with clumsy mushroom capitals upheld low ceilings,
and daylight stared in through a blank expanse of windows in thin steel sashes. Oliver had never cared for
the beauty which had been Martin's lifelong preoccupation; it almost appeared that he suspected and
feared its appeal. He seemed deliberately to avoid any
kind of architectural grace or ornament. He talked a
great deal of rather aggressive theory to Martin about
a building expressing its purpose in its design and construction; about continuous vertical support, lighting
units, economy, floor-space, and ventilation; about the
calculated strength of steel, and the surface texture of

concrete, and artificial stone. Martin told him once in a fit of impatience that he was more of an engineer than an architect, and found that he took it as a compliment. He was very successful, he worked like a slave, and it appeared that he had no other interest. He spared himself as little as he spared the men who worked for him and his temper was more uncertain than ever. He did not turn it on Martin, but everyone else had to suffer from it.

Martin suspected that a good deal of this arose from the difficulties of his domestic situation. The Barford marriage had not turned out well in the end. There was no child; and Dorothy Barford declined from a fretful, dissatisfied, inevitably neglected wife into a hysterical semi-invalid, who tried one doctor after another, collected treatments as if they were bric-à-brac and talked of little but her ailments. The Lovells had watched this situation develop, and done their best to avert it; Letty in particular had been astonishingly kind to Mrs. Barford, had encouraged her to move into London and had tried to find her friends; but the woman was a difficult subject for kindness. She mistook it for patronage, was awkward, touchy and always on the defensive; she did nothing to help her husband professionally or socially. Martin pitied her; he realised her disappointment, her thwarted affection for the man she had married and her hopeless incapacity to deal with him; he had even once or twice ventured the ungracious task of mediating between the two of them, but found it impossible. Oliver would not criticise his wife or defend himself from her whining accusations. He received advice in silence, paid for her medical consolations without comment, and appeared

to take refuge at the office from the dissatisfactions
of his home. He was occupied with clients and interviews all day long and spent half the night in the
drawing-office. If he had other consolations they did
not appear for some time to the innocent Martin, who
was startled to hear his daughter say bitterly one day
to her mother, "Mrs. Barford has only herself to
blame if Oliver runs after other women. What's the
use of a whining invalid to him? They haven't lived
together for years. She's a complete hypochondriac,
and she makes him miserable by her perpetual complaints; but he can't get rid of her and she's no inten-
tion of getting rid of him. She may complain of his
behaviour, but she'd keep her claws in him whatever
he did. I've no patience with her; there isn't a thing
the matter with her except a wish to be noticed. She
pretends to be dying about once a week, but she'll out-
live all of us."

Letty protested, "The poor woman's very unhappy." She always defended Dorothy Barford, and
she began to tell Martin a long, involved, unconvincing story about Oliver's attentions to the wife of one
of his clients. Stacy got up and went away; no doubt
she had heard it all before, and knew as much about
it as her mother did. Martin cut the recital as short as
he could; it was not his business, but it did not surprise
him when he came to consider it. He had long expected
something of the kind, and dared not, from the shelter
of his own marriage, criticise Oliver's mistakes. He
only hoped that the gossip had not distressed Stacy.
She was busy and apparently contented; she had at the
date of this conversation embarked on the fourth year

of her training, and she was actually putting in three
weeks as an assistant at the office, during her Easter
vacation, in order to get practical experience. She was
undoubtedly efficient, but not particularly tactful, and
she got on surprisingly badly with Oliver, who had
been unenthusiastic from the first about her appearance there. He was inclined to criticise her work, and
there was a definite quarrel on the day after Letty had
told her gossip to her daughter. Whether the two matters were connected Martin could not at the time decide. Stacy was undoubtedly in the right; she argued
Oliver down, proved him wrong over some detail in a
specification and triumphed, perhaps a little excessively, over his sulky surrender before she departed.
Martin was worried by the young man's scowl at the
door which Stacy had practically slammed behind her;
he thought, "Those two are always quarrelling nowadays. It makes life pretty difficult in this office. I wish
they wouldn't do it. Sometimes I wish I hadn't let her
come here. Oliver always had a bad temper, but it
seems to be getting worse, and Stacy has been pretty
trying lately. She certainly doesn't exercise much
feminine tact on us, in fact she bullies the staff worse
than Oliver does. I suppose that's what he means when
he complains that she's getting masculine. But there's
a lot of that sort of thing about the world nowadays,
most women don't take to authority naturally or
gracefully." He was obliged to admit, not for the first
time, that he was horribly sorry for Stacy and her
friends, going valiantly about together in threes and
fours, calling each other heartily by their surnames
and trying to pretend that they did not want anything

better than each other's company; and he said suddenly
to Oliver, "If Stacy's husband hadn't been killed she'd
have turned out very differently."

"Oh God! yes," said Oliver, with a tormented look.
"I know that"; and he got up and went out through
the same door that Stacy had shut two minutes earlier.
Martin heard him swearing at one of the draughtsmen in the drawing-office, and probably this relieved
his feelings, for Stacy and he were fairly affable to
each other for the few days which remained before she
went back to Bedford Square.

Martin began to wonder what was going to become
of her. She was going up for her finals at the end of
another year, and he had no misgivings about her getting through them; what he did not see was where she
could go afterwards. He supposed that he could em-
ploy her for a time as an assistant, and she could at
any rate stay in Bedford Row until she had completed
the six-months period needed for her diploma; but he
was afraid after this three weeks' trial that she and
Oliver Barford were not going to pull well together
permanently.

Martin himself was much less busy than he had
been. He could not persuade himself that it mattered
to him if Oliver's factories took up more than their
just share of the draughtsmen's time. It was not often
that he had the chance to build a house; he found himself obliged to depend much more upon small additions and alterations; he told himself that people had
no money for his kind of building nowadays. They all
wanted to live in flats and hotels, and their wives
shirked the difficulties of housekeeping and the expense
of nurseries; the old ten or twelve bedroom house was

a drug in the market. There was a fashion for antiques, too, which hit the architectural profession in a tender place; people did not want to build a new house, they wanted to buy a tumbledown pair of village cottages or a windmill or a Martello tower, and convert it into something inconveniently picturesque with the help of an interior decorator. Oliver was speculating in the only kind of architecture which had any future.

"And I suppose I ought to have done the same thing after the war," Martin told himself ruefully. "But I hadn't the sense to see which way the wind was blowing, and now I'm too old to change."

It was the first time he had said such a thing to himself, and the sound of it frightened him. It looked to him as if he were too late to help Stacy. She would have to find a partnership somewhere else.

4

He and Letty still lingered in the Brunswick Square flat; it was after all convenient for the office and for Stacy's rooms, which were Martin's chief haunts. He had begun to think vaguely of retiring in two or three years, when Stacy had finished her training and settled down to work; he had a fancy that he might live in the country with Letty and come up to town now and again, and take to gardening and fishing. He had begun to find London noisy and fatiguing, and the traffic kept him awake at night and worried him in the daytime; he found himself hesitating for three or four minutes at a time before he dared cross Holborn or Southampton Row. He was beginning to get headaches when he spent too much time at his drawing-board;

and the glasses which an affable oculist in Harley
Street recommended did not altogether relieve the mischief. Martin supposed that it was one of the inevitable miseries of later life, though he seldom thought
of himself growing older, any more than he noticed the
changes in his Letty, who had shrivelled and sweetened
like a ripening apple during the past few years.

They lived the quietest of lives together, talked very
little but knew all each other's thoughts, and had sunk
into an indifferent, contented placidity which yet had
its own distinctive flavour.

Letty had become soft, sweet and vaguely maternal
again, as in the old days; the fretfulness of her middle years was over, for a few months Martin had her
to himself in what seemed afterwards to have been a
perfect, unforeseen, autumnal happiness. It ended with
so little warning that he scarcely feared for her before
he lost her; she mislaid her life with as much carelessness as she had daily mislaid her snake-skin-
handled umbrella, or her blue leather handbag, or the
new tortoiseshell spectacles which she would not wear
because she fancied that they spoilt the look of her
rosy, delicate, slightly wrinkled face. Her characteristic, absent-minded incompetence took her from him
just as actually and inevitably as if she had stepped
off the pavement once too often in her own unheed-
ing fashion and had walked in front of a taxi-cab.
Neither Martin nor Stacy could have prevented her
wandering off that January afternoon to a sale in Kensington High Street, spending all the money she had
with her in the hot, influenza-haunted showrooms, and
waiting for half an hour in the rain before she could
fight her way into the proper 'bus. She had always been

easily defeated in crowds, and she had never got into
the way of taking taxis when she needed them; she
liked to justify her extravagant, unnecessary bargain
hunts by economising her fare home; and as usual she
had postponed the resoling of her shoes. Cobblers'
repairs were another of her weak points. She arrived
home after seven o'clock, exhausted, wet and chilled.
Martin for once was angry with her, and said, "These
rubbishing sales aren't worth going to if you come
back in this state." Letty was too tired and depressed
to defend herself; however, she cheered up considerably later in the evening. She undid all her parcels for
the amusement of Stacy, who was dining with them,
and had a long feminine consultation with her daughter about the propriety of shingling her soft, curly,
silver-gold hair. Martin said, "I do hope you won't,"
but the two of them only laughed at him; "I really
think I must," said Letty, "I don't want to turn into
a dowdy old woman." She had seldom looked brighter
or prettier, to Martin's mind; her lips and cheeks were
flushed with colour, she twisted her head about before
the mirror like a robin.

Martin remembered afterwards how gay her chat-
ter had been. He remembered too that she had talked
to him about Stacy, when the girl had left them, with a
rare, unusual understanding: and admitted, "You were
right about her, Martin; she was best away from us.
I think she's all right; I think some day she's going to
be happy." And she had said another thing which he
never forgot, "I want her to find some man who'll
make her as happy as you've made me." The kiss she
gave him was sweet and untroubled; he hardly noticed
the burning warmth of her lips.

It happened, neither oddly nor unusually, that he
had to spend the next day in the country; he went down
with a client to prospect a hill-top site in Sussex. When
he came back late he found Stacy at the flat, and saw
from her face that something had gone wrong. She
told him, "Mother's got 'flu; she's rather bad," but
this did not immediately alarm him; Letty had committed such imprudences before, and had taken no
great harm. He went in to visit the invalid, and found
her flushed, fevered, excited, talking and coughing a
good deal; he persuaded his daughter to spend the
night in her old room, which had become the spare-
room of the flat, but it was only because their daily
maid, a recent vexing economy of Letty's, went at
nine. He did not even wait to see the doctor next morning; he was busy and Stacy had volunteered to take the
day, which was Saturday, away from the office. Over
the week-end, however, his wife became steadily worse.
It was one of those epidemic, broncho-pneumonic
cases, with a rapid serious effusion into the lungs, which
practically drowns the patient; Martin was unable to
realise the gravity of the case before it was over.
There was the inevitable, timeless, dateless confusion
of a serious illness, the midnight visits of doctors, the
rustling aprons and perpetual conversation of nurses,
the trays, kettles, oxygen cylinders, dislocated meals,
the impotent anxiety and the hours of unoccupied waiting. He hardly saw Letty; they wanted to keep her
from talking, and she would not lie quiet when Martin
or Stacy was in the room. She was terrified at first,
she kept on asking Martin what was the matter with
her, and why he looked so worried; she took a dislike
to one of her nurses, and whispered in her hoarse,

panting, changed voice that he must get rid of the woman. Later she lost her strength; she lay gasping on her pillows, livid and exhausted, with her mouth open and her eyes half-closed. She recognised him still, and watched for his coming, and implored his help with her frightened, animal eyes long after she was unable to speak to him; even on the day when she died she managed to give him a fluttering, pitiful smile. He believed that she knew then what was happening to her and meant to leave him some last reassurance.

At the end there was nothing. He sat beside her for the last hour, but she did not open her eyes, and there was no returning pressure in the fingers which he clasped with his own; merely the sound of that difficult, failing, faltering breathing which presently came to an end. They told him that his wife was dead, but though his mind assented his heart could not believe them. Stacy took him away, there were dreamlike condolences and formalities from doctors and nurses; it was a bright January Sunday, and the bells were ringing for the eleven o'clock service.

Oliver came round to help Stacy with some funeral business or other, they shut themselves up together in the dining-room. The nurses were packing boxes and telephoning about taxis; the blinds of the flat were drawn down and the door of the bedroom was shut. Martin had been to see his dead wife lying there among her pillows with her lovely, infantile, exhausted smile, and come out and shut the door behind him. There was nothing left for him to do, and nowhere for him to go; he felt as if his life had ended with hers. He went out and walked about the empty, sunny, chilly streets. He had very little recollection after-

wards of how he spent that Sunday, or by what unconscious steps he came to wander into the dusty, deserted
drawing-office in Bedford Row. Oliver Barford found
him there, late in the afternoon, behind the drawn
holland blinds, which he had neglected to pull up; he
had taken out his pencils and instruments and he was
making a mechanical, meaningless, useless attempt to
work out the plans for the Sussex house.

XI

STACY got rid of her Fitzroy Square rooms after her
mother died, and came back to live with her father.
The lease of the Brunswick Square flat had eighteen
months to run and she had less than a year in which to
complete her training; she would have liked to remove
her father from the poignant associations of the rooms
where he had lived with her mother, but it seemed difficult and unreasonable to anticipate the move which
would in any case have to be made during the following winter. Father and daughter entered upon a queer,
suspended existence; at first they made no plans. Stacy,
no doubt, had her thoughts of the future, but she did
not speak of them; she would not allow herself to look
beyond the date of her finals. Martin found himself
incapable of looking forward; his thoughts went back
over the bright forgotten past, the colours of which
had revived strangely with his loss, or fixed themselves
in the aching empty present. He experienced all the
miseries of an amputation; when the first agony had
died down there was the perpetual, cheating, torment-
ing illusion of immunity, as cut nerves suggest the presence of a severed limb, so fancy told him twenty times
a day, Letty will want to hear about this; Letty will be

sitting by the fire when I open this door; Letty has just gone round that corner ahead of me, if I hurry I can overtake her. For many months he could not adjust himself to a life without her; he understood for the first time how such a shock can deaden feeling and extinguish hope.

Stacy was ultimately his salvation; her vivid life and anticipations carried him forward; he began to think of her future, though he cared nothing for his own. She gave him all the time she dared; she worked beside him through their solitary evenings, she made excuses for seeking his instruction and advice. He began to take his old pleasure in the workings of her mind, and in their community of tastes and interests; she thawed him gradually back to some sense of revived existence. Inevitably, he was much alone with her; she was too busy and he too sad for company, but she kept his older friends about him dutifully, and in particular he noticed a better understanding between her and Oliver Barford, who came to the flat as he had never done in Letty's time. The two of them had established a quieter, less resentful companionship; they had ceased to quarrel so flagrantly, though they still spoke their minds to each other without disguise.

Stacy's finals were at the end of the summer, and she passed them easily though not with all the distinctions that had been expected of her; Martin knew that this was his fault, she had been too occupied with him to do herself justice. She was to do her six months' assistantship in Bedford Row. Oliver had suggested it himself, he was busy on a new block of flats and had plenty of work for her, and after that she talked of finding some other opening. Meanwhile Martin and she were going

abroad for six weeks. He had originally suggested the
Low Countries, but Stacy, who was in a critical temper
after her struggle with the examiners, had protested,
"Oh! don't let's go to Belgium. I can't stick Belgium.
The country's as bad as Essex, all brickfields and glass-
houses and suburban villas and market-gardens. The
towns are dirty and noisy, and the galleries are full
of great, vulgar pictures by Snyders and Jordaens,
and the peasants are sulky, fat, stupid brutes with
sallow skins, who can't talk any civilised language
properly and grumble at all your tips. I loathe Belgians.
I had enough of them in the war."

Her father thought of his earlier trips abroad, and
protested uncertainly, "I used to think some of the
buildings were rather jolly."

"Oh! no, they're not." Stacy dismissed Flemish
architecture promptly and with her usual decision.

"Brussels is exactly like the Cromwell Road, with
trams and cobble-stones thrown in. Ghent is just a
manufacturing town, with a few stinking canals and a
silly little property castle and a church or two left
over in the middle of the chimneys, and half-a-dozen
gabled houses scraped to within an inch of their lives.
Louvain and Ypres are simply restorations. As for
Bruges, it ought to be transported to Hollywood, and
used as the background for a film. It's nothing but a
faked, patched-up, rotten unconvincing show for
tourists, full of tea-shops and Tauchnitz editions, and
fraudulent old women selling machine-made lace, and
artistic idiots sketching in smocks and sandals, and
motor-boats stirring up smells in all the canals. It's
far too late in the day for self-respecting people to go
to Bruges."

Martin tugged at his beard, and decided in his own mind that his daughter must have overworked hopelessly for her finals.

"Where would you like to go?" he murmured feebly. But Stacy did not seem to know. However, she brightened up a little, in the course of a discussion which ranged over most of the Continent of Europe, and was finally brought to admit that she would not mind going to Venice and Rome.

"I shouldn't mind going to Rome, either," agreed Martin. "I haven't been there since I was twenty-three. That's how I came to meet your mother. She came out with Granny Stapleford to look at the galleries, and they stayed at the pension where I was living. A cheap, stuffy place on the Pincian, it was, I remember. I wonder whether it's there still."

"I expect it is," said Stacy, "a decent pension doesn't usually go out of commission or change its name, even if it changes hands. I suppose the woman who kept it then must be dead, though."

"Signora Pellegrini? Certain to be by this time." Martin felt a small shiver creep over him, which betrayed itself in his voice as he said, "Good God! it's over thirty years ago, before you were ever born or thought of."

"Should you like to go there again?" enquired Stacy timidly.

"God forbid!" He excused the vigour of his denial by adding apologetically, "I'm getting too old for the discomforts of a cheap students' pension and that's all it ever was or could be. We'll go to the Flora."

"Won't Rome be rather hot at this time of year?" Stacy appeared to be repenting of her suggestion.

Martin, however, insisted; he had an obstinate, painful wish to revisit the place where he had first seen Letty.

"We can go to Venice first for a fortnight, till it's cooler," he said. "I'd like to see Rome again before they spoil the place by driving arterial roads through all the interesting slums. Oliver doesn't want you back till the beginning of October, and I'm in no hurry myself. And," he concluded soberly, "there's a penny of mine in Trevi fountain still; that means I'm destined to go back to Rome before I die." He did not tell his daughter how Letty's penny had been fished out again, and she had said that she would never return; it was one of the silent recollections which were driving him back to that brown rubbish-heap of antiquity, but he could not talk of it.

2

They got away by the middle of August, and went first to Venice, where Stacy was supposed to be lazy and recover from her studies; but she was in her most irritable and energetic mood. A less indulgent father would have said that she was definitely peevish. She said that San Marco, with its pinnacles and statues, illuminated by the arc-lights of the Piazza, was exactly like a wedding-cake, and that the ornamentation of its ogival arches was only fit to be broken off and crunched in lumps, like icing-sugar. She complained that the last two windows on the rosy wall of the Doge's palace were out of line with the others, turned up her freckled little nose at the tender, trembling colours of the reflected palaces on the Grand Canal, declared that the Bridge of Sighs ought not to exist anywhere but on a picture post-card, and refused to admire anything except the domes and nautilus-buttresses of Santa Maria della Salute, which Martin had always definitely disliked. She said that the mosquitoes kept her awake at night, that the veal and macaroni of the pavement-restaurants gave her indigestion and that her balcony on the Grand Canal overhung a *traghetto* where the boatmen came and went all night long shouting and singing. She insisted on buying a bathing-dress and going out on the sweltering, crowded deck of a steamer to the Lido, as a change from too many picture-galleries filled with heavy Bellini peasant-Madonnas, gross Bordone beauties and school-copied Tintorettos; but as soon as she got there she complained that the sand was dirty, and the Adriatic too shallow to swim in and full of obese trippers. "Really," said Stacy on the return journey, averting her eyes from the mirage of rosy towers floating incredibly between glittering sky and gleaming water, "one might as well go down to Southend on the Golden Eagle." Her father thought that he guessed what was the matter with her; she needed a gondola, and a young man in it to make love to her, and, failing that, nothing would please her. An old lady in their hotel had said to him, "How delightful for your daughter to go about with you always!" and the words had struck him coldly; he wondered whether Stacy did not desire something better.

In Rome she seemed happier, and they spent a pleasant three weeks prowling about his old haunts, and discovering much that he had missed on his earlier visit. If Stacy could not share his recollections she forced herself at least to be good company; she was

critical, appreciative, and instructive, and Martin enjoyed her alternations of prepared superiority and unguarded enthusiasm. He was proud of her elegant,
dandified air as she strolled beside him, upright and
alert, casting a slender shadow across the sunlit pavements, or propped her elbows opposite to him across an
iron table outside a café, or raised her proud head to
stare up into the frescoed ceiling of a palace or a
church. The aureate weather of a Roman September
had painted her cheeks and lips as it painted the vine-
leaves on the trellises of the Aventine; she was all
scarlet, brown and gold above the black-and-white
dresses in which she mourned her mother. He was
amused to see her draw the dark, roving eyes of the
Pincian loungers after her as she walked with her unconscious swagger to the parapet overhanging the
sunset city; he liked to feel her clutch his arm outside
a window in the Corso, full of Piranesi drawings, coral
ornaments or worn mediæval brocade. She was interested in everything, the trouble, after a day or two, was
really that she was interested in too much. She wore
him out. When he had been in Rome before, with her
young mother, he had been the one who strode tire-
lessly everywhere on his long legs, while Letty trailed
behind him, turned plaintive at the end of the afternoon, complained that standing tired her back, and
begged for cakes and tea when her eyes and neck ached
from a surfeit of architecture. Now it was her daughter
who walked him for what seemed endless hours over
the dusty pavements, who trailed him through one
church after another, up and down innumerable staircases and round and about the interminable maze of
crowded noisy streets, disdaining the little carriages

with their rattling wheels, broken tasselled harness,
sheepskin rugs and active fleas. Also she had caught
the prevailing taste for baroque, and kept her father
lingering for hours over everything which he had been
taught in his young days to condemn as decadent and
ostentatious. He was prepared to enjoy gardens laid
out with sweeping staircases and clipped ilex arcades,
or fountain-grottoes of artificial rockwork where
bearded river-gods reclined among spouting Tritons
and sea-monsters; but he could not bring himself to
tolerate churches where a detached façade, top-heavy
with gesticulating statues and unbalanced stucco
arabesques, dwarfed the mean brick nave behind it,
and where the interior was a tasteless confusion of
twisted barley-sugar columns, chapels frescoed and
gilded like stage boxes, ecstatic saints fluttering on their
pedestals in coloured marble draperies and tombs
where skeletons emerged from carved porphyry curtains. He persisted in thinking these acrobatics merely
vulgarly tiring; and he found that he had forgotten
how much there was to see in Rome, how widely the
palaces and galleries were separated, and how steep
and inevitable were the Seven Hills. He could not
remember that he and Letty had ever noticed their
existence, or that the streets in the old days had been
half so noisy or crowded. Stinking and dirty they had
been, of course, but so they were still, for all the talk
of improvement, as soon as he and Stacy left the Corso
or the Via Nazionale; and the jangling of trams and
hooting of innumerable cars were added to the
jostling and shouting of the Roman crowd, which
somehow did not amuse him quite as much as it used
to do. He decided that the place had not really changed

for the better in spite of the Napoleonic silhouette and crossed double V's stamped on every available wall and the black shirts and tasselled caps of the hawk-nosed youths who ogled Stacy at street corners. His daughter laughed at his regrets and went so far as to tell him that they were a sign of advancing years; she teased him when he groaned conventionally over the Vittorio Emanuele monument, "Come, Father, Imperial Rome must have been exactly like that, when the temples were new; all gilding and marble and bad statues, winking at you in the sun. The Romans had no taste in public buildings; they simply wanted an enormous barrack stuffed with loot, or a great, fat, triumphal arch; size was the chief thing they cared about. They weren't artists; they were good constructive engineers who used slave-labour because they couldn't get machinery. Vitruvius would have revelled in steel girders and reinforced concrete, he'd have admired a gasometer or a suspension bridge, and the roof of Paddington Station. Roman temples are officialdom, not genuine religious emotion; what their architects were really interested in was practical, useful, municipal stuff, law-courts and waterworks and theatres and public baths. All the good things in the galleries here were stolen from Greece; all that's left on the Palatine is just the concrete core of the walls and the brick centring of the vaults. The marble and mosaic, and painted surface ornamentation has been torn away and burnt for lime, or used to decorate mediæval churches. People are misled by ivy and weathering and picturesque decay; they haven't a notion how vulgar the original palaces must have been. Nero would have loved that frightful memorial on the

Capitol. I expect his Golden House was exactly like it."

Martin was amused by her sweeping generalisations; but he was tired by an exhausting afternoon among the imperial palaces, and he merely sipped his vermouth, and said, blinking mildly, "Their domestic architecture wasn't so bad. They understood comfort as nobody else has done till you come to the Americans. There's a lot to be said for a Roman villa; central heating, perfectly adequate plumbing, nice, handy little rooms opening off a courtyard facing south, a big living-room between the court and the garden, with sliding doors that you could open in the summer and a colonnade to dine out under. It's the perfect plan for a small country house."

"A bit chilly for England," said Stacy, yawning, for she also was a little tired with sight-seeing. "All marble and mosaic, with no outside windows, and nothing but the court to sit in. Besides, I hate a bungalow house, all on one floor. I like to go upstairs to bed."

"Nonsense. They had windows all right, and balconies, and roof-gardens, and an upper story, but they kept that for the servants. You wait till you see the new excavations at Pompeii. We must make time for a day down there, whatever else we miss. It's astonishingly vulgar; the Deauville or Brighton of those days, preserved in ashes." And he continued, in a somnolent voice, "I read a letter once in *The Times* from a man who said it was his dream to buy the site of a Roman villa and reconstruct it. I wonder if he ever did it. I wish he'd employed me."

"How was he going to furnish it, do you suppose? I

can't think of anything comfortable," Stacy said. "Just
marble seats, and boat-shaped lamps, altars to the
family gods, and loops and swags of evergreens, like
classical orgies on the films—Messalina, you know, and
Quo Vadis." They laughed, and Martin considered.
"First Empire furniture, I should imagine. Récamier
couches and marble-topped tables with Sphinx carya-
tides and so on; rather jolly. One could have great
fun working all that out. But I've never got hold of a
client with such an original notion. Mine have all
wanted to copy an Olde Englishe cottage from the
Ideal Home Exhibition, or a sweet little Queen Anne
house that their uncle's widow had just built at
Purley."

Stacy said, "My God, yes," with the perfunctory
profanity of her generation, which had long ceased to
shock her father; and he continued, musingly, "I suppose you're right about the public architecture. It must
have been heavy stupid municipal stuff, all gold and
bronze and marble, and central heating."

"Like Oliver's bank that he's so proud of," concluded Stacy with a grin, and finished the vermouth
in her glass.

She was beginning to recover from the strain of the
past year, and to be refreshed by her holiday; Martin
was satisfied by the change in her. He could not discover the same revival of spirits in himself, but for him
the case was different; he knew where his own trouble
lay. There was a small, plaintive ghost trailing round
after him through the long, hot, crowded days and
waiting for him through the long, hot, empty nights;
a ghost with a sweet, punctual, bewildered smile for his
enthusiasms, clinging hands which he could feel, so

nearly, between sleeping and waking, and lips which smiled, but never spoke. He could not lay that ghost, though he went down by himself one stifling afternoon to the Forum, while Stacy thought that he was resting, and sat in their corner beneath the Palatine cliff, and remembered what he could. The sky was as blue and hard as ever behind the broken columns, there were even three or four flowers in the grass, the colour of a girl's blue eyes; but he had no reason now to pick them, and he left them to wither. He thought, "She did her best to make me happy, I hope I made her as happy as I could." He buried his face in his hands and sat there a long time as if he were praying; but he was only trying to remember the look in her eyes. It was fading month by month; and soon it would be gone for ever.

Stacy was waiting for him in the hall of the hotel when he came back, full of reproaches. "You never said you were going out. You ought to stop indoors in the afternoons, not go wandering about in the sun. I can't imagine where you've been"; but that he did not tell her.

3

They went back to London at the beginning of October, and Stacy began her daily attendance in Bedford Row. Oliver seemed to find her more useful than at one time had appeared likely; he kept her hard at work over his drawings, and did not complain of her as much as her father had expected. Martin himself was busy that autumn and could not keep as close an eye on her as he had meant to do; but he gathered that she was settling down, and congratulated himself on her improved looks and cheerfulness. She did not neglect him, in spite of Oliver's demands on her time; she had endless plans for his amusement and diversion; she made him buy a car for her to drive him about in, and she involved him in the purchase of a week-end cottage before the year was out. The plan had been an old one of his, but she revived it. "We can perfectly well afford it if we content ourselves with a couple of rooms in one of the Inns of Court for the inside of the week," she declared. "It would do you all the good in the world." The actual discovery was his, a Wiltshire mill-house which he inspected for a client, and fell in love with on his own account.

He saw it first on a mild October afternoon very shortly after his return from Rome. The village proved to be an irregular line of thatched stone cottages. He found the mill at its upper end, built upon an island in the Wylyebourne. To the north of the island was a straight, sluggish leat, a row of five sluices and a whirling, roaring mill-pool; to the south of it twin streams embraced a kitchen garden and a neglected orchard. The mill-house was a long, narrow building, with two rows of cobwebbed, small-paned sash-windows and five dormers in a hipped roof, yellowed with lichen; there was a dentil cornice under the wide eaves, interrupted by swallows' nests and a projecting crane in the gable-end, for lowering sacks of flour.

He crossed to the island by a wooden bridge, leaning long enough on the white rails to see a two-pound trout quivering above the amber gravel in the tail of the race; the current was so clear that he could have counted the spots on its freckled sides. Another fish

turned over as he watched between the strong thrust
of the sluice-water and the returning eddy. Martin
walked between the currant-bushes to the doorway
with its blistered white paint, shell hood and simple
graceful proportion. "1720," he thought, "or 1730,
too good for a mill. Wonder what it was before that."
The doorstep was a semi-circle, cut from half a mill-
stone.

He unlocked the door, and went in. There were
three rooms on each floor in the domestic part of the
house, opening out of each other, lofty, large and filled
with bright reflections from the water. One had a good
marble chimney-piece and a simple moulding with lions'
heads at the corners. In the same room were a couple
of semi-circular recesses with shelves for china or glass.
His trained eye saw where a couple of windows had
been blocked up to save the window-tax; they would
have to be opened again if the house was to be restored for the client he had in mind. The lower rooms
had shutters folding into the wall, and window-seats
of a convenient height for kneeling upon; he looked
down from them into the glaucous green complexities
of the mill-race with its whirling, wrinkled, glassy
shapes; the light and thunder of it filled the empty
rooms. He explored the mill itself, which had an air
of being a later addition; the turbine was still in place
below a trap-door, but the stones and machinery had
been removed from the lower story; above were a
couple of attics which could be converted into extra
bedrooms or bathrooms, without much trouble. He
went down the tangled garden between the neglected
borders, where pot-marigolds and Michaelmas daisies
had overrun the box-edging of the paths, he smelt the

late, loose-leaved autumn roses, he counted the white-washed trunks of the burdened apple-trees, he rested on the shaky circular seat round the trunk of the wal-nut tree, and pushed through a thicket of brambles to the place where the twin streams married again be-neath a weeping-willow. The cheerful solitude of the place entered into his very heart; and though he thought, as always, "I wish Letty could have seen it," he found peace in the hour which he spent there.

Back in London that night, he said to his daughter, "I saw a nice little house down in Wiltshire this after-noon."

"Did you? Where?" She was always interested in his discoveries.

"Up the Wylyebourne valley, on the edge of Salis-bury Plain. Funnily enough, it's called Martinmill. The village is Berwick St. Martin, one of several Berwicks in the neighbourhood, all with Saints' names."

"I know that part of the world," said Oliver Bar-ford, who had been dining with them that night and was smoking on the other side of the hearth. "I was at Tilshead for a bit in 1915. It's pretty beastly round the camps, but there are some jolly little villages. I used to like looking at the local cottages when we went out for a route-march. They were mostly flint and stone chequer-work, or cob and thatch, and they used to cheer me up considerably after Army huts."

"You never had to live in one," Stacy pointed out crossly. "Phil and I had one for a whole winter in 1917, when he was at the flying school. It was ex-tremely damp and cold and crowded, and Phil was always swearing because he knocked his head on the beams. It was fearfully cold and I had to do most of my own housework. There wasn't anywhere much to walk because of the camps, and the wind never stopped blowing on those awful downs. I've got no use for Salisbury Plain."

Martin had not heard her speak of her husband or her married life for years. He saw that Oliver was perplexed by the frown on her forehead, and the angry, unhappy look in her eyes; in defence of his own discovery he said, "This isn't really on the Plain at all. It's a good way further west, more in the Shaftesbury direction." He gave them a description of it, more for the sake of diverting Oliver's attention from Stacy than for any other reason. "I thought at first it might have done quite well for Lady Trayle," he concluded. "She wouldn't mind spending money on doing up something really picturesque. But it turned out not to be large enough; she'll do better with Annis Court. I couldn't make more than five bedrooms out of this place, whatever I did, and there's no room to build."

Stacy's interest had been caught by his details.

"What does the man want for it?" she enquired.

"Twelve-fifty, the agent said, but I daresay he'd come down to a thousand. It's been empty some time, and water-mills are a drug in the market nowadays."

"And there's a turbine in the cellar developing 70 h.p. and you didn't buy the place yourself at once?" exclaimed Stacy. "Good heavens, Father, you're missing the chance of a lifetime. Send the man a wire to-morrow morning at eight o'clock."

"Why, what in the world should I do with it?" said Martin, puffing at his pipe and blinking at his daughter with his mild, peaceful eyes.

"It's perfectly obvious," said Stacy, in her own impetuous, enthusiastic fashion. "Buy the house cheap, put the roof in order, and give the rooms a lick of paint, then electrify the whole place, and sell it at an enormous profit. What will it matter if the site's a bit damp, when you've got electric fires in all the rooms? Just think of the fun you could have with it! All the water pumped and heated by electricity, electric cooking-stove, refrigerator, vacuum-cleaner, iron, electric washing-machine and electrically heated blankets if you like. Wash and polish your car by electricity, charge your own wireless accumulators and everybody else's in the village. Why, you could run a place like that with one servant. All you have to do is to stand by and smoke your pipe while the machine does the work. Turn the ground-floor of the mill into a garage and a workshop, and make a couple more bedrooms or bathrooms out of the attic and the loft. It'll be just the size of house that everybody wants. And it's the perfect neighbourhood, two hours from London, with a cathedral city to shop in and half the Army for neighbours. You could get four thousand pounds for it by the time you'd finished with it, even if you didn't want to stay there."

"Stacy, you are a fool," observed Oliver with a yawn. "Fancy going off the deep end like that about a house you've never seen."

"I'm not a fool. It's a very good plan. You only crab it because you weren't clever enough to think of it yourself." This was merely the perfunctory growl and spit of a puppy and a kitten brought up on the same hearth-rug, and as such Martin treated it, remarking placidly, "It seems to me rather a good notion. I don't know where Stacy gets all these ideas." He smiled at his daughter's bright face.

"Out of bloody little house-keeping magazines,"
growled Oliver, who seemed exhausted and morose. He
had been working hard and would have to go back to
the office again presently for another two or three
hours. Stacy was unruffled; she lit another cigarette
from the stump of her first, enquiring with interest,
"What's the fishing like, Father?" He had mentioned
it went with the house.

"Oh, about enough to amuse oneself with in the
evenings," said Martin. "Just what you can do off the
two sides of the island, and in the mill-pool. A few big
fellows in May-fly time, and nothing doing the rest of
the year. All that part of the Wylyebourne was
poisoned with camp-sewage and blown up with Mills
bombs when the Australians were in camp on the edge
of the Plain. It's never been much use since, though I
suppose it'll recover eventually unless the food supply
has gone too. It was fairly good once upon a time."
But he added thoughtfully, "I saw a fish under the
bridge as I went over that would go two pounds."

"Well, I think you'll be a fool if you let the place
slip through your fingers," said Stacy, looking cross.
"Besides, look at the name, Martinmill. It must be
meant for you."

Oliver laughed shortly, got up and knocked his pipe
out into the hearth.

"You're not going yet, are you?" said Stacy, with a
discontented expression. "I want to talk this over
properly."

"Well, you can do it without me," said Oliver. "I'm
going back to struggle with that elevation of Ritchie's.
The fool's put in the whole day on it and got it all
wrong, and the owner's coming in at ten to-morrow

to see what his new house is going to look like. I shall
be up till three drawing it all out again. I don't know
what use these articled pupils are now-a-days. I'd
rather have a boy from the Northern Polytechnic, at
three pounds a week, who hasn't got any fancy notions
and does what I tell him. Young Ritchie's full of his
own half-baked ideas, and if I don't watch him he slips
in a bit of his own as soon as my back's turned, but he
can't get a simple drawing right for me."

"I'll come round and finish it for you," offered Stacy,
rising.

"No, you won't. You'll stop at home and go to bed.
I don't want you getting in my way half the night. I
want the place to myself," Oliver snubbed her with
determination, and said good night to Martin; and
Stacy sulked, but went out into the hall of the flat with
him to say good-bye.

She shut the door behind her; but it did not latch,
it swung slightly ajar. Martin, lazy and sleepy by a
hot fire, did not get up to close it: he thought that
his daughter would be back again before he found the
draught troublesome. He heard the two of them moving about outside, and then he heard Stacy's voice,
always clear and now raised and sharpened by some
urgent irritation. "You were a brute, Oliver, to crab
the whole thing like that. Couldn't you see that I
wanted Father to live there himself? We must do something about him; he can't go on moping like this."

Martin sat upright, he was taken aback by his
daughter's tone; but a moment later he was even more
startled by his partner's reply; Oliver was answering in
a voice as caressing as his former accents had been
harsh, "You little idiot, of course I could. Your face is

like a pane of glass when you're trying to be diplomatic. That's why I pretended to think it was a rotten
notion. The old man would have turned pig-headed
at once if we'd both crammed it down his throat. You
never did know how to get your own way out of a man.
Leave it to me; I'll fix it for you." Their voices died
away in an intimate murmur; Stacy gave a little uncertain laugh; her father could almost have imagined
that she had been kissed behind that swinging door.

There was a bright, unusual colour in her cheeks
when she came back again; in an instinctive attempt to
provide her with a way of escape Martin said
hurriedly, "So I'm to buy the mill-house for you, am
I?"

Her colour deepened, but she said bravely, "You
heard that, did you? Yes, I've quite made up my mind.
We'll go down and see the place next week-end." Her
eyes were uncertain and defensive; he thought with
anxiety, "Of course, they think I'm getting old."

4

Stacy had her way over Martinmill without any
assistance from Oliver Barford. She and her father
moved into the house that Easter, and spent a picnic
week among new paint and packing-cases, carrying
furniture from room to room, and eating their way
through the immense case of tinned food which Stacy
had rashly brought down in the car before she realised
that tradesmen's carts called daily. Martin pottered
about hanging his pictures, arranging his books on the
new library shelves and sorting his fishing tackle against
the opening season. Stacy hammered down carpets and

stained floor-boards and reddled brick floors and
hearths; then she drove into Salisbury, came back with
a clattering load of garden tools, an armful of Dutch
rose-trees and some damp bundles of wilting seedlings,
and made a determined, ignorant attack on the
neglected garden. Her father used to look out of his
window, which stood open in the fine April weather,
and see her forking up his tangled borders, and slash-
ing his rose-trees to the roots; she wheeled away loads
of rubbish to the orchard, and built a bonfire whose
smoke drifted half way down the village street. She
would drag him out by the arm and walk him up and
down the uneven brick paths to instruct him. "This
place hasn't been touched for years. I'm going to clear
out all those beds in front of the house, and put in
new rose-trees, and get lavender plants for the edging.
I shall have a hedge of sweet-peas behind the roses,
and put all the vegetables beyond them out of sight of
the windows. I've put in three rows of peas, and broad
beans, and scarlet runners already; I shall get in the
first lettuces to-morrow, and carrots and beetroot next
week, and after that I shall sow a fresh row of peas
and beans every week-end we come down. I don't mean
to buy any vegetables this summer; I shall take back
a basket from here every Sunday night. There are all
sorts of things down by the hedge, parsley and thyme
and a whole bed of mint, and two rows of raspberry
canes, and a lot of currant bushes. I found a rock-
garden this morning, buried in grass; you can weed
that out. The orchard has got plum-trees and pears
as well as the apples, and there's a mulberry tree, and
something that might be a quince. Of course, they all
want pruning frightfully, but I'm afraid we're a bit

late for that, the sap's rising. I wish we'd been able to get the house sooner. I shall have a great go at them all next year."

Martin glanced at the neat, empty beds, where no green showed except a border of daffodils, shaking in the east wind; he said gently, "I hope you won't make my orchard too tidy. I rather like the moated-grange effect."

"Oh! we must get the place into good order," said Stacy, disregarding him. "Next autumn I'll order a whole lot of those streaky Dutch tulips and plant them in the grass. I shall make a herbaceous border under the hedge, and a bog-garden down by the backwater, with stepping stones and Japanese irises and bamboos and pink water-lilies. Don't you think that'll be rather nice?" She squeezed Martin's arm, and he smiled indulgently; he had a great weakness for his daughter when she was laying down the law on a subject about which she knew nothing. It pleased him to think of her as young, and hopeful, and in need of protection.

"You can do anything you like," he promised, "as long as you leave me a decent fishing-path, and don't clear out the reeds too much. I must have some cover when I'm after trout. Of course, if your Japanese irises get in my way when I'm trying to land a three-pounder I shall trample them under foot." Stacy laughed and told him scornfully, "I should think this place would about stand an eight-inch limit. If you get a three-pounder you'll have to have it stuffed for the front hall."

They had waxed the red-brick floor of the hall, and put a grandfather clock in it and an oak trough which had come out of the mill, and they had hung up

Martin's fishing-rods on a rack by the stairs. They had
made themselves a stiff Victorian mahogany dining-
room, with red twill curtains and family silhouettes in
maple frames and a sliding shutter in the wall to open
into the kitchen; and across the hall they had made a
room which was too elegant for a library and too
studious for a drawing-room. It had a great many
white bookshelves, two semi-circular recesses full of
Wedgwood china and blue Bristol glass, some faded
white-and-gold French chairs and couches, covered
with striped primrose silk, and long blue taffeta curtains at the windows which overhung the mill-pool.
Upstairs there was a green bedroom for Martin, a
yellow bedroom for his daughter, rather more
frivolous, and a pink spare room for visitors; they were
all fitted out by Stacy with flowered curtains and cheap
furniture concealed in spotted muslin; and there was
a small bathroom with a sloping roof. It was an extremely attractive house, and Martin and Stacy delighted in it.

The village of Berwick St. Martin went down from
the mill in a straggle of flint and chalk cottages, with
either thatch or stone tiles on their roofs and thatched
copings on their garden walls. There was a church,
dedicated to St. Martin, with walls of chequered flint
and chalk, squat pillars under dog-tooth capitals, a
square tower with a couple of round-headed windows
in it, some fragments of fifteenth-century glass and a
graveyard with yew-trees among the tombs. Martin
acquired a family pew in this church, beneath a seventeenth-century monument to some naval worthy; it
was ornamented with a fulsome epitaph, marble flags
and guns, and dimpled cherubs, wiping away carven

tears with marble handkerchiefs and putting their heads
together to gossip over the record of the deceased.
There was a group of almshouses beyond the church;
and where the bridge crossed the water-splash there
was a little round stone lock-up, with a beehive roof,
which had fascinated Stacy from the first.

Martin leased the fishing of the water-meadows
opposite the mill, and bought a load of old tarred rail-
way-sleepers to bridge the carriers. They were dumped
into the mill-head, and Martin watched them duck
down through the sluices, and go spinning through the
mill-pool to where Stacy waded knee-deep in the
shallows, retrieved them, and pushed them down-
stream. It took the whole of one May day with a
strong wind blowing the down off the willow-catkins,
and cuckoos calling in the hot sunshine, before the last
of the ditches was bridged; and after that Stacy and her
father put in another heavy week-end cutting and
splashing among the trailing banks of water-weed, and
poling the floating masses away through the runs between the flowering white cresses. They were very wet
and exhausted by the end of it, but the performance
amused them vastly. Martin learnt to drive his own
car under Stacy's scornful supervision, grinding
majestically up and down the village, and hooting con-
tinuously; when time was an object and there was a
train to catch she drove him at her usual whirlwind
pace into Salisbury, bringing his heart into his mouth
at every corner of the twisting lanes.

They went up and down to Martinmill for week-
ends all through the summer of 1925. The shaking
poplar foliage turned from copper to green, the apple-
trees blossomed, and the thin, red leaves of the wild

peppermint began to smell strong in the wet places at
the bottom of the orchard where the marsh-marigolds
grew. Green clumps of plants which Stacy could not
recognise came up in the borders, and neat rows of
vegetables under her wire-tunnels in the kitchen garden;
the slashed rose-trees, which had been nothing but dry
sticks, began to put out shoots and leaves. The house
martens came back, with a flash of white throat and
blue shoulder, and began to gather mud from the river
bank to repair the old nests between the dentils of the
cornice. A pair of red-beaked, squawking moorhens
reared a brood of chicks at the bottom of the island;
starlings infested the gutters, and a crooked apple-tree
in the orchard contained a nestful of gaping beaks,
defended by a ruffled, scolding mother thrush with
raised wings and puffed breast. The swifts began cutting black crescents in the air as they hawked for flies
above the water, and the trout began to rise more and
more regularly as the days lengthened and the weather
grew warmer and the duns began to hatch. Martin
caught three one week-end, and four the next, and
Stacy fluked a two-pounder on an alder in the mill-race,
and was delighted with herself for doing so. Oliver
Barford came down and slept in the rose-garlanded
muslin-curtained spare room, whose innocent pink-and-
white draperies were peculiarly inappropriate to his
taste. Martin understood him well enough to realise
that he liked the house, though he limited his comments to Stacy's gardening errors and some minor de-
fects in the electrical plant. However, he borrowed
Martin's spare rod and caught three trout on the spent
gnat, and appeared to enjoy a couple of quarrels with
Stacy about formal gardens and French cookery.

June wore on to yet more beauty, with a sudden
blatant explosion of scarlet poppies in the garden
which temporarily ruined all Stacy's colour-schemes;
she had not planted them and they appeared to be an
inheritance from former owners, as was the plague
of Canterbury bells which followed them. The
chestnut-tree by the gate stood upon a carpet of its
own red blossoms, and the first roses came out on a
wet week-end, when the mill-pool was pitted with rain
drops and the flowers beaten down by the south-west
wind. A whirling storm of bees round the eaves one
Sunday morning resolved itself into a velvet lump on
one of the apple-trees, and the fascination of watching
it hived kept Martin from church. July turned the
garden into a coloured tangle of sweet-williams and
foxgloves and lupin-spikes, overtopped by twelve-foot
hollyhocks with fifty fat buds up their stalks; the
loose-leaved cabbage roses spilt their petals everywhere. Stacy wearied of picking peas and beans to fill
her greengrocery basket for London, of bending her
back and pricking her fingers in the hot, sweet alleys
between the currant bushes and raspberry canes; she
complained that all her lettuces had gone to seed together. The roads were heavy with the honey-scent
of lime-blossom and white clover. The water-meadows
steamed in the sun, and swarmed with poisonous
horse-flies; there was no more fishing to be done before
the evening rise. An August thunder-storm laid Stacy's
garden in ruins and shook down the green apples by
hundreds into the orchard grass; it brought the river
into the garage and sent a roaring brown stream of
waste water from the road through the dining-room
and kitchen, to leave a flood-mark on the skirting and

find its level in the mill-pool. The storm detected a number of leaks in Martin's eighteenth-century roof, but did not destroy his affection for the house, though he grumbled to Stacy that it was a foretaste of what would happen every winter. He loved the place better with each succeeding month.

XII

STACY continued to work in Bedford Row throughout the following winter and spring. There was a suggestion that she might go into partnership with a fellow student, but she did not seem to be taking much trouble about it; she told her father that there was no hurry and that she was finding her present experience useful. Oliver Barford, rather unexpectedly, had said to Martin, "Why don't we keep her with us altogether?" but Martin had felt oddly unwilling to act on the suggestion, and it had lapsed. He had given up the Brunswick Square flat at the end of the lease and had taken a set of queer tumbledown attic rooms in Lincoln's Inn, with cracked, dilapidated panelling, sloping ceilings and a twisted staircase; there was just room for the two of them to eat and sleep there in the week, but all their treasures had gone to Martinmill. It was to these rooms that Martin returned one wet March evening, troubled and grave, with unexpected news for Stacy. He had been trying to wrap it up for her all the way home, but when she saw his face she demanded immediately, "What's the matter?"

He could not think of anything then to say to her except the truth, or as near to it as he could come, "Something about Oliver's wife."

His daughter shrugged her shoulders, "Nothing very serious can have happened to that woman. Just another of her fancies, I suppose." Her unconscious callousness jarred upon her father; he silenced it with, "Much more than that, I'm afraid."

She gave him a bright, wild stare. "Not—not——"

He said, "Yes, dead by now," and avoided her look; its desperation frightened him.

"I never thought that could happen," said Stacy under her breath; then, with a choking gasp and on a rising note, "But it hasn't . . . she couldn't. . . . Oliver told me she'd never been really ill. Why, I saw him only this morning." She was in too much agitation to wait for what her father could tell her. She had been away from the office all that afternoon on an errand of his, choosing slabs of green marble in a mason's yard, and she had gone straight home to Lincoln's Inn instead of to Bedford Row, where she would have run into the story her father had for her.

"The doctor rang up for him about half-past four. They'd only just found her. She was supposed to be resting." He moistened his dry lips, and got out the words, "She poisoned herself."

They stared at each other; Stacy with an indescribable accent, murmured, "I didn't think she had the pluck. What did she take?"

"Chloral, I believe."

"Ah! I thought it wouldn't be anything painful," commented Stacy, in the same peculiar tone; and then she demanded, "Are you certain it wasn't accidental? She slept badly, you know, and the stuff's tricky. He told me she was in the habit of taking it; that was one of his troubles. She may just have wanted to get some rest."

"I'm afraid not," said Martin unwillingly. "I haven't seen Oliver again, but it's all here, unfortunately." He gave her the wet, crumpled newspaper he carried. "There are letters, she blames Oliver for making her life unhappy, she hints about other women." Stacy gave a bitter, furious exclamation, "She would do that. She always had to have the last word. She used to make up stories, and reproach him with them; she was insanely jealous. It wasn't all true, though some of it may have been. She's thrown all the mud she can, and left him where he can't defend himself."

Her father hardly knew her. He protested, "Stacy, don't talk like that about the woman. She's dead"; but Stacy overbore him, crying, "I don't care what's happened to her, I only care about what she's done to Oliver."

Her voice broke on the name in a way which told him everything; she demanded with fierce sarcasm, "Has she mentioned me?"

He could only gasp and shake his head. "I wish she'd had anything to complain of. I've done my best. I've behaved honourably and fairly. I've kept myself free all these years in case something should happen; but now it's too late, he's got over it."

Her father was horrified; he had never seen her like this; he stammered, "I thought you had."

"I only put a good face on it," declared Stacy, with a pale, dreadful smile that shocked her father, and then she said what was for him the worst thing of all, "Are you certain she's dead?" He ordered her to be quiet then in a tone which he had never used to her before, and she obeyed him; she sat with her head turned away from him and her chin sunk in her hand; he dared not imagine her thoughts.

Quite late in the evening the doorbell rang, and they looked at each other with an instant apprehension. They were alone in the flat, with Stacy's daily maid gone home, and it was not a time of night at which they were accustomed to casual visitors. Martin felt an immediate conviction that the summons had to do with Oliver's trouble, and he realised that his daughter shared it.

"You go," faltered she, after a moment's hesitation; it was the only time in her life that he ever knew her flinch from a difficulty, and it gave him the measure of her agitation.

He went out into the passage and opened the door himself; it took him some time, for the bolts were shot and the oak fastened for the night, but he was in no way surprised to find Oliver himself waiting outside, very pale in the light of the overhead lamp, and breathing hard as if he had run up all four flights of stairs with something behind him.

"I had to come," stammered he, supporting himself with one hand against the door-post. "I had to talk to someone." His eyes were bright with exhaustion; he stared round him desperately. Martin drew him in, and shut the door behind him; he brought a waft of the raw night air with him from the well of the open staircase. The sleeve of his coat was soaked with rain; he could hardly stand. Martin thought only of getting him to the warmth of the fire, he pushed him into the sitting-room, forgetting Stacy.

She had shrunk back against the wall as far as she
could get from the door; she was supporting herself
there with her hands behind her. There was no colour
in her white, distracted face, but there was a strange
light upon it. Oliver stopped dead when he saw the
girl, he put out his hands and muttered, "Stacy!" It
was at once a cry for help and an unconscious betrayal.
Stacy answered it immediately, coming to him with outstretched arms as frankly as a nurse or a mother. She
was as tall as he, and at that moment stronger; she
took his weight against her shoulder, and guided him
into her father's chair; she knelt beside him, murmur-
ing over him as if he were a lost child. Her father
had not the heart to stay and listen; he went out of
the room unnoticed, and shut the door upon them.
Standing in the hall and staring at the wet foot-marks
on the carpet, he realised, in one intolerable moment,
that he had lost his daughter. There might be all the
miseries of the inquest before Oliver, the gossip and
newspaper paragraphs and publicity, he might be unconscious as yet of his own feelings, and Stacy might
defend herself with all her old, incalculable, shrewish
vigour; but sooner or later the two of them would
come together, as certainly and simply as they had done
to-night. "It can't be helped," said Martin out loud,
and started at the sound of his own voice.

2

Matters fell out much as he had expected, with a
little more delay and difficulty, but with an inevitable
progress towards the August week-end when Oliver
came down to Martinmill, with a black band of mourn-

ing on his arm and a look of queer excitement on his
ravaged, sulky face, and settled his affairs with Stacy.
He followed the girl about all that Saturday afternoon
without getting her alone once; she was being characteristically perverse and sullen, she would not look
him straight in the face or talk about anything except
the produce of her garden and the state of the fishing.
She made him take out a rod with Martin after tea,
in spite of her father's mild protest that they would
do no good before eight or nine, and the most that she
would do was to promise that she would leave her
daffodil-planting after supper, and come down the
meadow.

"But I don't suppose there'll be anything doing,"
she said crossly, "and I don't know how I'm to spare
the time. I've got a thousand bulbs to put in this week-
end." She seemed to think that much more important
than receiving the proposal from Oliver, a foregone
conclusion to which Martin had already given a rueful
and unnecessary consent. "I can't stop her marrying
you," was rather the tone he had taken, though he had
softened it with his weary smile. He now suggested
tactlessly, "I should have thought Oliver could have
helped you with your daffodils."

"I would if she'd let me," grumbled Oliver, "ke a
sulky schoolboy.

"Oh, Oliver would make a muddle of the whole
show," said Stacy. "He doesn't know anything about
gardening."

"No, and doesn't want to," retorted Oliver, looking
at her as if he would have liked to give her the shaking she deserved. At the moment, however, he submitted, accepted the borrowed rod, and followed Martin

down into the steaming, unsheltered meadow, where
the cows were switching impatiently at the flies and
the level sun was flinging long shadows from the old
and rusty sorrel, the seeding thistles and tall nettles
turning brown. It was a poor fishing evening, too bright
as Martin had said, and too early for the rise; Oliver
cast carelessly over the one or two small fish moving,
and put them down; he hung up in the willows across
the stream and the uncut brambles at the bottom of
the orchard; he sweated in the evening heat and cursed
the stinging midges and flies. Martin perfectly understood the reasons for his bad temper, but did not find
him any the better company on that account; it was
less from pity for the young man who was to be his
son-in-law than from a wish to be alone that he proposed to Oliver, about seven o'clock, when they were
at the bottom of the second meadow, "You might go
back and tell Stacy I shan't come in to supper."

Oliver brightened perceptibly at the suggestion,
mopped his hot forehead, and said, as if in apology,
"It's not much use sweltering down here for the next
couple of hours."

"No use at all," agreed Martin, "and much too hot
to work. You take Stacy by the scruff of the neck and
make her stop her idiotic gardening and give you
something cold to eat and drink. You and she can fish
the island stream after supper if you like; it'll be cooler
then. Tell her to leave me something on the sideboard;
I probably shan't come back till about half past ten."

Oliver glowered at him between suspicion and gratitude, swallowed something and seemed about to speak,
but could not find his words. He walked rapidly away
up the fishing-path, through the late summer jungle of

reeds and willow herb, as if he had made up his mind
to stand no more delays. Martin could see the tall,
moving point of the rod long after he had lost sight
of the man. "By the time I go back to-night they'll have
come to an understanding," he reflected, without the
satisfaction that the words deserved. He went right
down to the bottom of the last and longest meadow:
he wanted to put as much distance as possible between
himself and the house. It was cooler there; a fallen
willow had blocked the boundary-stream with its
branches, and there was a not too uncomfortable seat
upon the main stem, in the shadow of the pointed,
silvery leaves. He spent an hour there, smoking his
pipe, feeding his mind on the solitude of the evening
and imagining that he was facing the situation; but in
reality all that was over. He had already anticipated
Stacy's loss; she had made up her mind, as he very
well knew; she would take her happiness into her own
greedy, capable hands once more, and he did not grudge
it to her. He honestly believed that she and Oliver
would reward each other for the past; he had done
what he could to bring them together. He was only
thinking under the willow tree of a little girl who had
said, "Drawing at school is silly," of an obedient
schoolgirl who had delighted in his lectures, of a grown
woman who had come to him in her troubles. These
were fond, habitual recollections, he dwelt upon them
disconnectedly and found in them his comfort. He
sighed at last and knocked out his pipe and decided
that it was late enough to fish up to the house. The
meadows were deliciously cool and fragrant with
meadow-sweet. The grass gave underfoot with a juicy
crunching, the rushes whispered above the sliding

stream and there was a breeze which only they could feel. Martin heard the querulous, creaking notes of the sedge-warblers, creeping like mice up and down the reed-stems; a moorhen squawked, ducked her red bill under and dived with the precision of a mechanical toy. A water-rat slipped into the stream and swam across, lying as flat on the water as a fur skin nailed to a board; it nibbled through the stem of a green weed, brought a leaf back in its mouth, and entered its hole in the bank, quite unconscious of the watcher. Little fleets of hatching duns came down the sunset stream with their wings erect like sailing ships, they fluttered, and struggled and rose glittering into the golden air. He saw first one trout and then another splash after them, a hungry fingerling jumped right out of the water; but Martin waited for the sucking, spreading ring with the bubble in it, that came under the over-hanging grasses of his own bank, where he knew of a fish. It was a difficult place to cover; the reeds ahead of him drooped above their own reflection, and they had been insufficiently cut behind him, but he was in a wind-less corner and his first underhand cast was well-judged. The current set in towards the bank; it took the neatly-dropped and cocked fly with it, and slowly straightened out the slack of the cast, but the fly drifted down and over the fish without dragging. Martin held his breath as it sank, then tightened his hand. There came a sudden, vigorous resistance, the line ran down stream, the rod curved and shook, there was a splashing and threshing in the water. He coaxed and humoured the struggling fish to the bank. When it floated exhausted on its side he slipped the landing-net beneath it, climbed back out of the reeds and over the barbed wire into meadow again. There he detached the hook, killed and then weighed the fat, freckled, silvery thing and cleansed his hands of slime in the cold dewy grass. An ounce over the two pounds was a good beginning for the evening. He found with a start that he had forgotten about Stacy and Oliver. Well, they could manage their own affairs; he was too old to do more than leave them free. Better pleased with life he went on up the meadow. It had grown a little darker while he was kneeling over his fish; the horizon was rosy all round him, but the sun had gone. A heron, flying back to roost, went over him with a loud and menacing call; he heard, a little later, the lovely, tremulous hooting of a barn owl and saw it winging up and down the meadow; the great bird came quite close to him as he stood motionless among the reeds, its round, cat's face stared into his. Then he disturbed five wild duck paddling in a carrier, they quacked and wheeled and flew off in a high curve. Once, about half way up the second meadow, he glanced nervously over his left shoulder, because he thought that with the tail of his eye he saw something watching him; but it was only the pale, enormous face of the full harvest moon, just risen and not yet luminous, standing above the eastern horizon. As he crossed the stile into the upper meadow a bat circled round his head and almost touched his face. He caught two more fish on the same blue-winged olive, then, before the moon grew bright, changed to a small dark sedge; the fish were rising all round him for ten minutes as if the water were boiling, but he only caught one more in the time; then with a gradual decline, and one or two last dropping splashes, everything became quiet. The moon rose clear of the trees

and painted long shadows across the field; he saw her
light reflected in the windows of his own house as he
approached it. The apple-trees of the island chequered
the moonlight on the foam of the mill-race, but down-
stream there was a light mist curling off the water
already and he felt the chill of it touch him as he
walked a little stiffly over the plank bridge. He saw the
flutter of a woman's dress in the orchard and thought
to himself, "Stacy ought to know that it's no good
going on fishing once the mist begins to rise."

Then he saw the two of them standing together
under the laden apple-tree. They had come to the end
of their journey. Oliver had his arms round Stacy, and
she had yielded to them altogether, she was unconscious
of anything beyond. Their contented murmurs and
caresses mingled with the voice of the stream, they
were deaf and blind to all but each other. Martin went
by them in silence and unobserved on the wet and dewy
grass.

3

Oliver and Stacy were married that autumn. They
had not delayed their marriage as long as convention
demanded, but they were hungry for each other; Stacy
said that they had waited years enough already. Martin
saw his daughter married this time; to his surprise
and disappointment she chose the same ten o'clock
registry business as before, but she had not inherited
her father's religious feelings, and had a boat-train
to consider. Martin found time, in the middle of all
the forms and signatures and brisk official procedure, to
wonder whether his daughter was deliberately exercis-
ing the recollection of her first stolen marriage to

Philip Giffard, or whether Oliver had simply wiped
all that out of her mind; he had a passing vision of an
aeroplane falling down the sky and leaving a trail of
smoke behind it as evanescent as the memory of the
man falling with it. Stacy flung her arms round him,
she was as red as a rose. Martin decided that she had
forgotten everything, and he was glad of it. Oliver
was much more moved; he looked horribly pale and
nervous; he wrung Martin's hand and promised, "I'll
make her happy." There was no Letty now to remind
Martin of how he had once said the same thing to
her, but Martin himself had not forgotten. He said
to Oliver, "If Stacy's got anything of her mother in her
she'll make you a good wife."

Oliver took her away; they were in a gay, excited
hurry, they were going to Sweden together to look at
new buildings. That was the fashion of 1924. In
Martin's time it had been Greece or Italy, but all that
was out of date. He walked back to Bedford Row by
himself and reflected that now he was altogether alone;
but it seemed an ungracious thought for Stacy's
wedding-day, and he put it away for later.

The young people were not away very long; funds
did not permit of it. They sent him picture-postcards
of whatever architecture they supposed would be most
to his taste, neat little four-square island castles with
turrets, capped by bulbous lead spires, ruined mediæval
cloisters, or houses with steep-pitched roofs and crow-
stepped gables; they came back resolutely refusing to
admit their enjoyment of solitary lakes, white summer
nights, waterfalls and pine-trees. To hear them talk
you might have supposed that they had spent their
honeymoon looking at factories, saw-mills and concrete

bridges in Stockholm. Martin thought these objects of their pilgrimage ugly and uninteresting, though he was prepared to confess his admiration of the dark red walls, Venetian arcades, gilt cupola and menacing tower of the Stockholm Town Hall; it seemed to him a magnificent building.

"I'd like to have a look at that," he told his daughter on her return, "but then it's more the sort of thing to which my eyes are accustomed."

Stacy said, "Yes, it lets you down gently," and tried to make him appreciate her photographs of an odd kind of public building, a library or what not, which to his classical prejudices looked like a cross between a packing case and a gasometer. However, Stacy and Oliver apparently thought well of it. He was more concerned to see how they looked themselves, and was deeply content with their sunburnt, cheerful absorption in each other; it was early days to tell, but he thought that their marriage would prove a success.

They settled down temporarily in a top-floor flat in Torrington Square, where they had four spacious, inconvenient attic rooms with sloping ceilings, elegant Georgian fireplaces, barred windows with a view into the plane trees of the public garden, and a nursery gate at the top of the stairs for which they subsequently found a use. Oliver had chosen the flat because of its convenience for Bedford Row, and Stacy spent more time at first in the office than in her own home. She had begun to get work of her own to do, and even if it did not fill up all her time there was plenty that she could do for Oliver, who was so busy that he hardly knew where to turn. Martin came and went between his chambers and Martinmill, and found himself happier than he had expected. He saw plenty of Oliver and Stacy, who were cheerful company and seemed thoroughly satisfied with each other and evidently considered their marriage a great success. They still quarrelled occasionally, not altogether to Martin's surprise; but he was astonished and amused to find Stacy becoming docile, and even condescending to humour and manage her dictatorial young husband. Oliver was lordly and authoritative in public but somewhat henpecked in private; he amused Martin by patronising Stacy's architectural efforts and changed his former note of criticism into an admission that she was sometimes very useful.

"But she'll have something else to keep her busy next year," he told Martin, with a sheepish grin. Neither that first son of theirs, however, nor the boy who followed him two years later, kept Stacy long away from work. She proved to be the vigorous, detached, efficient mother that Martin had expected. She managed her husband and her house, her children and her work, with the same cool, cheerful certainty and absence of worry. Martin waited, expecting her to betray some sign of effort, but he waited in vain. She did not turn a hair; there seemed no necessity for her father to be anxious about her. The young people grumbled a good deal about the difficulties and disappointments of their profession, but as far as Martin could tell they were not doing badly. Oliver had plenty of his own class of work to do: he had two banks in hand, he was designing a block of flats near Victoria Station, and had nearly finished a cinema in Maida

Vale of which he was immensely proud. Stacy was getting herself a reputation for designing compact,
manageable little houses in the suburbs, with a garage
on one side of the front door, a sitting-room on the
other, running water in the four bedrooms, electric
fires, metal casements and wood-block floors. If she had
any other ambitions she concealed them and seemed
perfectly content with her domestic line. Her elevations, however, had caught a certain Prussian flavour
which startled her father's old-fashioned taste, and she
had built herself a staring white week-end cottage for
her family on top of a cliff near Dover which he found
very hard to admire. It was designed for reinforced
concrete in the best Le Corbusier manner; it had two
stories with a flat, railed roof, an asymmetrical series
of windows like letter-slots piercing the corners of the
building in a manner which disturbed all Martin's
notions of stability, and a bulging, oval sun-parlour on
the south-east angle which reminded him of a stranded
houseboat or the front of a two-decker tram. It had no
garden in the proper sense of the word; ("I'm not
going to be a slave to a sweet-pea hedge, as I was at
Martinmill," said Stacy); it stared from a blinding
white concrete terrace across miles of grey sea and
creeping ships to the mirage of the French coast.
Martin definitely disliked the exterior. Once inside the
copper-sheathed door, however, he was obliged to
admit the clean emptiness and mechanical perfection
of the wind-swept holiday place, with its naked concrete walls, its sliding doors and fitted furniture of
unpolished wood, its angular metal tubing chairs and
tables, its tiled and rubbered floors. There was nothing
in the house which could be destroyed by sun, or salt

air, or the casual Oliver, or Stacy's two vigorous, un-
manageable little boys. Martin was mildly amused to
find that his daughter had not been able to discipline
his grandsons. They were just as obstreperous as she
had been at their age, and she found even her grandmother's methods useless with them. Made wise by
time, Martin appreciated their health and vigour, and
relied on school to knock their impudence out of them.
Meanwhile they ran wild all summer in bathing suits,
became as hard and brown as driftwood, adored their
mother and respected no one but their father, who
could always keep them in order when he chose and
was absurdly proud of them. The elder was an Oliver,
Noll or Nolly for short; the younger, Nicholas Martin,
had christened himself Bunny, and refused to be
known by any other name. They were nice children, and
Martin was very fond of them, though he never
thought them as original as their mother had been.

He found himself spending more and more of his
time at Martinmill. His practice had dwindled further,
but he did not make any very serious effort to increase
it; he found himself growing peacefully, even lazily,
content with small jobs up and down the country and
a weekly visit to Bedford Row, more for the amusement of discussing professional points with Oliver and
Stacy than for the sake of anything he actually found
to do there.

He found time to compose a book which he had kept
at the back of his mind for years. It was based on his
old holiday jaunts with Stacy and it was an outline of
English architecture for children who might have her
enquiring mind and hungry imagination. There was a
good deal of miscellaneous historical information

mixed up with it, and he succeeded in transferring to
paper his own paternal, enthusiastic way of talking.
Stacy's children were too young for it, but Oliver, who
had stolen a chapter or two, unexpectedly approved
of it, and gave it some exceedingly amusing illustra-
tions. With these embellishments it found a publisher,
and surprised Martin by selling extremely well.

"There's no doubt about it, father, you've found a
new vocation," said Stacy, mockingly. "You'll be able
to spend the rest of your days writing variations of it."

Martin was resolved not to fall into that tempta-
tion, but he cast about him for other subjects, and
found them. His visits to London became more and
more intermittent, he gave up the Lincoln's Inn
chambers, and his practice slipped away finally, while
he sat in the mill-house, and buried himself contentedly
in books and drawings. He sighed for actual bricks
and mortar no longer. Stacy and her family came and
went, he made one or two short journeys abroad to
give himself fresh subject-matter; he took and enjoyed
a post as lecturer on a voyage to Crete and the Greek
Islands and up to Constantinople; he spent a winter
in Spain. He learnt to know the round of the year in
the Martinmill water-meadows, and subsided into a
quiet country life. Stacy declared that he not only took
in the local paper but read it; she made fun of his
placid retirement but she was really quite easy in her
mind about him, and sighed with relief to think that
he was happy once more.

4

In the winter Martin became a little rheumatic, and
reluctantly obeying his doctor and his family, went to

take the waters at Bath, whence he wrote enthusiastic
pages to Stacy.

"You were quite right. This place is just my period.
I go purring round, enjoying it; I collect pilasters and
friezes and Ionic colonnades and other elegant
features. The houses are all built of that delightful,
moth-eaten kind of freestone which turns brown and
black and streaky where the weather gets it. Most of
the city is pure middle eighteenth-century. I had no
idea the Woods were such good architects; they did
some astonishing things. My hotel has a rusticated
ground-floor, with Corinthian columns running up two
stories above it, and a cornice and a balustrade to
finish off with. It looks down an immensely long street
with a piece of stage scenery at the end, a house like a
Greek temple with a portico and urns and wing-
colonnades. There's a delightful bridge by Robert
Adam, with little shops all along it, hanging over the
river like bird-cages. There are squares, and circles,
and diamond-shaped piazzas; the place is full of good
town-planning notions. My doctor lives in an extraordinary Circus, which reminds me of the Colosseum
turned inside out. It has a continuous entablature running round the houses, a different Order for each
story, and a balustrade finished off with acorn-finials.
It's full of doctors; I understand it's called the Pill
Box locally. There's a gigantic Royal Crescent, with
huge columns dividing one house from another, and at
least two subsidiary crescents; the whole place goes
staggering in terraces up the side of the hills as if
gravitation didn't exist. The older streets have the most
absurd, romantic names, like Ainslie's Belvedere and
the Vineyards, the Paragon and Lime Grove; the later

ones are hopelessly dated by being christened Albany, or Brunswick, or Caroline, or Albert.

"There are whole terraces of the kind of Regency house which I am beginning rather to admire in my old age, all bloated bow-windows and cream-coloured plaster, like a piece of Brighton; and there is a good deal of what I call Crimean architecture in the suburbs, nice little low twin houses with flat slated roofs and striped green-and-white tin verandahs, the kind of place that's called Inkerman Villa or Alma Cottage. And when I come out from drinking my two glasses of tepid yellow water in Nash's Pump Room it makes quite a pleasant change to see the west front of a perfect Late Perpendicular Abbey, with a Jacob's Ladder running up each side of the West Window, and headless stone angels, all as drunk as lords, falling up and down the rungs."

It was not until the very end of the letter that he gave himself away by admitting, "I must say the hills are rather trying. I do my best to tread them down under my feet, but they take my breath away." But Stacy never got as far as the end of that page. She had glanced through his letter on a busy day at the office, and merely reported to Oliver that her father had written one of his long-winded letters about the Bath architecture, and seemed to be enjoying himself.

"Just the right kind of holiday for him," said Oliver. "Do him all the good in the world, probably. I don't think he's been looking at all well lately."

"Oh! he always gets a bit down in the mouth at the end of the winter," said Stacy, carelessly, "and I daresay Martinmill is a bit damp for him, at his time of life; but he loves it so, there's no moving him. He'll

be all right when he gets the rheumatism boiled out of
him. Next year we must make him go abroad again."
She added, with her short, hard laugh, "I only hope
he won't let himself in for marrying some sympathetic
boarding-house hag. Father is terribly defenceless
where women are concerned."

Oliver shook his head, and declared, "Your father
will never marry again."

Stacy protested, but he was obstinate.

"The old man would never look at anyone again
after your mother. You simply don't begin to understand the hold she had on him; it was extraordinary."

"Yes, it was," agreed Stacy, thoughtfully. "According to modern ideas, he ought to have got tired of her
almost at once. She didn't understand one word about
the things he liked, she wasn't any help to him in his
career, she didn't even make him comfortable at home,
and she wasted his money. She was one of those women
who neglect their husbands as soon as they've got their
children."

"You and she never really understood each other,"
said Oliver gravely, as if explaining the edge in her
voice to himself. "She was an extraordinarily sweet,
good woman."

"She never had any use for you," Stacy pointed out,
a little spitefully.

"No, we weren't out of the same pack of cards,"
admitted Oliver, without resentment. "But I saw
things about her that you didn't."

"She could always get round a man," declared Stacy.
"She spoilt them, and let them do exactly what they
liked. That was why Aubrey turned out such a little
rotter. There was no chance of her spoiling me that

way. She was fond of me, I suppose, but she never managed to make me feel it. Her life was all wrapped up in Aubrey."

"Your father's never been the same since she died," said Oliver. "Some sort of a spring broke in him when he lost her."

"That's true," his wife agreed, and she added with a queer, sideways look, "You and I wouldn't be such fools."

"Time will show," said Oliver grimly, putting his arm round his wife, and kissing her with a rough, careless certainty. "Perhaps we haven't got it in us." He was devoted to Stacy and made allowances for her manner; she said a great deal that she did not mean.

The Bath doctor, as a matter of fact, had told Martin, "You ought not to climb too many hills at your time of life."

When Martin had protested, "I'm not senile yet," he had become impatient, and persisted, "Four years of the war meant ten years of ordinary life. You've always worked your brains hard, and led a sedentary existence and burnt the candle at both ends, from what you tell me; you're the nervous, highly-strung, conscientious type, that takes life hard, and worries and struggles over what can't be helped. You've been having these headaches and giddy fits on and off for years without paying any attention to them, and you've gone on driving yourself when you ought to have rested. Now you've got a throbbing pulse, a twisted temporal artery, and a blood-pressure that'll have to come down before I say good-bye to you."

He was the gloomy, bullying type of specialist, who has a great contempt for his patients' intelligence and

believes in frightening them into docility. He had been
very successful with a certain hysterical type of woman
patient, but he was unnecessarily alarming to Martin,
who began to worry about his own symptoms, and to
lie awake at night counting the pulsations of the thick,
tortuous, radial vessels at his wrist. However, a return
to the quiet life of Martinmill and the placid, experienced ministrations of a country doctor who was far
more interested in the cross-fertilisation of sweet peas
than in the lives and deaths of his patients, proved the
best prescription for Martin; he watched Stacy's
daffodils reappear among the apple-trees, went out
fishing as soon as the season opened and began to write
a new book about mediæval monasteries and their
planning. He slept longer and better, and assured his
daughter and son-in-law that Bath had done him a
great deal of good. Stacy believed him if Oliver did
not; she had never been very observant where other
people were concerned.

"Father's looking much better for his cure," she
decided and was satisfied.

XIII

IT WAS IN THE MIDDLE of September, 1931, that
Martin went up to London to look at Oliver's latest
building.

Stacy and the boys had been down for the week-end
by themselves because Oliver had only just returned
from a trip to America and was too busy to accompany them. The little boys had enjoyed themselves
greatly, chasing chickens, eating blackberries and doing
their best to fall into the tail of the mill-pool, just as
their mother would have done at their age, while Stacy,
admittedly a little tired and overworked but very
pleased with life, lounged through a long Sunday
afternoon in the hammock under the walnut-tree, and
kept a casual but effective watch upon their performances while she recounted family news to their grandfather.

Martin was ready enough to be idle with her; it was
a warm, sleepy afternoon; the bronze leaves of the
beech-trees were turning rusty at the edges, but the
willow-leaves made gold and silver crosses against the
sky, and the chestnut-tree had gone up in a blaze of
orange and rose. Stacy's voice was as cheerfully content
as the lisp and murmur of the river among the

withered reeds, or the cooing of pigeons on the tiles of the mill-house.

"We've been tremendously busy all this summer. I shall be thankful to get the boys off to school again to-morrow. It's all very well to be successful, but one can have too much of a good thing and the last few weeks have been desperately heavy going. Really, Oliver and I might almost as well be divorced for all I see of him by day or night when he's got a big job on. Since he's been back from the States he's been head over ears in the new building." She laughed derisively and quoted, "If anybody calls, tell 'em I'm designing St. Paul's." Then she declared, "It's a mercy I'm not the old-fashioned type of wife. I have got something else but his behaviour to think about."

"Are you fairly busy yourself?"

"I've got quite as much in hand as I can manage," said Stacy with all her old self-satisfaction. "Oliver can turn up his nose at my domestic stuff as much as he likes. I pull my weight in the boat. The office can't live entirely on his shops and banks and competition-work. That sort of thing may be a very good advertisement, but it's pretty chancy. Mine is the kind of stuff that pays."

Martin smiled, but made no comment; he had long decided in his own mind that Stacy's work was not of any very lasting importance, though she made a good deal of fuss about it. It was competent, practical and untainted by any amateurish weaknesses. She knew her business and he respected her for it; but he understood and pardoned her slight continued professional jealousy of her husband. Oliver had something powerful and inimitable about his clumsy, ugly elevations which she would never equal; some day, when Martin, perhaps, was no longer there to see it, the younger man would build himself an enduring monument.

"I'm glad," said Martin, "that you're doing so well. You make me feel very old and out of date, idling down here." He added thoughtfully, as he bent his head towards young Noll and Bunny, who were trailing a hopeful line from the anchored weed-cutting punt, "Which of them is going to carry on the family firm?"

Stacy said firmly, "Neither of my boys is going to waste his time on architecture. It's the Cinderella of the professions and there's absolutely no money in it. I shall find something better to do with them than that."

Martin was not offended, he merely smiled. "You're talking just as your mother used to talk," he observed, with affection. "I took it more seriously from her than I do from you. I don't believe the itch for bricks and mortar has worked itself out in the family yet. Young Noll was demanding information about my new garage from the workmen yesterday, and apparently making sense of what they told him. Come now, Stacy, are you really sorry you ever took it up?"

His daughter laughed, blushed and shook her head. "No, the job's got me altogether, just as it has Oliver," she admitted. "Nothing else would have suited me so well. I don't quite know why I find it so fascinating. I suppose it's the blend of practical, historical and artistic, the general mix-up of beauty and tradition with sheer everyday common-sense, which gratifies and fulfils every side of one's nature in turn. There's a solid sense of achievement about finishing a building.

It satisfies the creative instinct. It's like," she concluded seriously, "producing a healthy child."

Martin said thoughtfully, "It gratifies the human wish for survival. We don't last long ourselves and our children may leave us or disappoint us, but the things we make last longer than we do. I like to imagine people living in good, sound houses built by me, after I'm dead and buried. It gives me a pleasant feeling of vicarious immortality." He smiled and admitted, "Of course, one's mistakes are horribly permanent, too. There's a dreadful house somewhere in the Chilterns, the first I ever built. I should rest more easily in my grave if I knew that was burnt down."

Stacy laughed, squeezed his hand and said, "You've got fewer mistakes to your account than most people; I should think you might lie quiet." The idle saying melted unnoticed into the flowing breeze of the autumn afternoon.

She went away with the children next morning in a car crowded to the doors with luggage. She was taking them back to school, and they seemed quite undisturbed by the prospect. She drove Martin as far as Salisbury, and left him there to go up to London for the day and look at Oliver's new building.

"Of course, you won't like it any better now it's up than you did in the drawings," she teased him. "I'm not even sure that I like it myself. And you're certain to disapprove of his new cantilever construction. But Oliver's frightfully pleased with himself over the whole thing. You'd better see if you can take him down a peg. I think he needs it." Her smile was maternal and lovely; she still adored her husband. Noll and Bunny waved their hands to their grandfather in a way which delighted him, as their mother swung the big car round in a swift, effective curve; Martin watched it slide away down the steep approach, and vanish among the traffic. He thought as he turned into the station, "They're a happy family. Funny now to think how I used to worry over Stacy. She made a lot of mistakes to begin with, but she's worked out her life all right; she's got a devoted husband who can manage her and look after her and make her happy, a couple of children who amuse her, and work that she enjoys. I don't need to trouble about her any longer. She's off my hands." And with an odd, unexpected impulse of self-congratulation he told himself, "If I haven't done much else I've made a good job of Stacy."

The journey to London was hot and the carriages were crowded with returning holiday makers; Martin had to stand most of the way in the rocking corridor and was sorry he had not waited for another day or a later train. The suburbs of London struck him as peculiarly dreary; he had not been to town for almost a year, and he had forgotten just how depressingly dingy and haphazard were the southern approaches to the city, how melancholy the miles of grey and brown terraced houses, flat slate roofs, clumped and squatting chimney-stacks, railway embankments, advertisement hoardings, gasometers and telegraph wires. Emerging from the station he wished himself back in green Wiltshire. The dry September pavement sweltered under a grey, oppressive sky; there was a little irritating wind blowing, which did not temper the heat, while it swirled and scattered the gritty dust and paper underfoot. Martin had meant to walk across the bridge for his own favourite view of the river, but his heart failed him. He took a taxi; then repented it when he found himself caught in the slowly moving lines of traffic across Waterloo Bridge. "This business is a scandal," he thought, "it ought to have been settled months ago, but now they've finally messed up the Charing Cross scheme Heaven knows what will happen." The scaffolding spoilt his prospect up and down stream; he missed his glimpse of St. Paul's. He puzzled for a moment over a couple of unfamiliar white towers, like chunks of wedding-cake, down in the smoke of the east; then placed them as Adelaide House and the Port of London building. He had never realised that you could see them from that point, they disturbed his recollection of the misty Thames. The top of Bush House looked aggressively square and threatening as he approached the north shore. "But all London's getting altered," he sighed to himself as his taxi worked through the confusion of the Strand, which was so much worse than he remembered it, and drove up Regent Street.

The fat, domestic, yellow curve of Nash's design had changed and swollen into buildings which were displeasing to his reluctant eye; he thought them overwhelming and ostentatiously gross. There was a great mass of scaffolding at the bottom of Portland Place, concealing the prow of a bulk as arrogant as a battleship; and in the streets beyond it there seemed to be an astonishing amount of demolition and reconstruction going on. He passed the hoardings and scaffolding of countless red, many-windowed blocks, towering flats or offices, breaking the old sky-lines and rising and receding above the narrow street. However, the house to which he was driving, unknown to Oliver or Stacy, with its wide shallow steps, its wrought-ironwork railing, and the five or six brass plates beside the dignity of its fanlighted Georgian door, had long outlived its builders and changed but little in a hundred and fifty years. The circular dining-room, where he waited, still had its curved mahogany doors with their elaborately fluted columns and classic entablature; the specialist's consulting room had kept its own delicate detail of medallion and pediment and cornice on which Martin strove to fix his disturbed attention.

"Of course, you take a professional interest in these things," remarked the specialist absently, tapping and sounding and looking judicial over his findings. Martin tried to make some rational reply.

"They tell me the ceiling is a good example of its period," said the great man with condescension. "I don't know much about that kind of thing myself, but my wife likes it."

Martin lay on his back on the slippery oilcloth couch and stared up at the precise, attenuated Adam design of masks, skulls and garlands above him, but he did not really see them.

"Your own doctor tells me, Mr. Lovell," the specialist said, "that you wish me to be perfectly frank. I can only say that in your case a quiet life is imperative. Any unexpected or excessive strain might have the most serious consequences."

He was kind, composed and unmoved; no doubt, thought Martin rebelliously, he pronounced a death-sentence every day.

"The condition of your heart and arteries really does demand the utmost care," continued the bland, sympathetic voice which vaguely irritated Martin, and later, in response to an enquiry, "You do really wish me to be perfectly frank? Of course, if it's a matter of arranging your affairs, and you wish to know how you stand, then I am bound to be open with you. I could not really say exactly how long you have to live, perhaps with great caution two or three years; but any imprudence might bring on a fatal attack. Yes, without warning. The matter really lies in your own hands."

Martin was curiously unmoved by the pronouncement. He heard a voice which he supposed to be his own remarking thoughtfully, "Well, I don't know what I've got to wait for. My wife and my son are dead; my daughter's married and provided for; my work's finished." The specialist began explaining away his pronouncement; curious, thought Martin, how these fellows hated committing themselves.

He listened and looked at the ceiling and thought that he would remember its pattern for the short remainder of his life.

2

It was after one o'clock when he emerged from between the fluted columns of the classic doorway; the autumn sun beat down upon his aching head, the shimmering, unshaded perspective of Harley Street made his courage weaken. He thought confusedly of one fact only in a reeling world, "I shall be late for Oliver's lunch." He drove to the office without noticing anything by the way; he was trying to think, or rather trying not to think, of what was to become of him.

The brown eighteenth-century house in Bedford Row looked much the same as it had done when he first entered it, forty years earlier, except that Oliver, or more probably Stacy, had recently ordered the dilapidated panelling of the staircase and first floor to be painted a delicate, lily-leaf green. The front room, with the marble chimney-piece and the carved festoon of flowers, which had been old Nick's office, and later Martin's, was crowded nowadays with the orderly mass of Oliver's sketches and catalogues, and filed letters. He was interviewing an unpunctual client there, and Martin had to wait in a little cupboard which, in his own day, had been a store for filed drawings, but was now converted to Stacy's personal use. Her father sat there for ten minutes, listening to the murmur of voices next door, and thinking as much of her young days as of anything else, while he stared unseeingly at a framed drawing of a house of hers on the wall, and rejected the consideration of the specialist's verdict.

Oliver came in by and by, very much pleased with his interview, and in his usual authoritative hurry.

"No more time to waste; come out at once and I'll tell you our news at lunch. Stacy and the boys got to you all right, I suppose? She'll kill herself one of these days, tearing about your curly lanes as if they were the Great West Road. I always tell her there are more right-angled turns on the road to Martinmill than anywhere else in England, but she never listens to anything I say nowadays."

Martin was accustomed to Stacy's and Oliver's perpetual criticism of each other, he had come to consider it a sign of their mutual affection.

"You're about the only person she does listen to," he observed, rising rather stiffly to follow his son-in-law out.

"Oh! I can manage Stacy," said Oliver blithely, and with truth. He stuck his head in at the door of the drawing-office, gave some vigorous instructions to an unseen pupil within, and swept Martin away to their belated lunch. He was in great spirits, and talked all through the meal, without noticing any preoccupation or inattention on Martin's part.

He had lately been to the United States for two months to look at modern American architecture, and had come back roaring mad with excitement over the things he had seen. He talked to Martin of streets like geological fissures, splitting the arid cliffs of masonry, blunt masses of stone which gaped into a thousand windows, of pale, naked towers which scraped the clouds from the sky, and flung their long shadows across half a city. Martin thought at first that the drawings and photographs which he produced were hideous; the buildings seemed to him like heaps of packing-cases, or blocks of pale, sliced honeycomb, buttressing a stack of factory chimneys; it made the back of his neck ache to look at them. Then he too caught fire, and was mesmerised to Oliver's enthusiasm.

"I take off my hat to the audacity of those fellows. You've no idea of the risks they run, pushing up seventy or eighty stories on a set of calculations that are nothing more or less than guesswork. How do you suppose a man's to work out the wind-bracing of a tower like that one? I've very little confidence in all their equations about slope-deflection and gridiron-support, wind-pressure, load and stress, and so forth. I tell you I've been up at the top of one of those places and felt it swing like a ship at anchor. It fairly made my blood run cold, and I flatter myself I've a good head for

heights. Think of the games they play with all these
new materials. They've just put up a great black-and-
white brick tower, all metal wings and wheels, with
fourteen arched pinnacles covered with polished
chrome steel. How's that going to stand the rain driving on it, and the sun eating into it? Nobody knows
what sort of state it'll be in after ten years. Of course,
you can try these games with a decent dry climate, and
a rock foundation. You daren't do it on London clay
and river mud, with soot and wet weather biting and
scaling your surfaces away. All the same I've come
back crammed with ideas about new materials, black
glass, artificial stone, all their queer new sheet-metal
alloys, chromium, aluminium and nickel steel and so on,
fireproofing treatments, and compressed seaweed for
sound-proof partitions. And I've learnt no end about
modern planning. There isn't an inch of rentable space
wasted in those big office-buildings in the States, I can
tell you; but I found out the trick of it. You start by
planning the lift-shafts, clump them all in the core of
the building and let them drop off in groups at each set-
back. Then you fit in all the service installations in the
windowless space round them, the ventilation shafts
and drainage, the telegraph and telephones and heating systems; finally, you plan your rooms round the
outside. That's how I shall start next time I get my
chance of doing a big building. I've absorbed some
pretty good notions about treating a façade, all tiers
of glass and metal windows going up and up between
plain piers of brick or stone, with nothing to break
the stream-lines. I'm going to drop all the old imitation
constructions of sham pillars and arches supporting
nothing, and to begin designing in plain blocks. The

stepped pyramid is the thing to go for in the future.
I wish I could have got out to the States before I did
the plans for this newspaper office of mine that you're
going to see this afternoon. I could have made ten
times the job of it with all I've learnt in the last two
months. Oh! well, I shall have to save it all up for the
next one. I've got plenty of time before me."

The last phrase revived Martin's unconscious
picture of sand running out in an hour-glass. Resting his
aching head on his hand, he said, "I'm afraid you're
managing to spoil my crawling, crumbling London for
me. Everywhere I've been this morning I've come
across some building that's all out of scale and dwarfs
its neighbours. You're altering all my skylines for me
and narrowing the streets into trenches. I used to think
the most characteristic thing about London was the
little low terraces, with their mild, dirty, brick fronts,
and the way nothing emerged from the general
humility except an occasional church spire. Now
wherever I go I see some towering white eyesore, with
pillars and plate-glass windows going up in vertical
lines, story after story, just as you describe, or a big
block of flats like a gingerbread cake, or a shop-front
in stripes of nickel and black glass. Soon I shan't be
able to recognise the place. Of course, I'm affected by
the fine solidity of it all, the mountainous look; there's
something about mere size that's bound to be impressive, and I do approve in theory of the blunt masses
and the absence of ornament. But it's all on too big a
scale for me, and it's come too late. I can't quite get
hold of the notion you young people are driving at and
I wish it had happened earlier in my time. I should
like to have waited and seen what you'll make of

London." His voice was an involuntary betrayal, but Oliver missed it.

"You can't stop a thing growing," said he, getting up and stretching himself with what seemed a gesture of unconscious power. "Wait till you see what we've done with the place in ten years' time."

Martin controlled a slight, inadvertent recoil. "I doubt whether I shall be taking much interest in architecture in ten years' time," he said slowly. "However, let's get on and see what you've made of this building of yours."

Oliver had his own car waiting, he drove as swiftly as his wife, but less dangerously; however, nothing could hurry the traffic of Chancery Lane and Fleet Street, and Martin had plenty of time to study the growth of Oliver's newspaper building before they arrived.

The work on the excavations had been in progress for over two years, but there had not been anything to see above ground and Martin had not visited the site since the time when the house-breakers had been pulling down an earlier building. Though he was familiar with Oliver's queer box-like design on paper, he did not expect to approve of it in its final form. What he saw through the windscreen of the car was uninviting, dirty-grey concrete walls, a mass of the new tubular scaffolding which revealed the bones of the building so much more clearly than the old poles and planks, and the tall jib of the crane turning on top of everything. There were gaping slits for windows in what appeared to him an excessive proportion of glass to wall, and an odd blunt curved nose to the building like the stern of a cruiser. Some kind of a set-back at

the fifth story was obscured from him by a projecting
staging. The whole place had a blind, staring, unfinished look; it went up like a desert cliff by steeps and
ledges with little to break its grey monotony. The
central doorway, on which, as far as he remembered,
Oliver had concentrated his ornament, was still
boarded-up and hidden; he could not remember how
Oliver had designed it; something in black glass and
nickel steel, was it? or marble and green bronze? He
recollected an odd, Mycenæan effect, splayed jambs
and a plain, heavy moulding; but all that was only
represented as yet by an echoing, dusty space inside
the hoardings, some scaffolding supports, and three
wide shallow concrete steps with boarded edges. He
followed his son-in-law into that dark noisy place, and
smelt the old sour reek of mortar, sawdust, and earth;
he had been long deprived of it but its familiarity
caught at his throat and nostrils. He stumbled like any
layman over the loose planks underfoot and the ex-
posed pipes of the sprinkler-mains and electric con-
duits; he had to grope his way between the stacks of
metal window-frames to the concrete steps of Oliver's
winding central staircase. He was glad to sit down
and rest in the little boarded office on the first floor,
among the samples of marble and mosaic and artificial
stone, while Oliver hauled out his blue-prints and tracings, all grimed and gritty with cement-dust, and explained his new cantilever-construction and talked
about his difficulties.

It was a long afternoon for Martin, and somehow
more tiring than he had anticipated. He was out of
practice for these descents into cold, forty-foot
excavations, lit by glaring electric light, these climbs

from floor to floor among the skeletons of printing-presses, lifts and ventilating-shafts, the familiar hiss and clang of riveting and welding which deafened his aching ears, these long discussions of technical points between Oliver and the stout, cheerful clerk of the works, which left him forlorn and excluded. He disliked the dark, uncertain ascents of ladders and crossing of plank bridges, and sudden disturbing glimpses into unimaginable depths. His old fear of scaffolding had come back upon him tenfold with disuse and ill-health; he found it almost impossible to follow the two younger men into the upper, lighter stories where the skeleton structure admitted breadths of sky. When they took him enthusiastically out on to an unfinished balcony which jutted over the street, and pointed down at the traffic, the glance into that crowded ditch made his throbbing head swim. He drew back and confessed apologetically, "I'm not so good at this kind of work as I used to be." He had not the sense, however, to refuse Oliver's proposal that they should go up to the foot of the crane and see the view from there.

"Astonishing, really," said Oliver, "we're higher than anything except a few of the churches and, of course, St. Paul's." Martin liked the idea of looking at St. Paul's from a fresh point of view, but he had not realised how much he was going to dislike that last ladder, with the sky open all round him, the hot, teasing wind tugging at him, and the scaffolding seeming to drop back from him as he ascended. He was horribly conscious all the way up of an open space to his left, an interval in the scaffolding, and a well going right down into the basement of the building. He had incautiously glanced into it just before he put his foot

on the ladder. He had seen the diminishing intricacy
of its perspectives, with men crawling in them, and
water at the bottom, and his scalp had begun to
prickle. He tried not to remember it as he went up the
ladder, but the wind came at him in little, menacing
puffs and the ladder seemed absurdly to swing that
way; there was an awkward moment at the top when
he had to lift himself from the ladder to the platform
where the crane was rattling and wheezing as it turned
above him. Fortunately the burly clerk of the works
was behind him to give him a push at the critical
moment and Oliver's lean, powerful hand was stretched
from above to sustain him.

3

Once he was up and had solid planking under his
feet, instead of the open rungs of the ladder, it was
like being on the top of the world. He had been
familiar in his old working days with many such airy
points of vantage, and they had always given him a
sense of his own protesting, determined insignificance.
That feeling now returned to him in all its force. He
was above the general level of the flat lead roofs about
him and on terms of equality with the fantastic silver
towers of half a dozen Wren churches, blackening together in all their delicate detail, century after century,
under the tooth of the soft, wet, soot-laden London
weather. From the east he was overlooked by the
maternal, almost gravid mass of the cathedral dome,
with the dark and slender spire of its attendant church,
lifted before it like an indicative gesture to command
attention. There were clouds coming up from the south-

west to threaten the square, round or octagonal temples and pinnacles of the churches; the flat roofs would presently be sluiced and drowned by thunder-rain. The Surrey hills were clear and dark under that heavy sky, but between him and their fine-drawn sky-line stretched mile upon mile of the crowded, smoking houses with which men like himself had filled the valley of the hidden river. It was as if he had been lifted up and pinned down under the mild gaze of the sky, to give his final account of his own work; and facing the end of his life, he admitted, "I've had my best moments out of the things I've built. They've meant more to me than Letty, or the children, or myself. Let them be my justification." He said to Oliver, lounging on a guard-rail beside him with the wind blowing his untidy hair, "You've made something that will last." It was more than the compliment for which the pleased and touched young man accepted it; it was the blind, grop-ing defence of himself and his kind against oblivion through the permanence of their work.

The afternoon was over; there was no more to see. It had grown chilly on the uplifted staging, and Martin became conscious of a throbbing in the temples of his aching head. He assented willingly when his son-in-law murmured, "Best, perhaps, be getting down. Jacobs wants to go." He took another look round and said, "I'm glad we came up here."

"Come again when it's finished," suggested Oliver cheerfully, and did not notice Martin's stare of doubt. He was glancing round before he left the platform of the crane and admitting carelessly, as if he had for-gotten the fact, "Yes, it's a good view. Stacy enjoys coming up here. She likes all the Wren churches."

"She and I used to go round and look at them when she was a little girl," reflected Martin, with a faint smile, "but that's a long time ago."

They went round the foot of the crane and came to the ladder.

"Better let me go first, Sir," insinuated the fat, cheerful clerk of the works. "Then Mr. Barford can give you a hand down. This ladder's a bit awkward-like at the top."

He turned and stepped briskly off the staging, as if into thin air; he descended until only his broad shoulders, red face and tilted bowler-hat appeared above the planking.

"If you'll just put your foot here," he suggested, laying his hand invitingly on the topmost rung and going down a step or two further.

Martin gave a last look round and upwards at the smoking expanse of roofs, the drifting cloud-wrack overhead and the skeleton arm of the crane; it seemed as if it menaced him like an uplifted finger. He turned with his face to the platform, gripped the upright of the guard-rail as the wind freshened about him, and felt with his foot behind him for the rung of the ladder. His son-in-law was just above him with outstretched hand, as he found it and went safely down a couple of steps. "All right now, aren't you?" the young man said, grinning cheerfully. "I'll be after you in a second. I just want to speak to the engineer." He waited for Martin's reassuring nod, then stepped back towards the cab of the crane.

It began to revolve at that moment, the engine rattled noisily and the arm of the crane began to sink. Martin's attention was distracted; he glanced involuntarily at the links of the chain, descending past his left shoulder, and their movements carried his eye downwards. He found himself gazing through the dreaded perspectives below into the very foundations of the building. The pool of water at the bottom blinked back at him, his aching head swam suddenly, his knees shook and everything turned green about him. He clung to the ladder and felt his hands slipping, he had time to call out, and to hear an answering shout from below. He opened his despairing eyes for one glance through the rungs of the ladder as he toppled sideways.

A strange, vivid recollection deluded his last moment. He thought that he saw his Letty, a girl again in a blue-and-white gown, trembling before him against the background of crossed poles and concrete blocks. She looked full at him and smiled as if to welcome him.

Then he lost his balance, and dropped from the ladder down past the scaffolding into the excavations.

Oliver, making one bound to the edge of the staging, was in time to see him fall and to hear the gasp of the clerk below, "My God! he's over!"

THE END